Carole Singer's Christmas

EMILY HARVALE

Emily Harvale lives in East Sussex, in the UK.
You can contact her via her website, Twitter, Facebook or
Pinterest

Author contacts :
   www.emilyharvale.com
   www.twitter.com/emilyharvale
   www.facebook.com/emilyharvalewriter
   www.facebook.com/emilyharvale
   www.emilyharvale.com/blog
   www.pinterest.com/emilyharvale

Also by this author:

Highland Fling

Lizzie Marshall's Wedding

The Golf Widows' Club

Sailing Solo

Acknowledgements

Thanks, as always, to my wonderful friends for their support and friendship.

Massive thanks to Karina of Miss Nyss www.missnyss.com for another gorgeous cover.

Grateful thanks to Christina Harkness for editing this novel and for her greatly appreciated input.

Heaps of thanks to David of DC Creation for all the clever things he does for my website, blog, launch events, bookmarks and designs. I don't know what I'd do without him. www.dccreation.com

Mega thanks to my Twitter followers and friends, Facebook friends and fans of my Facebook author page. It's really great to chat with you.

And to you, the reader, wherever you may be, for buying this book – Thank You.

Love,

Emily x

In memory of Charles Dickens for giving the world,
A Christmas Carol, and providing me with the inspiration
for this book.

***

Season's Greetings!

Thank you for choosing this book. I hope you're looking
forward to Christmas as much as I am. I simply adore this
time of the year. I love the sparkle of the lights; the colours
of the decorations; the glow of burning coals; the smell of
Christmas spices; the taste of mince pies warm from the
oven; the Christmas traditions: stirring the cake mixture
three times and making a wish, kissing under the mistletoe,
burning a yule log; the magic in the air; Christmas music
blaring in overcrowded shops; buying singing Santas and
dancing turkeys and the thrill of finding the perfect gift for
someone special; cold, crisp mornings and long, dark
nights; sipping sherry; knocking back the Baileys; spending
time with family and friends and telling ghost stories
around the fire; fond memories of those no longer with us. I
love it all. I hope you enjoy reading this book and it fills
you with the Christmas spirit! I wish you a Christmas and
New Year full of happiness, warmth and love.

By the way, the Geminids meteor shower mentioned in this
book is real. It takes place on the nights of December the
13th and 14th and is a spectacle well worth watching. I'll be
saying the rhyme in the book and making my wish. I hope
you will too.

MERRY CHRISTMAS!

CHAPTER ONE

'Carole!' Dominic yelled from the sitting room. 'Will you *please* come and sit down for just one minute? There ... there's something I need to ask you.'

Carole stopped in her tracks. She hovered on the threshold of the utility room, her eyes alight with eager anticipation. There was something about Dominic's tone. Was this *it*? Was he actually going to propose at last? They'd been dating for almost three years now. Surely, it was time? And she'd given him enough hints – not that Dom had seemed to notice.

She drew in a deep breath and hesitated for a few seconds before dropping the washing on to the floor of the utility room. Ignoring the flashback to her mother's house where piles of washing, magazines, books, pictures, shoes and empty wine bottles were akin to exhibits in the Tate Modern, Carole marched into the sitting room. The washing could wait. A few dirty clothes on the floor didn't mean she was turning out like her mother, and nothing was more important than this moment. She could sort the whites from the colours later.

'Of course, darling,' she said, smiling as she cast a reassuring glance around the room. She was nothing like her mother. Not even a speck of dust was visible.

'Come and sit here,' Dominic said, plumping up Carole's favourite cushion and placing it almost reverently back on the sofa.

He licked his lips and Carole watched him closely as she sat down. He always did that when he was nervous. This was it. This *must* be it! She would finally be able to get rid of the name that had been a weight around her neck for her entire life; the name that had made her the butt of so many jokes and stupid remarks especially around this time of year. Oh, joy of joys! She could finally bid goodbye, once

1

and for all, to the awful, horrendous, ghastly ... *CAROLE SINGER!*

She eyed Dominic hopefully. Why wasn't he getting down on one knee? Why was he pacing the room and rucking up the new rug she'd bought last week? And why do this now? As eager as she was for him to pop the question, their sitting room wasn't the most appropriate place to propose. She'd been hoping for the whole enchilada: a romantic dinner at a posh restaurant; roses; champagne; a violinist. No, a violinist was tacky these days; it would have to be a harpist. Oh, why didn't he just get on with it? She longed to be plain old, Carole Smith.

Well, she didn't long to be old. It was bad enough that she had almost four years on Dominic as it was and the fact that she'd be thirty-five next birthday just made things worse. Thirty had been terrifying but thirty-five! That was almost forty – and ... she was still single.

'Dominic?' she coaxed, in what she hoped was a sexy drawl. 'I won't bite, darling. You know you can ask me ... anything.' She gave him an encouraging smile.

He let out a long sigh, dragged a hand through his short brown hair and smiled sheepishly.

'The thing is this,' he said. 'I ... I know we agreed to spend this weekend together, Christmas shopping, but the lads have got tickets to see *Rob The Rich* on Saturday – in Manchester – and you know they're my all-time favourite band. I've been trying to get tickets for months, you know I have. Jerry is friends with one of the bands' sisters or something and he's scored us backstage passes. Can you believe that? I can't miss this, babe. I just can't! You don't mind, do you? Carole? Are you okay? You ... you're not angry are you? You know I'd understand if the roles were reversed and your friends got you tickets to see ... Michael Bubbly or someone.'

Carole's eyes met his. 'It's Michael Bublé, not Bubbly,' she said, not quite sure what had just happened.

2

'Whatever. It's okay if I go, isn't it? You can go and visit your gran. You've been saying for a few weeks now that you wanted to see her. I'll come down on Sunday afternoon if you want. Oh ... on second thoughts, that probably isn't a good idea. I expect we'll go for a few bevies after the concert and you wouldn't want me to get stopped for drink driving, would you? The coppers are really hot on that this time of year and alcohol stays in the system for at least twenty-four hours or something. Besides, it'd be a real rush to get back from Manchester and drive down to Sussex.'

'What?' Carole blinked several times as she tried to clear her muddled brain. How had Dominic gone from proposing to her, to telling her he was going away for the weekend – without her?

'What's wrong, hun? You seem to be on a different planet. I was saying that it would be best if I didn't come down to your gran's. She'll prefer to have you to herself anyway. And she never lets us share a room so there's no point in me driving all that way. I'm sure she doesn't like me even after all this time. Anyway, I'll be leaving on Friday evening and I'll be back late Sunday night, possibly early Monday – in which case I'll go straight to work. Why are you looking at me like that? ... Carole? ... Er ... isn't that your mobile ringing?'

'What?' Carole said for a second time. 'Oh, yes.' She stood up and grabbed her phone, snapping herself out of her stupefied state. 'Hi Gran. We were just talking about you. How are you?'

Dominic raised his eyebrows, tutted and strolled into the kitchen.

'Hello sweetheart. I'm fine thanks. How about you? Is ... is everything going well?'

Carole thought she detected a hint of tension in her grandmother's voice and instantly felt guilty for having left it so long between visits.

3

'All good here, Gran. Are ... are you sure you're okay? You sound a little ... tense.'

'No, no, I'm fine. Really. I couldn't be better. I suppose you're rushed off your feet as usual?'

'You know me, always making more work for myself than I need to,' Carole joked.

She knew she was a perfectionist when it came to her career as an illustrator and graphic designer and that she spent far longer on her drawings and designs than was absolutely necessary, but she could never let her work go out to clients until it was one hundred and ten per cent perfect – to her eyes. She also knew she devoted more time to the housework than most people, and cooking, and sewing and ... well, everything really. Anything she did, she did to perfection. That's just the way she was, or the way she had become.

'Yes, sweetheart. You take after your father in that respect. He was the same, God rest his soul. Everything had to be the best that it could be. It's a pity some of that attitude didn't rub off on your mother. How we all put up with her sometimes is beyond me. Have you heard from her this week?'

Carole sighed, remembering her father. He'd been dead for almost twenty years now but she still missed him dreadfully especially around Christmas time. He loved Christmas and everything that went with it, and now that she thought about it, so had she – until he passed away. She hadn't even minded the jokes about her name before that.

'I spoke to Mum yesterday. She's invited us all up to Scotland for the Christmas holidays. I'm not sure I can face it to be honest and Dom *really* doesn't want to go. We were thinking of saying that we wanted to have a quiet Christmas here, just the two of us, and that we'd be popping down to you as usual, but you know what Mum's like. I'm sure she'll try to badger us all into going. Of course, if you want to go, we'll come down and get you and drive you up

4

there.'

'Good Heavens no! Spend the whole of the holidays with my daughter? I may as well just give myself salmonella now. Louis Pasteur would have been proud of her! There are more bacteria thriving in her house than in any laboratory, I'm sure of it. Those germs would have me for *their* Christmas dinner, and as much as I love her, I really can't face it. Spending just one day tidying up after her was bad enough but at least when she lived in Essex, I could leave at the end of it and come home. I can't do that in Scotland. I don't think I'll ever understand why she and that new man of hers wanted to move all the way up there. Anyway, I'm staying put – and I've told her so in no uncertain terms.'

Carole giggled. 'Oh, Gran. I've yet to see the day when any germ – or anything else come to that – could get the better of you. You can't spend the holidays on your own though. That's awful. I'll speak to Dom and to Mum and we'll sort something out. Perhaps she'll agree to come down to you as usual.'

'Nick said that I should go on a cruise, find myself a nice young man and have some fun. That's not such a bad idea actually. But I won't be on my own if I stay here anyway. I've already invited Nick round for Christmas dinner.'

'Nick? Who's Nick?' Carole asked, unable to suppress a twinge of anxiety.

'He owns the new garden centre, Four Seasons Gardens, just outside of the village. I've told you about him.'

Carole bristled. 'This is the first I've heard of him, Gran. How long have you known him and why exactly have you invited him for Christmas dinner?'

'Nonsense, dear. I'm always talking about him. He moved to the village in the summer and he came and did some work on my trees. Now I know I told you about that. He was able to save my ancient apple tree, the one I was so worried I'd lose, and I'm certain that because of his skill

5

I've got more mistletoe on it this year than ever before.'

'Oh, yes. I vaguely remember you saying that you'd found a tree surgeon but you didn't say he'd opened a garden centre. That still doesn't explain why you've invited him for Christmas dinner though – or why he's advising you to go on a cruise with a man! Exactly how well do you know him?'

'Oh, Carole. Don't get all mother hen-ish. He's a lovely young man, and so handsome – in a rather moody and mysterious sort of way. I can't wait for you to meet him. I've told him all about you and–'

'Gran! What are you up to? You know full well that I'm virtually engaged to Dominic. Don't start your matchmaking with me and this ... Nick.'

'Sweetheart! As if I would. Actually, I'm thinking of keeping him for myself. Lots of older women have toy boys, don't they? He's a godsend, I can tell you. He's always popping in to see if I need anything. And I could sit and watch him work all day. Oh ... if only I were forty years younger.'

'Er ... how old is he?'

'He's thirty-six next month. On Christmas Eve, in fact.'

'Thirty-six! And he's always popping in? That sounds a bit odd to me. Where did he live before? What's his surname?'

'Carole, what are you suggesting? That he's after my money or something? He's not at all like that, I assure you. In fact, he's just the opposite. I had to ... Well never mind that. I'm telling you now if I was a girl of your age you'd have to fight me for him. He really is ... 'fit', as you youngsters say. He's like one of the Brontë sisters' heroes. You know the type – tall, dark and menacing on the outside but on the inside, all soft and gooey. And his eyes! They're as black as coal. Even his voice is sexy. The way he calls me Mitsy makes me feel like a teenager again. Gosh, I'm getting all wobbly-kneed just thinking about him!'

6

Carole wasn't sure she liked the idea of her gran getting the *hots* for a man more than forty years younger. She shook her head to erase the picture. She definitely didn't like the idea of this Nick calling her gran, Mitsy. Only family and close friends called her that.

'Hmm,' she said, 'I'm not sure I'd describe *Heathcliff* as soft and gooey.'

'No, that's true – but he was a man in love, and we all know how crazy love can make us. Oh ... sorry, sweetheart, I didn't ...' Mitsy's voice trailed off.

An even more unwelcome image popped into Carole's head; one that she hadn't had for a very long time and she coughed to clear her throat as if the thought were choking her.

'It's okay, Gran. That was years ago. I've forgotten all about that now. And you're welcome to this ... Nick. I've got Dom and I'm not interested in anyone else.'

'That ... that's lovely, dear.'

'Yes, it is. Listen, I was going to call you later as it happens. Dom is ... has to go away this weekend ... on unexpected business and I thought I'd come down and see you – if that's okay?' Carole lied.

Dominic was right about Mitsy not liking him and Carole decided it was better not to tell her that he'd changed their plans at the last minute and was swanning off for the weekend with his friends. She knew exactly what her gran would have to say about that.

'Oh! Um. Of course it's okay. You know you don't have to ask. I'd love to see you. It's been three months since I came up to stay for the week and it must be at least six months since you came here.'

'What? Has it really been that long? It can't be.'

'Yes, dear it has, but I know how busy you are so I'm not complaining. When are you thinking of coming down?'

'Um. Friday morning. I'll stay until Monday afternoon.'

'Perfect. I'm looking forward to it already. You can

7

finally meet Nick. But Carole, there's ... there's something I should tell you. Now I don't want you to get upset sweetheart and although Jutsdown is a village, you'll probably hardly even bump into one another but–'

'Gran? What is it?'

'Well, dear ... you'll find out sooner or later so I may as well just tell you. It was one of the reasons I rang, to be honest. Sebastian's back. And he's getting a divorce.'

CHAPTER TWO

Carole dropped onto the sofa and flopped back against the cushions, wondering if her heart would ever stop thumping. The news about Sebastian had come as a big surprise and she wasn't sure how she felt about it.

'So it's all settled then?' Dominic asked, returning to the sitting room with two large glasses of wine.

She glanced across at him. 'Sorry, what did you say?'

'I asked if your weekend is settled. Are you all right? You look as if you've seen a ghost. Nothing wrong with your gran, I hope.'

Dom handed her one of the glasses and she raised her head, meeting his pale brown eyes which, despite the hint of concern in his voice, were impassive.

'Thanks,' she said, noticing he'd filled the glasses almost to the brim as usual. 'Er ... no, gran's fine. It ... it was just something she told me about ... someone I used to know. It's nothing important.'

She forced a smile. That was the second time she'd lied in the space of fifteen minutes she realised; first to her gran about Dom, and now to Dom about her conversation with her gran. She must stop doing that or she really would turn into her mother.

'Good,' Dom said, sitting beside her and flicking on the TV, signalling an end to the conversation.

Carole stared blankly at the screen. Football didn't interest her in the slightest and under normal circumstances she would have got up and gone into the small second bedroom that served as her office, to continue working on one of her commissions, but these were not normal circumstances. Sebastian was back in the village of Jutsdown – and he was soon going to be single again.

Dom wrapped his arm around her, pulling her close and giving her a quick peck on the top of her head. In an attempt to put the brakes on her current train of thought, she snuggled up to him. It didn't help though. She just couldn't settle.

She wished she'd asked her gran for more details once she'd recovered from the initial shock. Instead, she'd pretended that Dom was calling her and told her gran that she would speak to her again later. She now knew that was a mistake, and it also dawned on her that she'd now told three lies, not two. She screwed up her eyes in self-disgust.

Her stomach seemed to be tying itself in tight knots and whatever it was that was rising in her chest and throat, it wasn't indigestion – she hadn't eaten anything since breakfast. She'd put on a few pounds recently and although she wasn't overly concerned about her weight, she did want to be able to fasten her trousers properly.

And Dom had made one or two remarks about her bottom 'looking big' during the last couple of weeks, and she didn't want him to think she'd let herself go *before* he proposed. Not that it looked as if he was ever going to. That thought took her mind down another path she didn't want to tread. Was it happening again? Had she spent the last three years of her life with another man who would, one day, just up and leave her without a word of warning, travel half way around the world, and marry someone else?

'Dom, you do love me, don't you?' she asked, resting a hand on his thigh and tracing imaginary little patterns with her finger. He didn't answer so she slid her fingers down the length of his thigh and back up again. 'Dom?'

Dom moved his leg and Carole's hand slipped onto the sofa. She straightened slightly so that she could see his face.

'What? Oh, yes, of course I do, hun,' he said without looking at her.

She placed her hand on his chest, slid it down to his waist and under his T-shirt and walked her fingertips upwards, leaning in to kiss him as she did so.

Dom slapped his hand over hers and tilted his head away. 'I'm watching the football, babe. Can we do this later?' he added, without glancing away from the screen.

Carole sighed deeply and slowly got to her feet. 'Sure,' she said, picking up her glass and trudging towards the kitchen. 'I'll go and make a sandwich. I haven't eaten anything since this morning.'

'Trying to lose some weight? That's good. Can you make mine a cheese and tomato ... with pickle? And use the white bread. I don't want that wholemeal, seedy stuff you like. It tastes like straw. And bring in the wine bottle will you, hun?'

Carole stopped in her tracks and sucked in a long, slow breath. A vision of hitting Dom over the head with the wine bottle leapt into her mind and she blinked, wondering where that could have come from.

'Yes!' Dom yelled.

She let out the breath in a heavy sigh and continued towards the kitchen. Dom's team had obviously scored, which was more than she had done.

***

Carole sat at the small pine table in the kitchen, deep in thought as she munched her sandwich. When she'd taken Dom's in to him together with the bottle of wine, he thanked her by smacking her playfully on her bottom. It was something he often did but this evening it annoyed her and she was now wondering whether it was because he'd failed to propose, or if it had something to do with hearing about Sebastian.

Unintentionally, she found herself comparing the two men. Dom, the man she loved now and whom she hoped would propose but hadn't, and Sebastian, the man she'd loved ten years ago who had proposed, and left her standing in the church with a broken heart, which she thought would

11

never mend.

And not just a broken heart but also an empty joint bank account. Although to give him some credit, he had sent her a cheque for her half a few months later – from Australia.

She still couldn't believe he'd booked a flight the day before their wedding, jumped on a plane the next day – their wedding day – and flown to a different hemisphere, just to avoid marrying her. The note he'd left, which unfortunately no one had found until after the humiliation of her arriving at the church, had given little by way of explanation and nothing in the way of comfort. It said simply:

Carole my darling,

I am so, so sorry for doing this to you but I really believe you'll thank me one day, and I hope with all my heart that in the future, we'll be able to be friends again. I wanted to tell you to your face but I can't bear the thought of seeing you upset, and your mum and Grandma Mitsy would skin me alive. It's better this way. I've had to use the money in our joint bank account but I promise I'll pay your half back to you as soon as I can. If you need it now though, just pop in and ask Dad to give it to you. I'm sure he won't mind.

All my love,

Sebastian.

At least that was one promise he'd kept, although the cheque came with another note, this time telling her that he hoped she'd 'moved on' and that he 'still couldn't believe it' but he'd just got married. Carole couldn't believe it either.

'Carole!' Dom called from the sitting room. 'Open another bottle, will you, hun? It looks like this game will be ace and I don't want to miss anything.'

She was tempted to suggest he reach out his arm for the remote, press the pause button and come and get the bottle himself – or his arse would end up as large as he thought hers was. But she remembered the pile of dirty clothes she'd dropped on the utility room floor earlier that evening and reasoned that, as she'd got to get up anyway, she may as well do as he asked.

'In a minute, Dom. I'm just finishing my sandwich.'

'Yes, yes, yes!' Dom yelled.

Carole knew he wasn't replying to her. 'That's just one of the many things I love about you, Dom,' she said even though she was aware that he couldn't hear her over the volume of the TV. 'The fact that we can have such meaningful conversations.'

She popped the final piece of her sandwich into her mouth, scraping the feet of the chair across the tiled floor as she stood up. Grabbing another bottle of wine and the corkscrew, she took them into Dominic. He eyed her curiously as if he didn't understand why she was giving him the corkscrew as well as the bottle. She placed both on the coffee table and marched out.

'I'm sorting out the washing, then I'm having a bath and an early night,' she said without looking back. 'Don't fall asleep in front of the TV again because I'm not coming down to wake you up.'

As she stuffed Dominic's boxer shorts into the washing machine, she wondered how the evening had gone from her believing she was soon to be Dom's fiancée, to her behaving like a nagging mother.

***

Fifteen minutes later, surrounded by fragrant bubbles of lavender and vanilla bath essence, which was one of the products in the latest of her mother's home-business ventures – and a rather good one, Carole had to admit – she dialled her friend Josie's number.

'I wondered when you'd call,' Josie said. 'Grandma Mitsy's told you about Sebastian, I take it.'

'Yes, she has. And I've got two questions for you. Why

didn't you call me and tell me he was back in the village and who the hell is this *Nick* guy who seems to be spending an inordinate amount of time with my gran?'

'Oh! Well I didn't tell you about Sebastian because the last time I mentioned him you nearly bit my head off, and you told me in no uncertain terms never to mention his name again. I only found out about it myself a couple of days ago, and as I saw him talking to your gran, I was pretty sure she'd call you and tell you anyway.'

'Talking to Gran! What do you mean, he was talking to Gran?'

'Precisely that. They were standing outside the post office stores, talking. Although neither of them looked particularly pleased to see the other, if you get my meaning. I kept out of the way so I have no idea what was said. Didn't she tell you that?'

'No. But she did say he's getting a divorce so I suppose she must have heard that from him, or possibly from someone else in the village.'

'Yeah. Everyone's talking about it ... Oh! Sorry. I don't suppose that's what you wanted to hear, was it?'

Carole tutted. 'Not really. But I suppose it's inevitable. Have you spoken to him?'

'No way! Besides, he only arrived at the weekend and I think he's trying to keep a low profile. Not that he's succeeding. He's back at his dad's estate agency. Rumour has it that his dad is thinking of retiring and handing over the business to Seb. That means he's here to stay, Carole.'

'Damn! That's all I need. Not that he means anything to me now of course. I'm with Dom and we're practically engaged.'

'You've been saying that for the past three months. Haven't you got him to propose yet? You're slipping, my girl.'

'Thanks Josie! So what else can you tell me about Sebastian?'

'Nothing. He's still gorgeous ... but I don't suppose you needed to hear that either, did you?'

'No. Oh, bloody hell! Let's change the subject. What can you tell me about this Nick?'

'Ah, Nick.' Josie let out a long, meaningful sigh.

'You sound like a gravy advert. Don't tell me you've got the hots for him too. Gran seems to think he's like some sort of romantic fiction hero.'

Josie sniggered. 'He is rather yummy. In a slightly scary, bad boy kind of way. Not that I think he is a bad boy. Although he may be a bad boy in bed. There's definitely something about him. And his eyes. They're–'

'As black as coal. I know. Gran's already told me. What is it about this guy? Both of you go all swoony just talking about him!'

'What can I tell you? Some men have just got it – and Nick's got it in spades ... and then some.'

'So he's good-looking,' Carole said. 'I think we've established that. But what is he like as a person and why is he spending so much time with Gran? Is he after her money or – God forbid – her?' She shivered involuntarily at the thought of it.

'Oh God, Carole! He's definitely not after her. Well at least I don't think he is. To be honest, he's rather secretive so I have no idea what's going through his gorgeous, sexy head. He seems to be quite a decent, friendly sort of guy but he doesn't divulge much about himself. And oddly enough, everyone in the village has just accepted him. It's rather strange now that I come to think about it. You know what we're all like. Eager to find out every little secret about everyone and if we can't find out any secrets, we make them up, but not with Nick.'

'Well that's weird. So there's no gossip about him? No juicy little snippets?'

'Nope. The only things I know about him are that he's single, mid-thirties and he bought the old plant nursery and turned it into a thriving garden centre in less than six months. He's always polite whenever I see him – which is actually rather a lot. I've developed quite an interest in plants and stuff, you know.'

'Plants! You? Now that's the most shocking news I've heard today. You can kill a floral display just by looking at it!'

Josie laughed. 'That's true. Which is why I need to spend so much time at the garden centre, getting ... advice.'

'Oh my God! Now I'm really worried. It was bad enough thinking he's got some strange power over Gran but if you're developing an interest in plants, it's more serious than I thought. It's just as well I'm coming down this weekend. I'll have to go to this new garden centre of his and meet him to find out exactly what's going on. It almost sounds as if he's got some magical powers or something!'

'Perhaps he's a white witch ... or warlock, or whatever it is male witches are called.'

'He sounds more like the devil incarnate especially as he seems to have both you and Gran drooling over him!' Carole wasn't completely certain that she was joking about that possibility.

'If he's the devil, Carole, I'll take Hell any day of the week. Please let me come with you when you go to see him. I need another excuse because I've got so many plants now my garden looks more like a jungle than it did when there were just weeds.'

'Hmm. No wonder his business is thriving. Okay, I'll be down on Friday. I'll go to Gran's first and I'll pick you up after work.'

'Great. I finish at four. I'll be waiting at the school gates. I think you're in for a bit of a surprise,' Josie said.

'I think this *Nick* will be the one getting the surprise, Josie. Oh, there's another call trying to get through. I'd better take it, it may be work. See you Friday.' She ended the call to Josie and, not recognising the number, adopted her business voice. '*Carole's Illustrious Images*, how may I help you?'

'Well you can start by explaining why you're not coming down until Friday.'

Carole sat bolt upright in the bath, almost dropping the phone into the rapidly cooling water. For one dreadful moment she'd thought it was Sebastian but she realised this man's voice was nothing like his soft melodic tones. This was granite, edged with ice.

'Who is this?'

'Nick. I'm a friend of Mitsy's and I'd really like to know what is so important that you can't drive sixty miles to look after your own grandmother when she has a broken leg and can't possibly look after herself?'

'W ... what? What are you talking about? Are you telling me Gran has had an accident? When? Where is she? Is she all right?'

The ice cracked a centimetre or two. 'Are you saying you didn't know? Didn't Mitsy call you this evening?'

Carole felt her backbone stiffen. 'Yes. Gran called me but she didn't say anything about a ... broken leg. Are you telling me that this happened before she called?'

'Spot on, Sherlock. It happened yesterday.'

Carole didn't like his tone. 'I don't think sarcasm is called for, Mr ... whatever your name is.'

'Nick. Just call me Nick.'

She could think of several other things she'd like to call him but she refrained from doing so. She needed to know about her gran.

'Well *Nick*, Gran didn't even mention it so how am I supposed to know? I'm not a mind- reader. It happened yesterday, you say. I take it Dr Edwards has been to see her and–'

'I took her to the hospital. They reset it and kept her in overnight but she insisted on coming home today. She told them that her granddaughter would come down and stay with her and I only agreed to bring her home on that basis. I can't be here twenty-four hours a day and–'

'You agreed to ...? Well! I think perhaps you're taking a bit too much responsibility for *my* family, Mr ... *Nick* and I am *so* sorry to have inconvenienced you! As for you not being with her for twenty-four hours a day, I should certainly hope not and–'

'Now who's being sarcastic? It's not an inconvenience. I'd happily look after Mitsy but I have a garden centre to run. I'm short-staffed at the moment and I can't physically be in two places at once. I also have a dog and you may not be aware of this, but Arten doesn't like dogs.'

Carole's mouth fell open. Of all the! Now this man was telling her the likes and dislikes of her grandmother's four-year-old cat, as if she were the stranger in this scenario.

'Of course I know that Arten hates dogs! And his name's Arkenarten. Arten is just his 'pet' name.'

'Pet as is 'cat' you mean?' Nick said, suddenly chuckling. 'I thought you'd named him after that dancer on *Strictly Come Dancing* until Mitsy told me about your fascination with ancient Egypt and that Arkenarten was your favourite of the Pharaohs.'

Carole was surprised not only by the fact that he had a very appealing laugh and that he knew of her love for the ancient Egyptian culture but that he had almost got the name right for one of the dancers on *Strictly*. This conversation was getting more bizarre by the minute.

'I think the dancer's name is Artem, actually. May I speak to Gran please and I'll sort something out with her.'

'She's asleep at the moment. That's why I'm taking the opportunity to call you now. She told me that you were coming down on Friday and that she'd be fine until then. But she won't, not on her own.'

'Look, there's no need for us to discuss this any further. I'm in the bath at the moment but I'll get dressed and come down right now.'

She glanced at her waterproof watch. It was eight-thirty p.m. She closed her eyes tightly and tried to think. She hated asking for favours at the best of times and to ask a favour from this man was going to take a lot but she knew she had no choice.

'Um ... I can be there in a couple of hours,' she continued. 'Is ... is it too much to ask for you ... to find someone to stay with Gran until I get there, please? You can ask Mrs Taylor. She lives at–'

'I know where Matilda lives, and I don't need to ask anyone. I'll stay with Mitsy until you get here. You haven't been drinking have you? Because if you have, I can stay here tonight and you can–'

'How dare you! You're making it sound like I'm an alcoholic or something! Who the hell do you think you are to lecture ... Sorry. That was rude of me and you are doing Gran and me a great favour. No, I haven't had a drink this evening. Well, I had one mouthful of wine but I didn't fancy it so I threw the rest away and had tea so ... I don't know why I'm telling you this. I'm fine to drive. I'll see you around eleven-ish. I just need to pack a bag and sort out a couple of things and then I'll be on my way. Is that okay with you?'

'That's fine. I'll be here.'

'Thank you.'

'There's no need to thank me, Carole. Drive safely. I'll have some hot chocolate ready and waiting.'

Despite the fact that he had disconnected the call, Carole kept the phone to her ear. His voice had changed completely during those last few moments and his words had been both strangely soothing and oddly troubling at the same time. This man seemed to know an awful lot about her, including her preference for hot chocolate in the evening, and she didn't like that one bit.

There was no time to think about that now though. She leapt out of the bath, wrapped a towel around her and

19

dashed downstairs to tell Dom that she had to go and stay with her gran not just for this coming weekend but for the foreseeable future, and that she'd be leaving straight away.

Astonishingly, Dom actually listened to her, probably because it was half time in the football match.

'So ... you're leaving tonight? And I might not see you for ... weeks?'

'Well, you can come and stay at the weekends. Not this weekend obviously because you're going to Manchester but next weekend and all the others – and for Christmas of course.'

'But your gran doesn't let us share a room! That means we won't be having sex for ... ages.'

Carole was tempted to say that they didn't have that much sex now but she didn't.

'We'll sort something out, Dom. I'll speak to Gran. I'm sure she'll let us share a room when she realises we'll be apart for so long. Don't worry. I've got to go though. There's no one else to look after her.'

'What about your mum? Surely Sarah could come down from Scotland and spend some time with her own mother?'

Carole thought that would probably be a recipe for disaster but she smiled encouragingly.

'Yes, I'll call her tomorrow once I see how Gran is. We'll organise something, Dom. Perhaps Mum and I can take it in turns to spend a week or so with Gran. We'll see.'

Dom smiled and grabbed the ends of the towel, tugging Carole towards him.

'Well we'd better have some sex now then, just in case.'

'Dom! I don't have time. I've got to ...' She didn't get any further.

Dom gave the towel one final tug and Carole landed on the sofa beside him, stark naked.

'You smell really sexy, babe,' he said, unzipping his trousers. 'I think your mum's onto a winner with this bath stuff. It's making me really horny.'

Carole wasn't sure whether she should take that as a compliment or an insult. Did she now need to use scented bath products to arouse her boyfriend?

A few minutes later, Dom's cry of 'Yes', *was* directed at her.

CHAPTER THREE

The village clock in Jutsdown was striking midnight as Carole pulled up in front of her gran's weatherboard cottage and parked next to a Land Rover, which she assumed must belong to Nick.

She got out of her car and stood for a few seconds on the gravel driveway, which was wet from the earlier heavy rain shower and bathed in the warm glow of light streaming out from every window. She had spent many years of her life here after her father's untimely death as she and her mother had moved in with her gran a few weeks later, both unable to stay in their family home that held so many wonderful but heartbreaking memories.

She assumed they would move back there one day but her mother sold the house just a year later and they spent the next few years moving from place to place, neither of them able to settle. Her gran's house had been her one haven of comfort in what had become an increasingly lonely world for a teenage girl with a mother who was growing more depressed by the day, but unwilling to admit she had a problem.

Carole pulled her shoulders back and tried to dispel such thoughts from her mind. She had no intention of taking a trip down that particular memory lane.

She grabbed her holdall and marched towards the white-painted diminutive front door, smiling now as happier memories welcomed her. She spotted the ball of black fur she'd named Arkenarten, curled up and balanced rather precariously on one of the many cushions piled on the window seat of the bijou study. That was the room where she had first begun to take her drawing abilities seriously, and she felt a tiny pull on her heartstrings, for Arkenarten, for the dreams of her youth and for the considerable debt of love she owed her gran.

She felt as if a knife were twisting in her chest. Her gran had done so much for her and yet, when her gran needed her, she clearly hadn't felt able to ask Carole to come and stay. What did that say about their relationship now? Carole shook her head as the feelings of guilt overwhelmed her.

The door burst open, making her jump back in surprise.

'Are you coming in or are you going to stand out there all night?'

She found herself staring up into a pair of large dark eyes and yes, she thought, they were as black as coal. They were framed by long lashes as dark as Arkenarten's fur; the face was definitely handsome but looked as if it had been chiselled out of a chunk of rock. His hair was the colour of burnt, roasted chestnuts: black but with flashes of deep red-brown as the light hit it. His tall, well-built body was hunched slightly in the doorway that he almost completely blocked, and an image of Gulliver in Lilliput sprang into her head.

'Well? You're letting the cold in. Perhaps you'd stop looking at me as if you've seen a spectre and come in so that I can shut the door.'

'What? Oh, sorry. It was a dreadful journey. Torrential rain most of the way together with patches of thick fog. That's why I'm late. It's taken me much longer than it should have.'

She stepped inside, babbling away to hide the strange feeling of nervousness she was experiencing.

'Really?' he said, taking her bag from her and tossing it onto the bottom step of the stairs. 'I thought perhaps it'd taken you a while to say goodbye to your boyfriend.'

Carole nearly choked. 'What ... what's that supposed to mean?' God! Did he know she'd stopped to have sex with Dom? This man really was the devil.

Nick shrugged his shoulders. 'You won't be seeing each other for over a week. Mitsy told me he's away this

23

weekend ... on business. You'd naturally want to spend some time saying your goodbyes. I know I would if you were my girlfriend.'

'Oh,' Carole said, trying to avoid eye contact. Something about the way he was looking at her made her feel very uncomfortable and he'd just reminded her that she'd lied to her gran about the weekend and Dom being away on business. Why hadn't she just told the truth about that?

'Well,' she continued, 'naturally we ... took a while, but I also had to pack my bag – the one you so kindly just tossed on the stairs. There could be something breakable in there, you know.'

He glanced from her face to the bag and back again. 'Is there?'

Carole stiffened and raised her eyes to his, tilting her chin up and tossing a long tendril of titian hair over her shoulder. 'No. But that's not the point. You shouldn't throw people's bags around as if they were ... sacks of compost or something.'

His eyes held hers for a brief moment before his lips curved into a strange smile.

'If that had been a sack of compost,' he said, 'I can assure you I wouldn't have thrown it. Compost sacks are known to split open and spill the contents all over the floor. I think your underwear is perfectly safe in that leather holdall.'

Carole felt the colour rush to her checks. 'My ...! Excuse me, but I'd rather *not* discuss my clothing with you. Where's Gran and how is she?' As she strode past him into the sitting room, she was sure she could hear him chuckling under his breath and it infuriated her.

Her gran was nowhere to be seen. She turned to face him and was disconcerted to see him leaning against the doorway, his arms folded in front of him, and his dark eyes watching her intently. The blue, red, white and pink checked shirt he was wearing hung open over a plain navy

24

T-shirt that strained across his broad chest and she had to stop herself from saying, 'Wow!' The sooner he left the better, she thought.

'Where's Gran?'

'Don't panic,' he replied more softly than before, obviously seeing the worry in her eyes. 'She's upstairs tucked up in bed. I was just going to make her a cup of tea.'

'How did she get upstairs with a broken leg?'

'I carried her. She's as light as a feather even with her leg in plaster.'

'Oh!' A vision of being carried up to bed by this man popped into her head but she quickly chased it out again. Her gran and Josie were right. He did look like a romantic fiction hero.

'Would you like a cup of tea or would you still prefer the hot chocolate?' he asked.

'Er ... hot chocolate, but there's no need for you to trouble yourself further. I can take it from here. You've got a dog, you said ... and possibly a girlfriend to get home to.'

'Just the dog. His name's Nicodemus. And it's no trouble.'

'Wasn't he a biblical teacher in Jesus' time?'

Nick raised his dark brows. 'My dog? Not as far as I know. I don't believe in reincarnation – or the Bible for that matter. You'd have to ask him.'

Carole tutted impatiently. 'Do you try to make a joke of everything? You know that's not what I meant. I meant Nicodemus was the name of ... oh, it doesn't matter. You can go now, thank you.'

Nick smirked, stood up straight and doffed an imaginary cap. 'Yes mi'lady. Thank you, mi'lady. I'll just say goodnight to Mitsy and I'll get out of your way.' He turned and took the stairs three at a time.

Carole leant her head to one side to watch the long, athletic legs make short work of the steep, narrow stairs, and she shook herself mentally. What was the matter with her? She was clearly overtired. Why was she ogling this irritating man's rear view when her darling Dom was now sitting in their house, alone and possibly missing her already?

As she walked into the kitchen, she realised just how ridiculous that thought was. Dom was probably fast asleep on the sofa, dreaming about his upcoming trip to Manchester to see *Rob The Rich,* whilst the TV no doubt was still blaring in front of his long, lithe, prostrate body.

And she was still thinking about Dom's body but not just *his* body, when Nick appeared at the kitchen door just a few minutes later.

'Mitsy's fast asleep and I didn't want to wake her. She knows you were coming down so there's no need to tell her you've arrived – unless you want to, of course. I'll be off if there's nothing else you want me to do for you before I go.'

Carole's cheeks burned as she felt her eyes travel the length of Nick's frame. She had no idea why but she was actually wondering if he would have only taken five minutes to ... say goodbye if he had been in Dom's place earlier. Too scared to speak in case her voice betrayed her thoughts, she just shook her head.

He eyed her curiously and grinned, as if he were reading her mind. 'Okay, I'll say goodnight then. I'll pop by first thing in the morning to check on you both. Pleasant dreams.'

'Er ... same to you,' she managed to say.

Nick disappeared into the hallway only to reappear at the door seconds later. 'It was lovely to finally meet you, Carole. Mitsy has told me so much about you that I feel I know you already. I'm glad we'll be seeing a lot more of each other.'

Carole watched in silence as the sexiest smile she'd ever seen spread across his decidedly kissable mouth and an image of them ripping one another's clothes off popped briefly into her head.

He turned and marched towards the front door and Carole grabbed the edge of the worktop to stop herself from running after him. Not that she really thought she would. Although ...

Good grief! She really was turning into her mother. She was now the sort of woman who chased after any sexy male she met – whether she actually liked them or not!

'Bye! And thank you!' she yelled seconds before she heard the front door close.

She made herself some hot chocolate and sat at the kitchen table, lost in thought until Arkenarten finally slinked in to greet her. He jumped up onto her lap, purring like a washing machine as Carole stroked him under his chin. He responded by rubbing his large furry head against her cheek.

In the space of just one evening, her emotions had been sent spiralling with thoughts of three very different men and she wasn't absolutely sure how she felt about any of them.

There was Sebastian, her past boyfriend and a man she still had feelings for in spite of saying she didn't. He'd broken her heart so badly that she had been on the verge of a nervous breakdown and if it hadn't been for her gran taking care of her, she probably would have had one. It had taken her years to get over him sufficiently to be able to start dating other men.

That's when she'd met Dominic, her present boyfriend and soon to be fiancé, whom she sometimes felt was more interested in his career, the television, his friends and, well everything else other than her. She had spent the last few months hoping he would propose but did she really, honestly want to spend the rest of her life with him? Especially now that Sebastian was back and would soon be single again. She loved Dom; she was sure of that, but not as much as she had loved Sebastian all those years ago.

And now there was this Nick. A man she knew nothing whatsoever about and had disliked from the moment her gran had mentioned his name – and having met him, felt that she probably still did. There was definitely something not quite right about him. He was almost too good to be true. He'd probably turn out to be one of those gigolos or something. A man who preyed on old and vulnerable women to get either their money or sex – or both. And yet she couldn't deny that from the first moment she set eyes on him, she had been ... mesmerised. That was the only word for it. Perhaps he really did have some strange magical powers of some sort.

She grinned at her own foolishness. 'Magical powers indeed. What am I going on about Arkenarten? And you are the most gorgeous male I know. I really wish all the others were as uncomplicated as you. Right, I think it's time you and I went to bed, young man.'

He jumped off her lap and headed for the door and she followed him upstairs. She looked in on her gran and saw she was sound asleep so she headed for the room that was considered 'hers'; one of the three spare bedrooms that overlooked the back garden and the ancient apple tree.

Arkenarten jumped up on the bed and stretched himself out, rolling over several times before curling up in the middle of the duvet.

'Typical man,' she said, getting undressed and falling into bed beside him, suddenly feeling too tired to even try to move him over. It had been a very peculiar evening and she had the strangest feeling that things were going to get decidedly more complicated from here on in.

CHAPTER FOUR

Carole woke with a start, unsure at first where she was but certain that she could hear someone moving about downstairs. She sat bolt upright and instinctively reached out for Dominic but remembering she was at her gran's, for some reason she glanced at her watch instead. The room was too dark for her to read the display so she fumbled for the lamp. Switching it on, she noticed in the dim light from the energy saving bulb, that Arkenarten was gone.

She heard the creak of the stairs and the sound of footsteps approaching her bedroom. She pulled the duvet up under her chin as if that might protect her, momentarily freezing with fear. It couldn't be her gran, not with a broken leg. The footsteps were sure; too steady and moving far too quickly. Should she try to get out of bed and hide? Should she ...? The knock on her half-open door was followed by a voice she vaguely recognised.

'Are you decent? May I come in?'

'Y ... yes ... no!' she shrieked, wondering why Nick wanted to come into her bedroom when it was clearly still the middle of the night.

The 'no' was too late. Nick shoved open the door and switched on the light.

'Good morning,' he said walking towards the bed and placing a mug of steaming coffee on the bedside table. 'Milk, no sugar. What's wrong? You look as if you've seen a ghost.'

'You scared me half to death! What are you doing here?'

'Apart from bringing you coffee, you mean? I told you I'd call in this morning. Did you sleep well? You look tired. It's early so you can go back to sleep for an hour or so if you want. I'm taking Nicodemus for a walk but I'll pop back before I go in to work.'

'Are ... are you always this ... jolly in the morning?' Carole asked, feeling rather irritated not just for being woken up at what she was sure was an ungodly hour but also because he had said that she looked tired.

'Sorry. Bad night?'

'Short night. What time is it anyway?'

'Five-thirty,' he said, grinning broadly.

'Five-thirty! Good grief! Do you usually wake people up at this time of night?'

'It's morning. And most of the people I know are usually wide awake by now. Mitsy was awake long before I arrived. She called me and asked me to bring a few things round.'

'What do you mean, Gran called you?'

Nick gave her a curious look but the grin was still firmly in place. 'I'm not sure I can give you a better explanation other than she picked up the phone and dialled my number.'

'Very funny,' Carole said, running a hand through her hair and getting it caught in a tangle. Damn, she thought. She could just imagine what her hair looked like this morning and for some absurd reason, she found herself wishing Nick hadn't been able to see her in such a dishevelled state. Which brought her to another thought; one she voiced this time. 'How did you get in? I'm certain I locked the door last night.'

'You did. I have a key.'

'You have a ...? Why doesn't that surprise me as much as it should? Did Gran give it to you?'

He tipped his head to one side and seemed to study her face for a second. 'No, I stole it when she wasn't looking.'

'There's no need for sarcasm.' Carole shifted her position but still clung to the duvet as if it afforded some protection from his dark, penetrating eyes.

'Then don't ask foolish questions. Drink your coffee before it gets cold.'

'Don't tell me what to do! But ... thank you for making

it.'

'My pleasure. It's a lovely morning,' he said, strolling across to the window and pulling back the curtains a fraction to reveal an almost completely black sky scattered with rhinestone-like twinkling stars.

Carole grimaced. 'How on earth can you tell that? It's still pitch black out there. Don't tell me. You have a feeling for such things. It's in your blood or something.' She grabbed the mug of coffee and took several large gulps. It was delicious she grudgingly admitted to herself.

He turned to her and chuckled. A deep, throaty, sexy sound that warmed Carole far more than the coffee did.

'No. I heard the weather forecast on the radio on my way over here. Dry, cold and sunny although there's a possibility of snow showers this evening. Perfect late November weather I'd say.'

'Hmm! If you like snow I suppose and not being able to get anywhere because the roads haven't been gritted properly. That's certainly not my idea of perfect weather.'

'I love snow, although I'll admit it may hold up deliveries but it doesn't stop me from getting where I want to go. Have Land Rover, will travel, or whatever the saying is. You're welcome to come for a walk with Nicodemus and me if you like.'

'Thank you but no. I make it a rule never to go out until the streets are properly aired and I can actually see where I'm going. As it doesn't get light until about eight a.m. at this time of year, I'm not venturing out before nine.'

The grin broadened. 'It's only twenty minutes until dawn but I accept it's not sunrise for another two hours so okay, I'll leave you to it. I'll be back in about an hour. Will you be up by then?'

'No.'

'You're not a morning person are you?'

'No.'

Their eyes met and the gleam in his made her stomach

feel as if it wanted to do a little pirouette. She wondered what he was thinking but she dared not ask. From what little she knew of him so far, he'd probably tell her, and she might not like what she heard.

'Okay, I'll see you later,' he said. 'By the way, I've fed Arten and I've brought some eggs and a jar of honey. They're on the kitchen table. I'll nip into Cindy's Bakery on the way back and pick up a fresh loaf.'

'Don't tell me the local shops are open at this ungodly hour? Or did you drive all the way to Tesco?'

He looked at her as if she were mad. Cindy's Bakery opens at six which is why I'll go there on my way back, but the eggs are from my hens and the honey, from my bees.'

'You ... you keep hens and bees?' This man was like no other she had ever met and she wondered how many more little surprises he had up his sleeve.

'Why is that so surprising?' he asked.

'Oh. Er ... no reason I suppose. I ... I've just never met a man who keeps hens and bees before, that's all.'

'Yes,' he said, 'it's a heady combination.'

She glowered at him. 'There's no need to make fun of me. I live in London remember, and, well, beekeepers and henkeepers are not something you see on the Tube.'

'How can you tell? You shouldn't judge a book by its cover you know. Lots of people are diversifying and keeping livestock or growing their own produce. Just because a person wears a suit to the office, it doesn't mean they aren't mucking out a pig pen in their garden when they get home.'

Carole shuddered at the thought of it.

'I take it you have an aversion to pigs, by the face you're pulling.'

Her head shot up and her eyes met his.

'No. Pigs are fine – at a distance of course. It's mud I have a problem with. Or dirt of any kind, come to that.'

The grin disappeared to be replaced by a questioning

32

frown. 'Really?' he said. 'You're not going to enjoy helping out in the garden centre very much then, are you? I must dash. See you later. There's more coffee in the pot downstairs.' With a final brief smile, he pulled the door to.

'Thank you ... I think,' Carole said, letting her head flop back against the pillow. It shot back up again as if she had suffered whiplash. 'What do you mean, helping out in the garden centre?' she yelled after him.

He didn't answer. All she heard was him calling out goodbye to her gran and the sound of his walking boots as they hit a few of the stairs which he was clearly bounding down.

What on earth had he meant by that, she wondered and where the hell did the man get his energy from? Her mind started to wander in a very unwelcome direction and she tutted at her own waywardness.

Assuming he was just being sarcastic with his remark about the garden centre and her helping out there, she savoured the final mouthfuls of coffee as she heard the front door close. She'd get up in a minute and go and see her gran she told herself, but she needed a few seconds to get her head together. What was it about this guy that made her feel so ... so ... uncomfortable?

And why had her gran apparently given him the run of the house? She couldn't stay in bed she decided; she had to go and see her gran and find out exactly what was going on.

***

'Hello Gran!' Carole said, dashing to her gran's bedside and hugging her tightly. 'What on earth happened to you and why didn't you tell me when you called yesterday? In fact, why didn't you call me as soon as it happened?'

Mitsy kissed the top of Carole's bent head and ruffled her long mop of titian waves.

'I didn't want to worry you, sweetheart. I knew if I told

33

you, you'd jump in your car and rush down and I know how busy you are so–'

'Gran! I'm never too busy to come to you when you need me. Please don't ever think that again. I know I don't come and see you as often as I should and I'm really sorry for that. I just don't know where the time goes these days.'

'I know, dear and it gets worse as we get older. Never mind that though. I'm fine, and Nick took really good care of me so there wasn't any need to trouble you. I told him I could cope on my own and that I could sleep downstairs on the sofa bed in the study but he wouldn't hear of it. I said that you were coming down at the weekend and I'd be fine but I knew he wasn't happy. I didn't know he'd called you though and I gave him a telling off for that but he means well so I can't be cross with him. Besides, it is lovely to see you, sweetheart.'

Carole couldn't imagine anyone telling Nick off, least of all her petite grandmother. She struggled to picture how he would have reacted to that – and failed.

'It's lovely to see you too, Gran. Are you sure you're okay? Are you in pain? Can I get you anything?'

'No, I'm fine. Honestly. I can't feel a thing and Nick's been giving me some of his home-made remedy. He swears I'll be up on my pins and dancing around the sitting room with him before I know it.'

'Dancing around ...! Just how well do you know this Nick, Gran? I mean, are you sure it's wise to let him have a key to your house? He gave me quite a start this morning when he brought me up a cup of coffee.'

Mitsy chuckled and patted Carole's hand. 'Coffee can be very scary dear, although not the way Nick makes it. His is heavenly, but then so many things about him are.'

'Gran, I'm serious! He behaves as if he owns the place.'

'Nonsense, Carole. He's a godsend. I don't know how I would have coped without his help these last few months and ... well never mind that. I think you've got entirely the wrong impression about him – and his intentions. You'll soon see he's one of the nicest, kindest men you're ever likely to meet. Good heavens, as you say, he even brought you a cup of coffee in bed this morning! How many men do you know who would do that?'

Carole thought about it. She couldn't remember the last time Dominic had although she'd taken him coffee in bed hundreds of times. Actually, she now realised he never had, but he worked long hours in his office in the City as a lawyer so he needed his sleep. She worked from home and, as he often told her, she could take a nap whenever she needed to. That sounded oddly patronising now that she mulled it over.

Neither had Sebastian, but they hadn't lived together or ever been in a situation where he could have done so. During the four years they were dating, he lived in the village with his parents, and Carole, at that time, lived in the village with her gran. Other than the few times they went away on holiday together, they were never in the same house in the morning. And, unlike Nick, Sebastian was never given a key.

'Lots of men do that, Gran. Coffee in bed is nothing special,' she said in what even she recognised as a feeble attempt to downplay Nick's apparent charms. 'You didn't answer the question though. How well do you really know him and why does he have a key?'

Mitsy sighed as if the weight of the world were on her tiny shoulders. Shoulders that, Carole was only now noticing, seemed even smaller and rather more fragile than they had the last time she'd seen them. A sudden horrifying thought crept into her mind.

'Gran,' she said, almost too scared to ask, 'are you unwell? Other than the broken leg, I mean. And how did you break your leg anyway?'

Carole watched as a faraway look crept into her gran's pale blue eyes.

35

Mitsy sighed again. 'I'm not as young as I used to be, sweetheart. Nothing works as well as I expect it to. I'm not ill but ... well, I did go through a rather bad patch, health-wise recently and my eyesight's not what it was and ... I do silly things every once in a while. I ... I have little accidents. The last three months have been particularly bad and if it hadn't been for Nick ...' Her voice trailed off on yet another sigh.

A dreadful, somewhat terrifying and bizarrely random idea popped into Carole's head from nowhere. She had thought this Nick seemed too good to be true – and perhaps he was. Not many men of his age – and looks – would spend their time with a woman old enough to be their grandmother unless they were either a relation, a saint or they could get something out of it.

She had often read about people who took advantage of vulnerable old ladies and ... hurt them, both physically and emotionally. Could it be possible that Nick was doing this to her gran? Victims of that kind of abuse were always too scared to speak out against their abusers and often gave the impression that the abusers were holier than thou and the victims were the ones in the wrong. Was that why her gran seemed so ... unsure of herself, so nervous?

She took Mitsy's hands in hers and squeezed them tightly. 'Gran,' she said as gently but firmly as she could, 'I'm here now and I'm going to be staying for the foreseeable future. If ... if there's anything you want to tell me, anything that is worrying you or anyone who is frightening you in any way, you can tell me and I'll deal with it. If ... if someone is forcing you to hand over money or something. I'll make sure you're safe, I promise you. No one will ever be able to hurt you again. Not Nick or anyone else.'

She saw the confused and startled look in Mitsy's eyes and the subsequent look of horror as Mitsy glanced towards the door.

Carole turned swiftly and a mixture of fear and anger took hold as she saw Nick, standing in the doorway, a murderous expression in his dark eyes and his jaw clenched so tightly that the muscles in his now ruddy face seemed about to burst out from under his skin.

Carole jumped up from the edge of the bed but still held one of her gran's hands.

'How dare you just barge in here without knocking!' she yelled, attack being the best form of defence in her opinion.

'Carole!' Mitsy shrieked. 'No!'

Nick's eyes travelled the length of Carole's body and the corners of his mouth curled in obvious contempt.

'I think,' he said, his voice cold and hard with clearly suppressed fury, 'you've been watching too much television. If you're actually suggesting that I broke your grandmother's leg or have hurt her in any way to get money from her, let me assure you, you're very much mistaken. I have no idea what can have put such a ludicrous notion into your head. I came back to ask if you wanted anything besides a loaf of bread whilst I'm at the bakery but as my presence seems unwelcome to you, I'll go. In future, I'll ring the doorbell when I visit – assuming I'll still be allowed to visit while you're here. Mitsy, you know where I am if you need me.'

He turned on his heel and marched from the room and out of the house in a matter of seconds, slamming the front door behind him.

Carole was shaking and she turned to her gran who seemed to be in a stunned state of shock.

Mitsy raised tearful eyes to Carole's face and in a strangled tone asked, 'What ... what just happened, Carole? What have you done? How on earth could you possibly think such a thing?'

'I ... well ... he just seems too good to be true and ... and he's only thirty-something and ... and very good-looking, and ... well, why else would a man like that want to spend so much time with ...?'

'An old woman like me? Is that what you were going to say? I'm shocked, Carole, truly shocked. To even think for one minute that I'd ever let any man control me or physically abuse me and not do something about it is beyond crazy, but to think that Nick had ... had actually hurt me. Stolen from me. That he'd broken my leg! Well! That's the sort of fanciful notion your mother would get. A real drama queen that one has become, but you! I had thought better of you, my girl.'

'I'm sorry, Gran! But try to see it from my point of view. I don't even know that you've broken your leg until I get a call from someone I've never met telling me to get down here and look after you because he's too busy, and when I get here, I find he's got the run of the place and you're looking like you ... well, less than your usual spritely self.'

Mitsy tutted. 'Of course, I'm not looking spritely. I've got a broken leg! And I'll admit I have lost a bit of weight over the last few months but I'd have lost a lot more if Nick hadn't been popping in with little treats for me and making sure I was eating at least one good meal a day. He's been an absolute wonder and how do you repay him? You accuse him of battering me! What's more, Carole, if he really *were* some felonious brute with evil intent, why the devil would he have phoned you and asked you to come and stay with me? That's the last thing he would have wanted. I'm very disappointed in you, Carole. Perhaps it's partly my fault for not telling you what's been going on with me and I realise I'll have to do that, but for now the most important thing is that you go and apologise to Nick. Without delay.'

'But ... Gran!'

'No, Carole! I mean it. I'm sure you meant well and I know you thought you were acting in my best interest but believe me, you could not have made a bigger mistake if you'd tried. You must apologise. Right now!'

CHAPTER FIVE

Carole trudged along the pavement, feeling very sorry for herself and more than a little foolish as the village clock struck seven on a cold, grey and overcast morning.

So much for a perfect sunny day, she thought, hugging her coat more tightly around her and burying her chin in the folds of the upturned collar. How she wished she had worn a scarf and gloves.

She wondered exactly how one apologises to a man for accusing him of beating up a little old lady when he was in fact, being more of a knight in shining armour. Damn the man! But he'd got the weather forecast wrong so at least he wasn't perfect, although to be fair, he had said he'd heard that on the radio.

'Oh! I'm so sorry,' she said, bumping into someone as she rounded a corner. 'I wasn't looking where I was ... Sebastian! Oh my God! Sebastian. It's ... it's you!'

Sebastian looked as shocked as Carole felt.

'Hello Carole,' he said, staring at her as if she were a mirage. He leant forward to kiss her on the cheek but missed and planted a kiss just behind her ear in her thick, wavy hair.

'Sebastian,' she said again, unable to say anything else.

'You haven't changed a bit,' he remarked as his bright blue eyes scanned all five feet four inches of her. 'What ... what are you doing in Jutsdown? Visiting Grandma Mitsy I guess. Did she tell you I was back? We bumped into one another the other day, just a day or so after I got home. I'm rambling, aren't I? It's just so lovely to see you.'

Carole gave her head a quick shake. 'Sorry, I'm not quite with it this morning. Um, yes I'm visiting Gran and yes, she did briefly mention that you were back but that's not why I'm here. I mean ... that is ... Gran's broken her leg and I've come to stay ... to look after her.'

'Really? When did that happen? She was fine when I saw her.'

'Yes. It happened on Tuesday apparently but I didn't hear about it until yesterday. And even then not from Gran. I came down last night and ... now I'm the one who's rambling.'

They stared at one another in silence for several seconds as if they were both studying a work of art and trying to read the hidden meaning behind the brushstrokes.

'I'm staying with my parents,' he said, 'and back, working at Dad's estate agency.'

'So Josie told me,' she replied.

He nodded. 'The village drums still work then?'

'Not as loudly as they used to but yes, they still work.'

Another momentary silence.

'You really do look wonderful, Carole.'

'So do you, Sebastian.'

'I ... I've often thought about you,' he said. 'Wondered how different my life would be if ... well you know.'

She nodded. 'Me too.'

'I made a big mistake.'

'Did you?' she said, silently praying that her voice didn't sound as eager as her heart felt.

'Yes.'

'Oh.'

'I ... I'm getting a divorce.' He stepped a little closer to her.

She swallowed and blinked several times. 'I heard.'

'Josie?' he asked.

'Gran,' she replied.

'Ah, I don't think she's forgiven me yet.'

'No, I don't think she has.'

Another step closer. 'Have you, Carole? Can you?'

'I ... I don't know. I ...' Carole looked deep into his eyes, and saw the old Sebastian.

'I've never stopped loving you, Carole. Some part of me stayed here when I got on that plane. The best part, I think. I've come back to see if I can find it.'

'Oh.' Her voice sounded strangled even to her and alarm bells were ringing in her ears. She realised it was her mobile and it was as if someone had poured cold water on a spark just as it was bursting into flame. 'Sorry,' she said, grabbing her phone from her bag and seeing Dominic's smiling face looking accusingly up at her on the screen. She had to save herself. 'It ... it's my fiancé,' she lied and she watched the colour drain from Sebastian's handsome face.

'Oh! I ...' he seemed lost for words now.

Carole smiled apologetically and answered the call. 'Hi Dom,' she said trying to sound relaxed but feeling far from it.

'Hi babe, how's things? I thought you might have called me to let me know you arrived safely.'

'Oh! Sorry dar ... Dom. It was an awful drive and I was so tired when I got here. I was going to call you later but ... I'm running an errand for Gran and I've lost track of time. Are ... are you on your way to work?' She stole a look at Sebastian from the corner of her eyes and thought that he was looking rather impatient.

'Yes. I've got meetings all day so I won't get a chance to talk to you until late tonight. Is it okay if I call around eleven? Will you still be up?'

'What? Er ... yes. Yes, that's fine.'

'Okay, I'll speak to you later. I ... I missed you in bed last night.'

'Really? I mean, yes, me too. Have a good day. I'll talk to you later.'

'Oh! Okay. You're clearly busy. Catch you later, hun. Love you.'

'Mmm. Same here. Bye.'

She pressed the end call button and raised guilt-ridden eyes to Sebastian's piercingly cynical, blue ones.

41

'Forgive me,' he said, 'and it may be none of my business, but it doesn't sound like *True Love* on your part. Our conversations were never that brief and we lived a five-minute walk from one another.'

Carole bit her lower lip and squared her shoulders. She felt a need to champion Dominic and oddly enough, to put Sebastian in his place. She hadn't seen him for ten years and yet in a matter of seconds, he'd managed to reignite feelings in her that she had thought were firmly under control.

'Our conversations may not have been brief, but your notes certainly were.'

She saw him flinch and felt a tiny pang of regret.

'Ouch!' he said. 'Well, I suppose I did deserve that. I'm really, truly one hundred and fifty per cent sorry for the pain I must have caused you, Carole. I ... I still don't know why I did what I did. I can only apologise ... and hope that you'll let me make it up to you.'

'It's fine, Seb,' she lied. 'It was a long time ago and whilst I will admit that I was devastated, completely, thoroughly and utterly, I'm over it now and I don't bear you any ill will.'

His eyes seemed to bore into her and she clung to her phone like a talisman warding off evil.

'I'm not sure that's what I was hoping to hear,' he said, his eyes affirming the sadness in his voice. 'I think I was hoping ... well ... it doesn't matter what I was hoping, does it? You're engaged and I'm clearly too late. Aren't I?'

She couldn't help but notice the inflection of doubt at the end of that sentence and her heart jumped on the opportunity.

'Well, when I said that I'm engaged, that isn't strictly true. What I meant to say is that I'm practically engaged. Dominic is going to ask me to marry him any day now and...' Her voice trailed off as she realised just how foolish her words sounded.

A beacon of hope lit up his eyes. 'So ... it may not be too late then? For me, I mean. For ... us.'

'Hello Carole! How lovely to see you again.'

Neither she nor Sebastian had heard his father approach them from the car park across the road.

'Are you staying with Mitsy for a few days?' he continued, clearly oblivious to the situation he'd stepped into. 'I hear she's had an accident and broken her leg. Do give me a shout if there's anything I can do, won't you? You two catching up on old times, are you?'

Carole smiled sheepishly. 'Um ... hello Mr Jarvis. It's good to see you too. Yes, I'll be staying with Gran for several weeks I should think. She needs someone to look after her.'

'Yes, she's not getting any younger. I was surprised to see her working at the garden centre to be honest but she seems to love it there and Nick's a fine lad. He usually takes good care of her. He must have been mortified when she fell off that ladder although why she was climbing a ladder I'll never know but you know Mitsy, never one to ask someone to do something if she thinks she can do it herself.'

'Yes, that's true. Gran's always ... wait a minute! Did you say she's been working? At the garden centre? And climbing ladders!'

'Yes, I thought you ... oh, she didn't tell you. Well, that's Mitsy for you. Must get on. Do pop round for coffee some time. Penelope would love to see you.'

Carole was too stunned to reply.

'So Grandma Mitsy's got a toy boy then?' Sebastian said after his father had walked on. 'I haven't met this Nick guy yet but everyone seems to think he's the best thing since sliced bread. He's only in his mid-thirties though, from what I hear. Is he after her money, do you think?'

'What? Sorry, Sebastian, I have to go.'

'Oh ... okay. May I call you?'

'Yes. Yes, any time.'

'I'll be in the pub tonight if you fancy joining me,' he said.

Carole was already hurrying down the road but she called back over her shoulder. 'I'll have to see how things go.'

Meeting Sebastian for a drink was not top on the list of her priorities right now. She had to get to Josie's before she left for school, and find out how long her gran had been working at the garden centre and exactly why Josie had failed to tell her that too.

**

'I thought you knew!' Josie said when Carole banged on her door ten minutes later, demanding to know why she'd kept that piece of news a secret.

'Based on what?' Carole asked, stepping into the hall of Josie's small, flint cottage. 'When I spoke to you yesterday I made it clear that I didn't know this Nick guy from Adam. Surely it must have occurred to you that if I hadn't heard about him, I also didn't know Gran was working for him?'

'Well, when you put it like that, I suppose it should have,' Josie said, leading the way into the kitchen where she had been having her breakfast. 'But I can honestly say that it didn't. Your gran's been in and out of there since the day he opened it, even before he opened it, come to think of it. At first she just seemed to be hanging around and ... well, I think I assumed she just liked the company, living on her own as she does. I don't know when she actually started working there. Or whether she really does. Perhaps she still just hangs out there. I know I would, given half the chance.'

Carole pulled out a chair and sat at the kitchen table. 'That's not helping, Josie. I'm supposed to be apologising to this guy for accusing him of beating up Gran and for possibly trying to steal her money or something and now I find out he's actually her employer! No wonder she—'

'Excuse me! Did you just say you accused Nick of violence towards your gran? And theft? Good God, Carole, that's almost funny! Nick? Violent? And a criminal?'

'Okay, don't make a big deal out of it. Gran's already read me the riot act. The point is – and I don't know how many times I have to keep saying this – I know nothing about the guy. I'm beginning to feel as if I've walked into a remake of *The Stepford Wives* or something. Everyone keeps telling me how wonderful he is but until yesterday, I hadn't heard his name more than once when Gran says she told me he pruned her apple tree. Don't laugh at that and don't make dirty jokes about my gran!'

'I wasn't going to! Although you must admit ... okay, I'm sorry. I'll shut up.'

'I'm worried, Josie and I'm convinced he's hiding something. I don't care what anyone says. I've just got a feeling about him. My insides are definitely giving me warning signals.'

Josie handed Carole a mug of coffee and sat down opposite her hugging a bowl of cereal to her chest. 'Are you sure that your insides aren't giving you some other sort of signals? Mine definitely go all weird every time I see him.'

'Absolutely not!'

'I can tell when you're lying, you know. You fancy him too, don't you?'

'No! I'm practically engaged to Dominic. I admit that I did think he was rather good-looking but if I fancy anyone other than Dom, it's Sebastian. God, I nearly threw myself in his arms just now in the middle of the street without giving Dom a second thought!'

'You did what?' Josie said through a mouthful of *Frosties*. 'Are you telling me you've seen Seb already? I thought you only arrived around midnight last night! Bloody hell, Carole, you have been busy!'

Carole tutted. 'I bumped into him this morning, on my

way to apologise to Nick. And I do mean literally, bumped into him. We got talking and ... well, I feel awful saying this Josie but it was just like old times. As if none of the last ten years have happened. And he even told me that he made a huge mistake and he's been regretting it ever since. He still loves me, Josie, can you believe it? Sebastian Jarvis actually still loves me.'

'Really? He told you that ... this morning ... in the street? He actually told you he still loved you? And that's a good thing because ...?' Josie didn't look convinced.

'Of course it's a good thing! Why wouldn't it be?'

'Well, because as you keep saying, you are practically engaged to Dom, the guy you're actually living with at the moment, so that's one minor problem. Then there's the fact that Seb does still have a wife, which leads me nicely on to the real crux of the matter. The guy left you at the altar ten years ago, ran off to Aus using money from your joint bank account, and married someone else a few months later. You're not seriously telling me that you would resume a relationship with a man who broke your heart without so much as a backward glance. And caused you to nearly have a breakdown, let's not forget.'

Carole glared at her friend. 'Trust you to remind me of that.'

'Well, clearly someone has to! Look Carole, don't get me wrong, I like Seb, I always did but you were devastated when he left. It took you years to get over him and whilst I'm not absolutely convinced that Dom is the love of your life, I think he's a far safer bet than Sebastian.'

'He made a mistake, Josie! Surely everyone's entitled to be forgiven for making a mistake?'

'Fine. Forgive him. Just don't get involved with him again, that's all. If you're having doubts about Dom, I can understand that but please, don't convince yourself that you're still in love with Sebastian because you'd have to be insane to feel like that.'

Carole sighed and hugged the mug of coffee. 'Then I think I have to say I'm insane, Josie, because that's exactly what I do think – and I'm not sure that I ever really stopped.'

Josie slumped forward on the table. 'And Dom? What about him?'

'That's the real problem, Josie. I love him too.'

'Oh dear God! It's not even eight o'clock in the morning! You've only been back in the village for one night, and I need a drink already. Look, I've got to get to work. Why don't I pop round this evening and we can have a proper talk about all this ... over a bottle of wine?'

'Um ... I think Sebastian asked me to meet him in the pub,' Carole said.

'And you're going? You're actually going on a date with Sebastian the day after you get here? What about your gran? I thought you were supposed to be looking after her.'

'Oh, that's true! Perhaps I'd better suggest Sebastian comes round to gran's instead. But it's not a date! Just to talk, that's all. Nothing else.'

Josie stared at Carole in silence for a full ten seconds.

'Your gran will just *love* that idea. Well, I think you're right about one thing. You really are insane. I'm going to work. Haven't you got some apologising to do?'

'Oh bugger! I'd almost forgotten about that.'

47

CHAPTER SIX

Carole had been to the old plant nursery on the outskirts of Jutsdown village, hundreds of times, as a child and young teenager. The nursery was one of her dad's favourite places and he'd taken Carole there to help him choose plants for the sprawling garden of their Victorian villa many times over the years.

After her father's death Carole avoided the place like the plague. Even when she and her mum moved back to the village to live with her gran again, she couldn't bring herself to visit it. It had taken all her will power to go there when she returned to the village after finishing her art and design course in Edinburgh. She was twenty-one, single and about to embark on the adventure of a lifetime – starting her own illustration and graphic design business from the study of her gran's house funded by the £5,000 her gran gave her for her twenty-first birthday.

This was a new beginning and as such, it was time to put the past behind her. Somehow she felt she needed to. And part of that meant visiting all the places she had known and loved; places she'd been with her dad; places where she'd been truly happy.

One of those places was the old plant nursery. It was as if this was the final ghost she needed to lay to rest. She walked through the gate that day, spotted Sebastian and took the first step on the path of what she later believed to be *True Love*.

They'd been friends for most of her life, of course. They both grew up in the village and Jutsdown wasn't exactly large. At the last count there were still only just over two hundred people living there. But she and Sebastian had never been anything more than friends – until that summer. That wonderful, glorious, blissful summer when she'd walked into the nursery to buy herself a plant for her new 'office'– just one plant – as a memento of her dad, and ... Sebastian had smiled at her.

His eyes were the brightest blue she'd ever seen; she couldn't remember them being that blue at school. And had his hair been quite so fair? Or quite that wavy? It fell in a tumble of curls across his suntanned temples.

She noticed he watched her move from one bed to another; one long wooden bench-table to the next until he asked if he could help. He wasn't working there; he too had just popped in, and his knowledge of plants was less than hers but his enthusiasm was infectious. He followed that up with an offer of a cup of coffee, followed by several long, passionate kisses, followed by–

'What have you come to accuse me of now? Trying to kill the cat?'

Nick's acerbic tone brought Carole back from her daydream with a rather unpleasant jolt and she almost forgot that she was there to apologise. She hadn't even realised that she'd walked through the open gates of the new garden centre and she looked about her as if she were drowning in an ocean with neither ship nor shore in sight.

'I ... oh ... ah ... um.'

Nick's dark brows arched. 'Smell the blood of an Englishman,' he said. 'Have you come here to quote historical quatrains and nursery rhymes?' Suddenly a smile crept across his mouth. 'Hmm. That's actually rather amusing I suppose as this was historically, a nursery – and I do sell beans, as it happens.'

'What? Oh, I see. Jack and the Beanstalk. But wasn't that "Fee-fi-fo-fum"? Anyway,' she said, shaking her head as if she thought the conversation were absurd, 'No. And I haven't come here to accuse you of anything either. Although having said that, I would like to know what my grandmother was doing up a ladder at her age and what her role here is, exactly.'

'Why don't you ask her?' he said, looking away from her, grabbing a bag of compost and tossing it onto his shoulder as if it were a speck of dust.

'Because I've only just found out,' Carole replied, screwing up her nose and stepping backwards as tiny black grains of earth like jet black flakes of snow fell from the corner of the bag.

'That doesn't explain why you're asking me and not her,' he said, disappearing into the distance in just a few long strides.

Carole followed after him sidestepping piles of upturned terracotta pots, lumps of wood, half open bags of bark, discarded, dirty tools and a myriad other hazards and affronts to cleanliness.

'Because I came here to apologise and bumped into someone who told me how Gran broke her leg. As I was on my way here anyway, I thought I may as well ask you.'

'You came here to apologise?'

The hint of sarcasm was evident to Carole but as she was busy negotiating her way between a rather grubby-looking wheelbarrow and a large shrub which wouldn't be out of place in a horror film about man-eating plants, she chose to ignore it.

'Yes,' she said, 'Gran was very upset and I think I may have possibly … arrgh!'

For the second time that morning, Carole bumped into someone because she wasn't looking where she was going. She hadn't noticed that Nick had stopped in his tracks. This time it wasn't such a pleasant encounter.

Her head hit the edge of the bag with a thud. Her flailing hands caught Nick sharply under his chin with a resounding *thwack.* She tried to steady herself but stumbled further, kicked over a half-full watering can and tipped forward, head-butting Nick firmly in his stomach.

Nick tried in vain to retain his balance and his hold on the bag of compost as both he and the bag toppled backwards. He was the only thing stopping Carole from falling flat on her face and she fell with him, landing squarely on top of him with her head coming to rest with some force, in the area of his crotch.

Carole's open mouth slammed shut on impact, causing her to bite the tip of her tongue and Nick let out a sound like nothing Carole had ever heard before.

It was several minutes before either of them could move. It was only when Carole realised that her face was within millimetres of Nick's groin and that the warm liquid she could feel between her teeth was blood, that she managed to roll over and scramble to a sitting position on the compost-covered concrete floor.

Nick rolled over too, bringing his knees up to his chest, his eyes screwed up in pain. Carole watched him in a daze, wondering whether she'd bitten off the tip of her tongue. Bizarrely, if she had, it occurred to her that she would never again be able to say the phrase, 'It's on the tip of my tongue.'

Nick moaned quietly and opened one eye. 'If that's your idea of an apology, please don't bother to apologise in future.' His dark eyes sprang open and filled with concern, and in spite of the pain he was clearly experiencing, he managed to pull himself up. 'Are you hurt? This hurts like hell but there's blood on your chin and, I'm pretty certain it's not mine.'

Carole shook her head and tears crept into her eyes. 'My tongue!' she sobbed, trying not to move her lips or teeth. 'I bit my tongue. Is ... is the tip still there?' She gingerly slid her tongue out between her lips.

Nick's brows creased and he managed a grin. 'Yes,' he said, 'it's all in one piece. I think you've just nicked it.'

Even Carole managed a slight smile at the absurdity of that statement. 'Nicked it on Nick,' she said, and their eyes met as they grinned awkwardly at one another.

Nick struggled to his feet. 'Come to the office with me

and I'll get the first-aid kit. You can use the sink in the kitchen area to get cleaned up. Does your tongue hurt? I've got some pain killers.' He held his hands out and taking her hands in his, he pulled her to her feet.

Carole felt an odd sensation shoot through her as his fingers closed around hers but it was nothing compared to the jolt her highly charged nerve endings gave her when he gently brushed some specks of compost from her cheek with his thumb. She pulled away as if she'd been stung by one of his bees and she rubbed the spot he'd touched with the back of her hand in an effort to regain her composure.

'Are you okay?' he asked.

She nodded. 'Yes. My tongue does hurt but I'm sure it'll be fine. My pride, however, may take longer to recover.' She glanced down at her favourite green coat, now covered in compost and she dreaded to think what else. 'I must look an absolute mess.' She brushed at the dirt but realised she was only making it worse.

'You look lovely,' he said.

Her eyes shot to his face and she was sure she saw him blush.

'Especially with that blood on your chin,' he added in a lighter tone.

'It's all the rage this season.'

'You wear it well,' he joked. 'It suits you.'

He turned and led the way to his office and she followed behind him, her eyes taking in every inch of him. His broad shoulders and his strong, oddly elegant neck; his dark, almost black hair with hints of dark chestnut where it had been lightened by the sun; his firm bum and his long, powerful looking legs which his jeans clung to in places she thought she probably would – if she were a pair of jeans.

Stop it, Carole, she silently rebuked herself. You seem to keep forgetting you're practically engaged.

'Are you okay with dogs?' he asked, turning to look at her, his hand resting on the doorknob of his office. 'I've got

52

Nicodemus with me and he can get quite excitable, although sometimes he's a bit of a wimp and timidly shrinks into the corner. Depends on whether he likes you or not, I guess.'

Carole nodded. 'I like dogs. Is he big?' she asked, envisioning the sort of dog Nick would have.

Something powerful, dark and mean looking she supposed, like a Rottweiler or Bull Mastiff. She braced herself. She had told the truth; she did like dogs but she'd just fallen over once today and she didn't relish the prospect of being knocked for six by an overactive solid mass of canine muscle.

She almost laughed when Nick opened the door and she came face to face with a svelte honey-coloured dog that looked something like a cross between a Doberman and a whippet. His sleek, short golden fur gleamed in the fluorescent light of the office.

'This is Nicodemus. Nicodemus meet Carole – and be nice.'

Nicodemus lifted one brow, glanced up at Nick then over to Carole, got up from his plush bed and gracefully trotted towards her, nuzzling her hand with a very wet, pink nose. His long slim, pointed tail wagged furiously from side to side, like a metronome at a rave and his tall pointed ears were bolt upright and had a rosy glow to them.

'Wow!' Carole exclaimed. 'He's gorgeous! What breed is he? Or is he a cross?'

'A mutt you mean, like me?' Nick said, smirking. 'No, he's a pure bred Pharaoh Hound.'

Carole tutted at his remark. 'He looks as if he's blushing,' she said, giggling at Nicodemus' enthusiastic greeting.

'They do. Pharaoh Hounds are unique in that their nose and ears go that rosy colour when they get excited. He clearly likes you.'

'And I like him,' she added, completely forgetting her

tongue or the fact that her coat was now having a dog's head rubbed against it. 'I've never heard of a Pharaoh Hound before. His head does sort of resemble Anubis' but he wasn't a Pharaoh, he was a god.'

'The name doesn't come from that. It's an ancient breed and it's believed that the Pharaohs kept them as hunting dogs. They love hunting and they're exuberant chasers. Having said that, they are quite calm, sensitive creatures and they're good with people including children, and other animals. Pretty much the perfect pet. They even get on with cats – apart from Arten that is, but that's because Arten doesn't like Nicodemus, not the other way around. Sorry, I'll get the first-aid kit. Move over, you mad dog,' Nick said tenderly. He grinned across at Carole. 'I meant Nicodemus, not you by the way.'

Carole smirked. 'Very funny,' she said.

He handed her the kit and nodded towards the open door of the small kitchen area.

'It's a bit of a mess in there,' he said, 'but it's one hundred times cleaner than the bathroom. That's full of dirty boots and towels and stuff. There's a washing machine in there so it's a bit of an all purpose area whereas the kitchen, well, I only use that for making tea and snacks.'

'I'm sure it's fine,' Carole said, taking the kit and stepping into the kitchen. She almost reeled from the shock and she couldn't stop the little gasp of horror escaping.

'I did warn you.'

'Not sufficiently,' she said ungraciously. 'I ... I think I'll wait until I get back to Gran's.'

Perhaps by some people's standards the kitchen may have just needed a quick wipe over with a damp cloth and a bottle of disinfectant but to Carole's eyes, it required nothing less than an industrial standard intense clean, possibly fumigation.

Nick was by her side in a split second. 'Don't be

ridiculous. There's nothing in here that'll kill you and you can't walk the streets with blood on your face. I'd offer to take you home but my staff won't get here for at least another half an hour and I'm expecting a big delivery.'

'I can wait half an hour,' she said.

He ignored her, grabbed her hand and rather ungallantly dragged her into the kitchen. He soaked a piece of kitchen towel under a spluttering tap and gently wiped away the blood as he held her chin softly between his fingers.

Much to her surprise, she let him.

***

'So,' Nick said, sometime later when they were sitting in his office and drinking coffee, 'didn't you say that you came here to apologise or something?'

Carole was eyeing her coffee mug warily. Not because it was dirty; she'd found the washing up liquid and had washed both of the mugs, the spoons and even the kettle and the taps thoroughly before allowing Nick to make the coffee. It was because her tongue was still tender and she wondered if hot coffee might just make it worse.

'Oh! I ... ah ... um–'

'I think we came in on that note,' he said. 'Don't worry, it's unnecessary. I was hurt though, I'll admit. To know that anyone could think that I ... but then the fact is, you don't know me from Adam, and unless Mitsy has told you as much about me as she has told me about you, you're entitled to wonder what my motives are, I guess.'

'Precisely! At last, someone who understands!'

'It's rather ironic that the *someone* is me,' he said, lounging back in his chair and studying her face over the rim of his mug.

She met his eyes briefly then glanced away, shrugging her shoulders before her eyes shot back to his.

'What do you mean, Gran's told you about me? What ...

what exactly *has* she told you?'

He met her gaze with a look of compassion and sat upright, leaning slightly towards her. She swallowed, fearing the worst.

'She told me about your dad; about how hard your mum found it to cope after his death; about ... about her failed relationships and the constant moving. She told me about how brave you were and how you studied for your degree; started your own business and how you've now got a successful career as an illustrator and graphic designer. She told me about Sebastian and what that did to you; she–'

'Okay!' Carole snapped, banging her mug down on the desk. 'I get the picture. She's told you pretty much my entire life story! Though God alone knows why.'

She couldn't stop the tears from trickling down her cheeks and she jumped to her feet and turned to leave.

'Carole,' he said, leaping from his chair and grabbing her arm. 'Please don't be upset by it. Mitsy is so proud of you and she loves you with all her heart. She gets pleasure out of talking about you and ...and I'm happy to listen. She doesn't mean any harm by it, you know that and I can assure you, nothing she's told me will ever go any further. I can promise you that.'

He handed her a tissue and she wiped her eyes. He was only inches from her and she could smell a faint scent of aftershave. She looked up and met his dark eyes.

'Don't worry,' he continued, brushing a wayward lock of hair from her face, 'your secrets are perfectly safe with me.' He winked at her and grinned mischievously.

'It seems I don't have any secrets, whereas you on the other hand ...'

He arched his brows. 'I'm not sure I have that many. But ask me anything and I'll tell you – with possibly one or two exceptions.'

She moved away from him, needing to put some space between herself and his undeniably tempting body as the close proximity was doing strange things to her temperature.

'Okay. Well for a start you can tell me your surname.'

His eyes narrowed and he shifted uncomfortably. 'Ah. Unfortunately, that's one of the two things I'm not prepared to tell you – not because I have a dark history or anything but simply because, like yours does for you, my surname causes me great embarrassment. I will promise you this though. I'll tell you on Christmas Eve.'

'Why on Christmas Eve? Why not now?'

'Two reasons. Firstly, by Christmas Eve we'll both know one another a lot better and ... I won't be so concerned about it, I hope. Secondly, that's my birthday and birthdays are a great time for wishes and revelations.'

'Really? Hmm. I don't know ...'

'Why? Because you think I'm hatching some sinister plan and by the time you find out my name and Google it, gaining access to my extensive criminal record, it'll be too late? Let me just say this. Mitsy knows it and she understands. If surnames are really that important, ask her.'

'I will,' Carole said, sitting back down. 'Why did you come to Jutsdown and where did you live before that?'

He slid his hands in his pockets, winced slightly and leant back against the wall.

'God, that still hurts. Okay, I came to Jutsdown because my sister told me about this nursery. She works as a property finder for her and her husband's TV production company and she happened to be driving through this village, saw the 'For Sale' sign and called me. She knew I wanted land to start my own garden centre and this of course, was perfect.'

'You've got a sister?'

'Yes. I'm not sure why that should be such a surprise. People do have siblings you know, even possible villains like me.'

'I don't. For some reason I just thought ... well, it

57

doesn't matter. Is she older or younger?'

'The same age. Her name's Mary and we're twins, although not identical fortunately for her. She takes after Mum and I take after Dad. It's good it wasn't the other way around really. Anyway, she and Harry, that's her husband, live in Epsom in Surrey.'

'And your parents?'

He shook his head. 'They've reverted to their twenties and are currently travelling the world spending all their retirement money but they too, have a house in Epsom. I've got to make a success of this place though because it looks as if Mary and I will be supporting them in their dotage.' He grinned. 'Next question.'

Carole was still getting her head around the fact that he had a family. She had no idea why but for some reason she had assumed that he was on his own and that was why he had latched on to her gran.

'Wow! Um ... oh, you didn't say where you lived before here.'

'All over the place. I found it difficult to settle – oddly enough until I saw this place. This probably sounds silly but as soon as I set foot on this land, I knew this was where I'd spend the rest of my days. It felt ... as if I'd come home. As if it had been waiting for me. It was apparently for sale for several years until I came along. Another point in its favour – I got it for a good price. But to answer the question, I've lived in London, Surrey of course, the United States and Canada. I worked my way around both countries for a few years, oh and Italy many years ago but the less said about that the better.'

'Misspent youth?'

'Unrequited love.'

'Now that I've got to hear about.'

'Not much to tell. She was beautiful. I wasn't. I had spots I seem to recall. Quite a lot of them actually.'

He shivered for effect and Carole burst out laughing.

'I find that hard to believe,' she said, scrutinising his clean-shaven, blemish free skin.

'It's true. I grew out of it, thank God. Although to be honest, I don't think it was just the spots that put Lucia off. I was also stick thin and a bit of a wimp.'

'Now I know you're lying!'

'I'm not. Honestly, I'm not. You can ask my sister when you meet her. It's all true.'

'When I meet her?' The idea of that seemed strange to Carole.

'Yep. She'll be down sometime in the New Year. Assuming you're still around here then.'

'Gran said she's invited you for Christmas dinner! Why aren't you spending it with your family?'

He shrugged. 'Mum and Dad will still be travelling. They're not big on the whole Christmas thing and Mary and Harry are spending this Christmas in the States with Harry's folks. Mary's just found out that she's expecting their first child and they want to tell the family the news in person, assuming everything's okay. It's early days yet and she's superstitious about telling too many people too early. So it's just me and Nicodemus this year.'

There were a hundred and one things Carole wanted to ask him. Things that were probably far more important than where he planned to spend Christmas but she was still coming to terms with seeing Nick in a family context and everything else just went out of her head.

'I'd better go,' she said suddenly. 'Gran's been left on her own for over an hour now.'

She headed towards the door, stopping to stroke Nicodemus on the way.

'Does Nicodemus just sit in here and sleep while you work?'

'No, sometimes he serves the customers but he's not very good with the card machine. Cash, he's fine with.'

Carole grinned. 'He probably tells better jokes too.'

Nick grinned back. 'That's not difficult. Sometimes my neighbour, Albert looks after him. Albert's elderly dog died just after we moved here so he loves having Nicodemus. Feel free to pop in anytime,' he said, stepping aside to let her pass. 'You'll need to learn a few of the ropes before Monday if you're still going to be taking over from Mitsy.'

'Taking over from–?'

'See you later. I've got to dash.'

A delivery lorry had pulled into the parking bay and Nick ran out to meet it before Carole had a chance to ask him what he meant. She considered waiting until he returned but two young lads cycled in and Nick waved them over. They were clearly *the staff* and what had been a relatively peaceful place just a few short minutes ago had now turned into a hive of activity. She decided she'd better get out quickly before she did get roped in to help.

CHAPTER SEVEN

'Did you apologise?' Mitsy asked the moment Carole entered her bedroom. 'Oh! Good heavens! What on earth has happened to you?'

For a split second, Carole was tempted to say that Nick did it – which in a way was true, but she could tell that her grandmother was genuinely concerned and this wasn't the time to be facetious.

'It was my fault. I wasn't looking where I was going and I tripped and fell in the garden centre. I'm fine though and so is Nick although we're both a bit battered and bruised. When I fell, I'm afraid I knocked him down too.'

To Carole's surprise, her gran sniggered.

'It's not funny, Gran. That place is an absolute death trap not to mention it's filthy.'

Mitsy tutted good-naturedly. 'It's a garden centre, dear. It can't possibly be pristine. As for it being a death trap, I've managed perfectly well without tripping over anything, almost every day for the last few months, and my eyesight is nowhere near as good as yours.'

Carole's head shot up at that. 'Almost every day for ...! Gran, I really think it's time you and I had a serious talk. Okay, I'll admit that I may have got the wrong impression of Nick but how exactly did you meet him and why are you apparently working for him? Mr Jarvis told me that you fell off a ladder there and that's how you broke your leg. No wonder you didn't want to tell me. What were you doing up a ladder at your age?'

'When did you see Justin Jarvis?'

'This morning on my way to the garden centre. I bumped into Seb and ...'

'Oh really? So you've talked to Sebastian, have you? And what did he have to say for himself?'

'I'll tell you about that later, Gran. I want to hear about you and your connection with the garden centre first.'

'Well, you'd better go and have a shower then and make us both a nice cup of tea. I hate to say this, sweetheart, but you are absolutely filthy and there seems to be something green in your hair.'

***

'Nick rang when you were in the shower, sweetheart,' Mitsy said when Carole took a tray of tea and biscuits into her grandmother's room forty minutes later. 'He wanted to check that you were okay. He's such a thoughtful young man and he said that your apology was one he'll remember for a long time to come. I'm so pleased that you were nice to him. You'll soon see just how mistaken you were about him.'

'What else did he say?' Carole asked inquisitively. Nick was clearly as good at bending the truth as she was but she was rather glad that he had.

'He's going to pop round at lunchtime and carry me downstairs, if that's all right with you. I don't want to be cooped up in here all day.'

'That's absolutely fine with me. Would you mind if I did a little bit of work this afternoon then? I've got one or two things on pretty tight deadlines and if you're happy to read or watch TV, I can get on with those.'

'Absolutely, dear. Don't you worry about me. I'll be fine.'

'Excellent. Well, let's hear the whole story then, Gran. Let's start with how and when you met him and work our way forwards from there, shall we?'

Mitsy sighed. 'Sometimes sweetheart, you're like a dog with a bone. You just won't let go, will you?' She smiled and patted one side of her bed. 'Come and sit up here with me and I'll tell you all about it.'

Carole curled up beside her and tucked one arm in hers.

'I think it was fate,' Mitsy said. 'I hadn't been to the old plant nursery in years but for some reason when I was out for one of my daily walks – it must have been around Easter time I suppose, I found myself standing at the gates. One of them was open so I wandered in and Nicodemus came bounding up to me. I didn't know his name then of course, but he was such a beautiful dog and I bent down to pet him.'

'I met him today. He is certainly gorgeous and very friendly.'

'Yes. Well, he was rather exuberant that day. Nick had spotted me and called Nicodemus away but it was my own silly fault, I lost my balance and toppled over. Don't worry, I wasn't hurt and Nick rushed to my aid. Despite assuring him I was fine, he wouldn't hear of letting me come home on my own and when we got here, he insisted on making me a cup of tea. We got chatting and he told me he was hoping to buy the nursery.'

'Gran! You shouldn't have let a complete stranger into your house.'

'Oh Carole. Don't start that nonsense again. I've always been an excellent judge of character and I could tell immediately that Nick was an absolute gentleman. It was one of the most pleasant afternoons I'd spent for a very long time, to be honest. And we really hit it off. I told him about the way it used to be and he told me his visions for the future. Not only did I like him, I liked his plans and I asked if he'd show me his drawings of the scheme. One thing led to another. He made the most delicious dinner for us both and–'

'Gran! You're not telling me that ... that ...' She couldn't bring herself to say it.

'Good heavens, Carole! Are you suggesting ...? How could you think such a thing? I know I told you that he's gorgeous and that if I were forty years younger you'd have to fight me for him but I'm seventy-six years old and I'm not about to have nooky or whatever you young things call it these days with a man less than half my age! Really, Carole! And as if he would either.' Mitsy tutted loudly. 'I'm very glad he didn't hear you say that, my girl.'

'I'm sorry, Gran but ... well ... it sounded as if that's what you were leading up to.'

'Well, I wasn't. So let me finish. We had dinner and some wine and he said that he'd better find a hotel for the night and I suggested he stay here. He said he couldn't impose. He stayed at The Manor Court Hotel and invited me to breakfast the next day.'

'Oh. And ... and then he bought the nursery and started work on it and I suppose you decided to go and help out.'

Mitsy sniggered. 'Something along those lines dear, yes. Although it wasn't quite that straightforward.'

'Why?'

'Well – and don't get up on your high horse before I've finished. Nick got the nursery very cheaply because it'd been for sale for such a long time and there are restrictive covenants on the land, as you probably remember, so it can't be used for residential development, but the surrounding land can. He didn't have the money for that land so he wasn't thinking of buying it yet. I offered to lend it to him by way of an investment – but that's not public knowledge.'

'What? He told me he got it cheap! And he never mentioned that he'd borrowed money from you! I knew it! I knew he was after something!'

Mitsy smacked Carole's hand. 'Stop it, Carole. You're getting the wrong end of the stick again. He didn't mention it because I've made him promise not to. I said I'd tell you in my own time, which I am doing now. And believe me, it was a battle to get him to agree. He said that he'd let it go and hope he could work around it or raise the money via his family later. I told him I'd buy it and he could accept me as a partner or I'd sell it on to him later. And that's what happened.'

'So he's now bought the land from you ... at the price you paid for it at least, I hope.'

'No. He offered to. He raised the funds about a month ago but ... well, you are so busy these days and Sarah had just moved up to Scotland to be with Jamie. I really needed something to get my teeth into. I persuaded Nick to let me remain a partner and help out in the garden centre for a few hours a day. He agreed and that, as they say, was that.'

'So you're actually a joint partner in the garden centre!'

'Yes. And I've never been happier. I pop in and out when I feel like it.'

'But it's been making you ill, Gran! You said yourself that you've been going through a bad patch. How could he let you run yourself ragged like–?'

'Do stop jumping to conclusions, sweetheart. The garden centre is what's been keeping me going. I planned to tell you all about it but for some reason, it never seemed the right time.'

'Why not? And why didn't you tell me how you were feeling? I didn't think we had any secrets, Gran.'

Mitsy raised her eyebrows as if she had some doubts about that. 'Perhaps not in the old days, sweetheart but since you've moved in with Dominic, I'm not sure you tell me everything quite like you used to. And that's fine. We're all entitled to keep our own counsel. The health issues weren't serious, and as for not telling you about the garden centre, I think I wanted you to meet Nick first. Perhaps because I thought you might get the wrong end of the stick,' she said with a sardonic smile.

'Now what makes you think I'd have done that, Gran?' Carole said, shaking her head. 'I'm so sorry. I'll try to think things through before I jump to conclusions in future. But you have been unwell?'

'Yes. I started to get some pain in my stomach. I ignored

it at first, of course. I wasn't eating properly and that was adding to my dizziness. I kept having silly little accidents and Nick noticed there was something wrong and insisted on me calling Dr Edwards. I had a stomach ulcer and I was also anaemic. I'm much better now. I've been on a course of treatment for a few weeks and everything is almost back to normal.'

'Gran! You really should have told me.'

'There was no point, Carole. And I didn't want to worry you.'

'And your leg? How did that happen?'

'My fault entirely. Nick has told me a hundred times that I am not to climb up ladders or lift anything heavy and such like but I wanted a box of labels and I knew they were on the top shelf in the office. I used the stepladder. It was only two steps but I missed my footing and slipped. I just landed awkwardly, that's all. It's only a fracture but they did have to reset it.'

'Oh Gran.' Carole kissed Mitsy on her cheek.

'I know you're really busy with your own work, sweetheart and if it's really too difficult then please do say so but I did suggest to Nick that you might be able to take my place at the garden centre – just for a couple of hours a day – or whenever you have a spare moment. Because of this,' Mitsy said, tapping her leg, 'I'll be out of action for at least a few weeks and Nick has rather come to rely on me, even if I do say so myself.'

Carole's head shot up. 'So that's what he meant by me helping out. Oh, good grief!'

'You're right. It's too much to ask, dear,' Mitsy said. 'You've been good enough to come and take care of me. I can't expect you to step into my job as well. I'm sure we'll be able to sort something out. Perhaps Sarah would be prepared to come down for a few days.'

Carole's mouth fell open in surprise. 'Mum! You'd ask Mum to help out in the garden centre. Gran, the place is a bit of a mess already. If Mum got her hands on it, it'd look more like the local refuse tip than a garden centre. I'll do it. I suppose I should anyway. After all,' she added, grinning, 'someone needs to protect your investment.'

***

'So when do you want to start?' Nick said, leaning against the kitchen door frame after depositing Mitsy on the sofa bed in the study. 'It would be really good if you could drop in for an hour or so either tomorrow or Saturday. It's the 1st of December on Sunday and people will be coming to order their trees and holly and mistletoe, so it'll be a bit too busy for you to get the hang of the tills and such like then. Mitsy usually works for a few hours in the morning but obviously, as you're doing me a huge favour I can work around whatever suits you. I realise you've got your own business to think about, so if it's really too much, I'm sure I can manage.'

'Well, I can come in early tomorrow if you like and we'll take it from there.'

He raised his eyebrows and grinned. 'By early, you mean after nine-thirty, I take it.'

She grinned back and handed him a mug of tea. 'No, I was thinking around seven-ish, if that suits you.'

'I thought you weren't a morning person?'

'I lied,' she said, adding under her breath, 'I seem to be doing rather a lot of that lately.'

'Sorry?'

'Nothing. Is seven okay?'

'Great. Do you have any old clothes that you're happy to get dirty?'

'I'm never happy to get my clothes dirty, old or otherwise, but I'll see if I can find something ... suitable.'

'I may have something at home that will fit you.'

She was horrified. 'If any of your clothes fit me, Nick,

I'll kill myself.'

'Still being a drama queen, I see.' He grinned and tilted his head to one side. 'I didn't mean my clothes. Mary left some of her old things at my place last time she was down. I'm sure they'll fit you and let's face it, she won't be able to get into them for several months. I'd say you're almost exactly the same size as her. Thirty-six, twenty-six, thirty...' He hesitated.

'Be very careful,' she said, blushing. He was spot on so far.

His grin widened. 'Seven.'

'Eight. And you were obviously being diplomatic, so thank you.'

'I wasn't actually.'

His eyes focused intently on her hips and she could feel her cheeks growing redder by the second.

'You don't look like a thirty-eight.'

'Really? Because an inch makes such a noticeable difference, does it?'

His dark eyes held hers and his grin widened even further. 'Some women say an inch makes all the difference.'

Carole sucked in her breath, not absolutely certain whether they were still talking about her hips or something else entirely. Her temperature shot up several degrees, giving the oven containing the casserole she was making for dinner, a run for its money.

'Mary's thirty-seven,' he continued, 'or at least she was, but I'm sure they'll fit you. I can bring them round this evening if you like when I come back to take Mitsy up to bed. And before you start thinking it's weird that I know my sister's precise measurements, it's because I've had them drummed into my head. The last time she stayed was when she'd just found out she was pregnant and she measured and weighed herself every ten seconds to see if she'd gained an inch or put on any weight.'

Carole couldn't think clearly. 'That would be good,' she said, 'if Mary wouldn't mind.'

'She won't. Okay, I'd better get back. What time do you want me this evening?'

'What? Oh, to take Gran up. Er ... whenever it suits you both.'

She suddenly remembered that she had been thinking of inviting Sebastian round for a chat. She obviously couldn't do that if Nick was going to be popping in, although just as he'd said he would, he had rung the doorbell this lunchtime. It was probably just as well anyway, she thought. Her gran disliked Sebastian after he ran off to Australia; possibly more than she disliked Dominic.

***

'You'll never guess who's in the pub talking to Sebastian,' Josie said as soon as Carole answered her mobile.

'Who?'

'Nick! They're standing at the bar, chatting as if they were long lost buddies.'

Carole felt the colour drain from her face. 'Really? Who started the conversation?'

'No idea. I've only just got here. I'm tempted to go over and say something.'

'Like what?'

'Just, hello or something, and that I didn't know they knew each other.'

'It's the village pub, Josie. The only pub. And Nick and Seb are about the same age so I suppose it's only natural that they'd strike up a conversation. Don't start making me get paranoid about it. Oh by the way, I've got some news for you.'

'Dom's proposed at last.'

'What? No, of course he hasn't ... I mean. It's nothing to do with Dom. I'm going to be helping out in the garden centre in place of Gran. I start tomorrow.'

'What? How did you wangle that?'

'I didn't wangle it, Josie. Gran asked me and I naturally said I would. He'll be very short- staffed otherwise and what with Christmas coming and everything.'

'Wow! Um ... I'd be happy to offer my services. He doesn't have to pay me – well not in money anyway. I'll take payment in kind.'

'I bet you would. I could put in a good word for you, if you like. He's coming round later to take Gran to bed.'

'I think you may want to rephrase that statement. I take it you didn't invite Seb round then?'

'No. You're right, it would upset Gran, and what with Nick coming back here and Dom calling me later, I think it's best if I take things slowly as far as Sebastian's concerned.'

'Bloody hell, Carole! I think that's the most sensible thing I've heard you say in months.'

***

Carole was working on one of her designs when she spotted Nick walking up the path at around ten-thirty that evening. Arkenarten was curled up on his usual cushion on the window seat and Mitsy was dozing on the sofa bed, her large-print book hanging loosely in one hand.

Carole dashed to open the door before he could ring the bell. She put her finger to her lips.

'Gran's dozing,' she said. 'I didn't want you to ring the bell and startle her.' She caught a whiff of aftershave again as he stepped into the hall. 'Did you have a good evening?'

'Yes, thanks. I went to the pub. How about you?'

'Working. Would you like some tea or coffee or ... hot chocolate?'

He smiled. 'Chocolate would be good. I brought a few of Mary's things as promised. See what you like and what you don't.'

'Thanks.' She took the small holdall of clothes and tossed it onto the bottom stair, grinning as she turned back to face him. 'Nothing breakable, I hope?'

'Only the glass slipper, Cinders,' he replied. 'I saw a friend of yours this evening.'

She held her breath but he didn't continue so she had to ask. 'Really? Who was that?'

'Josie. She's often in the garden centre. She says she loves plants but personally, I think she probably buys so many because she keeps killing them. Sorry, I suppose I shouldn't call one of your friends a plant murderer should I?'

'As opposed to me calling one of my Gran's friends a brute and a criminal, you mean? Josie will be the first to admit she's not very good with plants but she's eager to learn. Actually, that brings me nicely to a suggestion I have for you.'

'Oh?' He looked anxious.

She headed for the kitchen and he followed her.

'You said that you were short-staffed and although I'm happy to help as much as I can, I do have to look after Gran and I also have quite a bit of work on at the moment which I need to get finished in the next couple of weeks. Josie finishes work around four each day. She's a music teacher and she works part-time at the village school. She does have other pupils but she did happen to mention that she has a few hours most days and would be happy to volunteer her services in exchange for ... some free expert knowledge.'

'Oh, did she? What sort of expert knowledge?'

'What?' There was no doubt about it, this guy could definitely read people's minds. 'Oh, um ... the green-fingered variety. I mean plant knowledge. Stuff about plants.'

She could feel herself blushing and turned away to make

the hot chocolate.

'I'll have to check with Health and Safety. There're all sorts of regulations regarding employees – paid or otherwise. In case there's an accident or anything.'

'Hmm. Like Gran falling off a ladder and me tripping over a watering can, you mean?' She smiled but he looked deadly serious suddenly. 'That was a joke,' she said.

'Not from where I'm standing.'

'Oh, Josie's probably out of the question then?'

'I think so. It would be good to have the help but when things start to get busy, it's going to be very difficult to keep an eye on everyone and make sure they're safe.'

'Do you need to do that?' she said, handing him a mug of hot chocolate, his fingers sending tiny shock waves through her as they brushed against hers.

He gave her an odd look. 'I rather think I do.'

CHAPTER EIGHT

Carole slept fitfully. She had the strangest dreams but when she awoke, she couldn't remember any of them. One thing she could remember though. Nick would ring the front door bell before he came in. When she switched on the light and glanced at her reflection in the mirror, she was very glad of that fact.

Her long wavy hair was even more tangled than usual and she'd forgotten to take her mascara off last night after Dom had phoned. She now had Panda eyes. So much for smudge- proof, she thought.

She dragged on her dressing gown and headed downstairs to make coffee. She would need at least three cups – and very possibly a mild sedative – before she could face working amongst the dirt and debris of the garden centre for a couple of hours this morning.

She pushed open the kitchen door and wasn't sure what she heard first – the crunch of bone or the ring of breaking china. She definitely heard the moan of a man in pain.

'Oh my God, Nick!' she shrieked, poking her head around the door to see blood trickling from his aquiline nose. 'What are you doing here?'

'Bleeding all over Mitsy's kitchen floor,' he said, tipping his head back to stem the increasing flow.

'Sit down,' Carole said, grabbing a tea towel and holding it under the running cold tap before applying it to Nick's nose.

'Ow! For someone who accused me of beating people up, you're doing a pretty good job yourself.'

'I'm sorry! How was I supposed to know you were in here? I thought you'd ring the bell.'

'I would have, but Mitsy called and asked me not to, in case I woke you up. She asked me to drop in some milk because she thought you might not have any left.'

'Don't tell me ... it's from your cow, or possibly goat.'

'What?' he said, looking askance. 'No. The post office stores. They open at six.'

'Is it gone six?' Carole glanced at her watch.

'It's six-thirty,' he replied before she had a chance to read the display.

'And I said I'd be at the garden centre by seven! Are you okay? I'd better get a move on if I'm going to help you today.'

'I think you've done quite enough already.' He leant his head forward slowly and removed the tea towel. 'What happened to you?'

She saw the questioning look in his eyes as they scanned her face. She wasn't too pleased that he was obviously referring to her Panda eyes and tangled hair. So much for him being a gentleman. Mind you, she reasoned, she had possibly just broken his nose.

'This is what I often look like in the mornings,' she said, switching on the kettle. 'Get used to it.'

'I'd like to,' he said, 'if you don't kill me first.'

She didn't dare ask what he meant by that.

'I'd better get on,' he continued. 'I'll see you later. I've got an appointment so I won't be at the centre until around seven-fifteen, so you've got some time yet. Mind if I take the tea towel with me? I'll wash it and return it later.'

'What? Oh yes, that's fine. I'm really sorry about your nose, Nick.'

'I'll live, although I'll probably get a black eye and that may take some explaining to Mitsy.' He grinned at her. 'I'll leave that to you.'

He walked into the hallway and Carole leant around the kitchen door to watch him go. For some absurd reason, she loved watching him walk.

***

74

Carole showered and managed to untangle her hair before trying on the clothes Nick had given her last night. He was right about her and his sister being about the same size. The jeans, T-shirt and over shirt fitted her perfectly; possibly a little too perfectly. Mary obviously liked to show off her figure. The jeans were skinny-fit, the T-shirt clung to her like a second skin and even the brushed cotton over shirt seemed to cling around her bottom. She wondered whether she should try on something else but she was running late as it was and everything looked a similar style anyway.

She popped her head around Mitsy's door.

'I'm off, Gran. Will you be okay? Do you want me to ask Nick to take you down stairs?'

'No thank you. I'll stay in bed this morning. I'll be fine, sweetheart. You go and have fun.'

'Fun! In a freezing garden centre surrounded by dirt and goodness knows what else. Yeah. It's going to be a riot. Oh, I didn't tell you, I nearly broke Nick's nose this morning. Don't worry, he's okay but if you see him with a black eye later, you'll know why.'

Mitsy chuckled. 'I'm not sure I should ask how that happened.'

'Best not to. See you later.'

She dashed down the stairs and out of the door and was about to jump in the car when she saw Sebastian running towards her.

'Carole,' he called out. 'May I have a word before you go?'

'I'm running late, Seb. I was supposed to be at the garden centre fifteen minutes ago.'

Sebastian arrived at her side, breathless but as gorgeous as ever; possibly more so with his rosy cheeks, his dishevelled wavy blond hair and his bright blue eyes alight with enthusiasm.

'I just need a minute, Carole. Just one minute. I thought

you would come to the pub last night or ... or call me.'

'Sorry. So much happened yesterday and I had to work last night. I'm on some pretty tight deadlines. Besides, I couldn't leave Gran.'

He nodded. 'No. No, of course not. Look, what if I get Mum to spend the evening with her? We could go out for dinner and talk. I really think we need to talk, don't you?'

Carole knew her gran didn't like Sebastian but she had remained friends with his parents so she wouldn't mind that, apart from the fact that she'd know the reason for it and who Carole would be with. Besides, should she really be going out to dinner with her ex?

'Yes. But not tonight, Seb. What's the rush? I'll be around for at least six weeks. That's how long it'll take Gran's leg to heal and possibly a bit longer so there's plenty of time. Unless you're thinking of going somewhere.'

'No. No, I'm not going anywhere. You're right. There's time. It's just ... well, when you said that you thought your ... what's his name? Your boyfriend?'

'Dom. Dominic.'

'Well, when you said that you thought he'd propose any day now I ... I suppose I wanted to talk to you before that happened. I assume he'll be coming down this weekend.'

'No. He's going ... he's away on business. He won't be down until next weekend.'

Sebastian heaved a sigh of obvious relief. 'We've got all next week then. That's good.'

Carole was confused. 'I'm not sure what you mean, Seb. Are you saying that we need to talk before next weekend because whatever we discuss may have an impact on my relationship with Dom?'

He stepped forward. 'I think we both know the answer to that, Carole. If we're honest with ourselves.'

She swallowed and looked into his eyes. 'Are ... are you saying that you think we may have a future together? You and I? After all this time? You ...you think we can just pick up where we left off?'

He slid an arm around her waist and pulled her to him. Her breath seemed to desert her and she gasped for air.

'I would say ... almost exactly where we left off. All I could think about last night was holding you in my arms again. Making love to you. Kissing every part of your body. We were good together, Carole. You must remember that?'

'I do.' The irony of those words hit her like a wet fish and she managed to regain her composure momentarily. 'I've got to go, Seb. We'll talk next week.'

Before she knew what was happening his mouth was on hers in a kiss as demanding as it was passionate. It was a kiss of possession. A kiss claiming ownership and she wasn't sure if she liked it or not. It took her a few seconds to pull herself free.

'Seb!' She gasped for breath. 'What the hell do you think you're doing? You can't kiss me outside Gran's house after all this time. Especially not like that!'

'I'm sorry, Carole. I ... I didn't mean to kiss you. It ... it just happened. I want to hold you so much. I–'

'I've got to go,' she said, stopping him before he did anything else – before he said anything else.

She was confused enough already. She wasn't sure about the kiss but his words had stirred something inside her. If he wanted to pick up almost exactly where they had left off, that meant being engaged, possibly marriage, once his divorce came through, of course. And the absurdity of that thought brought a need for distance for now. Space for her to think.

'I'll call you next week, Seb and we'll see.'

She jumped in her car and raced out of the drive, glancing in the rear-view mirror when she reached the T-junction at the end of the lane. Sebastian was still standing there, staring after her.

***

Carole pulled up at Four Seasons Gardens and was surprised to see that Nick's Land Rover wasn't in one of the parking bays. The gates of the centre were wide open but there was no sign of life. Well, not human anyway. Only plant life.

She noticed that the mass of shrubs, trees, and plants appeared to be in some semblance of order and it surprised her for some reason. She remembered what the place used to look like in the old days, when it was just an old-fashioned plant nursery, and she smiled.

Nick's Land Rover appeared from nowhere and screeched to a halt beside her Toyota Aygo. She almost jumped out of her skin as the sound yanked her from her memories. She caught her breath and got out of her car smiling at Nick. He opened the passenger door of his vehicle and Nicodemus leapt out and bounded towards her.

'Good morning,' she said cheerily. 'You gave me such a fright just then. I was miles away, dreaming of days long ago.'

'I can imagine. You're late!'

Carole felt the temperature drop by several degrees.

'So are you. At least I've got an excuse. I had to–'

'Yes, I saw what you had to do. I didn't have you down as that sort of girl. Clearly, I was wrong.'

Carole blinked several times in bewilderment. What *was* he talking about? Realisation dawned.

'Oh my God! You saw Seb kissing me!'

'I couldn't really miss it.'

'Were ... were you watching me?'

He was lifting a box from the back of the Land Rover but his head turned towards her and a look of contempt swept across his face.

'Don't be ridiculous. You really do have a very vivid imagination, don't you? If you hadn't been so ... wrapped up in what you were doing, you might have seen my Land

Rover parked outside Matilda's cottage. She wants to have a Christmas tree planted outside in the front garden and we were discussing the best position for it when ... when she commented on ... your morning activities. I think she was even more surprised than I was – if that's possible.'

'Matilda saw me?'

'That would be a very definite yes. And she did watch. Every long minute of it. And gave me a running commentary.'

He grabbed the box and headed towards the doors of the centre whilst Carole stood, open- mouthed and shaking from head to toe. She wasn't sure whether it was from fear of the possible repercussions once her gran and everyone else no doubt, heard about it, or from anger at Nick's arrogant and holier than thou attitude. She decided it was the latter and stormed after him with Nicodemus following at her heels.

'For your information, Mr High and Mighty, that wasn't what I was going to say, or why I was late. I was late because, apart from oversleeping as you know I did, I had to clean up the mess you made on Gran's kitchen floor!'

He turned and glowered at her. 'The mess I made! Well, I'm so sorry about that but you were the one who nearly broke my nose let's not forget, and I did offer to clean it up but you said you'd rather do it because – and let me get this right – you'd "make a better job of it" than I would.'

'Well, it's true! You've only got to look at your kitchen here to see that cleanliness isn't high on your list of priorities. And I wouldn't have nearly broken your nose if you hadn't been loitering in Gran's kitchen at six-thirty in the morning without telling me that you were there!'

'Well, forgive me! You moan at me for waking you up and bringing you coffee in bed at "some ungodly hour" to let you know I'm around. Now you moan at me for not waking you up and telling you I'm there. It seems I can't win with you. Give me your mobile number and I'll send you a text message in future.'

'Don't be facetious. And you have my mobile number. You called me to berate me for not coming down to be with Gran, if you remember?'

'I didn't call to berate you. And that was your landline.' He opened the doors and marched through, letting them swing shut in Carole's face.

'Oh! Now you're trying to break my nose, are you?' She pushed the doors open so hard that one of them hit a stack of boxes, knocking them flying.

'I've got my arms full or haven't you noticed? I thought you'd come here to help, not to wreck the place,' he said.

'Wreck the place? I think you got there before me on that one.'

His eyes creased into tiny slits as he stared at her. 'I don't think this is going to work. This place is clearly an affront to your sensitivities. Perhaps you should go and see if there's anything you can help Sebastian with instead. I'm sure you'd find that more to your taste and that's obviously where you'd rather be. I just hope your soon-to-be-fiancé doesn't find out.'

Carole's mouth fell open as she gasped in surprise. 'How dare you! How dare you lecture me on something you know nothing about? For your information *Nick,* not that this is any of your business, I didn't kiss Seb this morning – he kissed me!'

'Is there a difference?'

'Of course there's a difference! Or has it been so long since you've kissed a woman that you can't remember? It takes two to kiss properly. This morning, Seb grabbed me and kissed me. I didn't kiss him back.'

'That's not what Matilda said.'

'I couldn't give a damn what Matilda said. Perhaps you should have watched instead of listening to gossip. Then you would have seen that I pulled away from him and got in my car to come here. If I'd known that I was going to be insulted, I wouldn't have bothered.'

He was still staring at her. 'You pulled away? Really? And that took you several minutes to do, did it? I told you, I got a running commentary.'

She sighed heavily. She had never felt like slapping someone as much as she wanted to slap him but she managed to control the urge. She'd already tried to castrate him and break his nose. If she slapped him too, she would be the one with the criminal record for GBH.

'Yes! It did. I was so surprised by it that I hadn't even realised he was kissing me at first. It took a while for me to get myself together and his arms were wrapped around me so tightly that it then took some time for me to break free. Why don't you grab an unwilling and unsuspecting female and kiss her and see how long it takes her to get away. I'll even time it if you want.'

She thought she saw something flash across his eyes and even a hint of a smile at the corner of his mouth but it was gone in a split second.

'I might just do that one day,' he said, turning away and heading towards his office, still holding the box in his arms. 'The only problem is I don't believe in kissing unwilling or unsuspecting women, especially other men's girlfriends, and definitely not when they're practically engaged. And if you're offering yourself in the role, you'd hardly be unwilling or unsuspecting, would you? Now as fascinating as this discussion is, I've got work to do. Stay or go, the choice is yours but if you're staying, you can pick up those boxes you so kindly knocked over just now.'

'Of all the ...! I wasn't offering myself ... although I can assure you, I'd be both unwilling and unsuspecting. I have absolutely no desire to kiss you and somehow, I can't quite see you in the role of an enthusiastic and desperate lover!'

Through his office windows, Carole saw him drop the box on his desk. She saw his head shoot up and his shoulders tense. He appeared to be mulling something over.

She stayed where she was and watched him for a few seconds, wondering if she'd said too much. She was about to take her coat off and go and pick up the boxes when he turned and stuck his head around the door frame. He looked almost comical.

'Are you saying Sebastian kissed you because he was desperate? That's not very self-complimentary is it?'

'What?' That wasn't very amusing in her opinion. 'I didn't mean he was kissing me because he was desperate. I meant he was desperate to kiss me. There's a big difference, you know. Huge! He said he'd been dreaming about me all night and he couldn't wait to hold me in his arms again, to make love to me like we used to, to ... God! Why am I telling you this?'

He scowled. 'Really? He said all that and you were still unsuspecting ... and unwilling when he kissed you. My, my. Didn't you believe him?'

'Of course I believed ...! Look, I'm not going to continue this conversation with you. I came here to work, not discuss my sex life. This may come as a surprise to you, oh Lord and Master, but what I do in my personal life really is no concern of yours. And ... not that that is what happened as I think I've explained in some detail, but if I want to kiss another man, I'll damn well do so whether I'm engaged or not. Is that clear?'

Their eyes locked for several seconds and her breath came in short sharp gasps.

'Practically engaged,' he said, grinning slightly. 'You're not engaged yet, or so I've been led to believe. And yes, that's perfectly clear. I'll bear it in mind for the future. I assume you're staying. If so, once you've restacked the boxes, you can make some coffee if that's okay with you. I'll be working on the beds out the back for about three quarters of an hour so I'll be ready for a cup by the time I finish that. I take mine white with no sugar.'

Carole tutted. 'It won't take me that long to stack the

boxes and make coffee,' she said with a hint of annoyance, taking off her coat and tossing it onto one of the chairs.

'I should hope not,' he replied, stroking Nicodemus who was standing by his side. 'But I'm guessing you'll want to give the kitchen a thorough going over before you even attempt to touch the kettle – and that will.'

'Very funny,' she said, even though she knew he was absolutely correct; that was exactly what she would do.

He glanced across at her and his eyes seemed even darker as they travelled the length of her body, stopping their journey at her flushed face.

She fidgeted, feeling somehow almost naked by the way he was looking at her.

'They fit,' she said, pulling at the hem of the tight T-shirt before realising that emphasised her curves even more.

'So I see,' he said, coughing as if something had stuck in his throat.

'Haven't you got work to do?' she added.

'What? Oh yes. Sorry, I was just wondering why those clothes look so much better on you than they ever did on Mary. It seems an inch definitely does make all the difference.'

He smiled down at Nicodemus, cocked his head to one side to indicate the hound should follow him and marched off towards the land at the back of the garden centre without another word, leaving Carole fuming in his wake.

'That man makes me so mad,' she said through clenched teeth.

She was sorely tempted to throw something at his back only because she was stupidly hoping that he'd turn round and smile at her the way he'd just smiled at his dog. And that thought made her madder still.

CHAPTER NINE

Carole felt very tired by the time she got back to her gran's cottage around midday. It wasn't because she'd been working so hard at the garden centre although she had certainly done that. She'd stacked the boxes, swept the very large floor space, moved piles of pots and plants and various other things to make more space and tidy around them, and then she'd cleaned the kitchen.

By the time Nick came in for coffee, he said he hardly recognised the place and asked if, like the animated version of Cinderella, she had a secret army of mice and birds to help her. She wasn't sure if he was pleased or not and when he took his coffee and went back outside, she thought he probably wasn't.

Nick asked one of his staff to show her how to work the cash register and take credit card payments and another to show her where things were. When Josie called her at eleven o'clock to ask if she fancied lunch later, she had the distinct impression that he was trying to avoid her. When he came in at twelve and told her she'd been there too long and she should go, she wasn't sure if he meant for her benefit or his.

'So you've still got feelings for Sebastian, have you, after all this time?' Mitsy asked the moment Carole walked into the cottage.

'Matilda told you then?'

'Did you really think she wouldn't?'

Carole shook her head and kissed Mitsy on the cheek. 'No. But I hoped I might get a chance to tell you first.'

'Well, as dear as Matilda is to me and as much as she assured me that she'd keep it to herself, I think it's safe to say that half the village already knows that you and Sebastian kissed and the other half will know by tomorrow.

Do you really think that was wise? Kissing him in broad daylight? Are you sure this is a road you want to go down?'

'I'm not sure about anything any more, Gran. Just a few days ago, all I wanted was for Dominic to propose and for me to become Mrs Carole Smith. I didn't have a care in the world other than that. Now ... I'm so confused, I don't know if I'm coming or going.'

'Do you want to talk about it, dear? You know I'll always be here for you. Whatever you do, you know I'll support you one hundred per cent.'

'I know you will, Gran. And I will talk to you but not just now. I need time to get my head together a bit and think things through. I will just say one thing though. Seb kissed me this morning and it was a complete surprise. I didn't know he was going to do it and I stopped it as soon as I realised what was happening.'

'That was very wise, sweetheart. Just be careful, though. Seb is a good-looking young man and we both know how much you loved him. How much we all loved him in fact, but people aren't always as they seem and, however well we think we know someone, sometimes they can take us completely by surprise. Now, how did you get on at the garden centre?'

'Quite well, I think. And it's a lot cleaner now, I can tell you that much. I'm just going to have a shower if you don't mind and then I'll tell you all about it. Oh, Josie's popping in for lunch if that's okay.'

'Of course, dear. It'll be lovely to see her. She's got a bit of a crush on Nick if I'm not mistaken.'

'How do you know that? Is it that obvious? Does ... does Nick know?'

'I should think so, dear. Josie does make rather a show of waiting to be served by him even when there are others available to help. He'd have to be blind not to notice that, although he's never said anything about it. He's very open about lots of things but not his love life. That's one thing he seems to want to keep rather close to his chest. He told me about an unrequited love in Italy but that's about it.'

'Lucia. Yes, he told me about that too, briefly. Haven't you asked him, Gran? That's not like you? You usually give everyone the third degree about that sort of thing the minute they set foot over the threshold,' Carole said, grinning affectionately.

'Of course I have. He just says that there's not very much to tell. Lucia broke his heart and whilst he's had a few girlfriends since, he hasn't found 'the one'.'

'And you didn't persist?'

'What more is there to say? The man's a true romantic, dear.'

'Really? Well, he doesn't seem that romantic to me. Sarcastic – yes. Flirtatious – possibly. Romantic – no.'

'Give him time, sweetheart. I'm sure Nick's got a few surprises up his sleeve.'

Carole headed towards the stairs to go for her shower. 'That's what worries me, Gran, although not in the way you mean.'

***

'I'm really sorry, Josie,' Carole said over lunch after telling her friend that she couldn't help out in the garden centre. 'It's a matter of Health and Safety or something. I suppose there's a cost element. He didn't really say.'

'Oh well. It's probably just as well actually. I've been asked to help out with the Christmas musical at the village hall so that's going to take up quite a bit of my time between now and Christmas Eve.'

'You don't sound very happy about it,' Carole said.

'I'm not particularly. I agreed to play the piano but now I seem to have been press-ganged into doing that, helping out with the costumes and acting as a script prompt, tea lady and God knows what else. General dogsbody, I believe

86

it's called.'

'You'll have such fun,' Mitsy declared with evident enthusiasm. 'I'll be helping as usual but I can't do as much this year because of this leg.' She shot Carole and Josie a mischievous look. 'Nick's agreed to help backstage so he'll be there every night they're rehearsing and also beforehand, moving things and suchlike.'

Josie brightened visibly. 'Really? Well, I suppose it's the least we can do, isn't it, to support the local community? And it's for a good cause, after all.'

'And what's that? The how to get Josie off with Nick cause?' Carole joked. 'Oh, don't look at me like that. Gran's known for ages that you've got a crush on the guy.'

Josie looked horrified. 'How?'

Mitsy tutted and grinned. 'Good grief, Josie. You couldn't make it any more obvious if you barged into his office naked and sat on the man's lap. Oh! Whilst we're on the subject, Carole dear, I know you're terribly busy and I really shouldn't ask but that's something you could do to really apologise to Nick.'

Carole spat out the mouthful of tea she'd just taken and even Josie looked aghast.

'Gran!'

Mitsy seemed confused and then burst out laughing. 'Oh dear, no! Oh Good heavens. I didn't mean you should sit on his lap, naked dear! That's the trouble with getting old. Things pop in and out of one's head, often with no connection to anything at all. No, no. I was thinking of the scenery and of Nick and that reminded me of the Christmas trees.'

Carole sighed with relief although she was having trouble deleting the image of herself sitting on Nick's lap ... naked.

'Sorry Gran, now you've lost me totally. Do you want me to draw some Christmas trees?'

'No, no. Well possibly. Nick's selling Christmas trees at

the garden centre and he's building a sort of archway for people to walk through and having a type of Santa's winter wonderland theme going on, with fake reindeer and suchlike – just to get the children excited. I was thinking it would be lovely – if you had the time that is, to paint a sort of stone effect entrance for the arch – as a surprise.'

'Oh I see. Um. Yes, I could do that, I suppose. It wouldn't take that long really. But ... how can I do it as a surprise when he'll be at the garden centre whilst I'm doing it?'

'Well ... this is just a suggestion, dear and please say no if you'd rather not. He'll be at the pub on Saturday evening. I know that because he's agreed to run the end of the month pub quiz. I've got keys to the centre and if you'll both help me into your car, we could go along on Saturday evening and do it then. Josie and I can organise the rest of the winter wonderland part whilst you're doing the archway. That way, when he gets in on Sunday morning, he'll see it and it'll be such a lovely surprise. What do you think?'

Josie sighed. 'I seem to have got myself press-ganged into spending Saturday night in a freezing garden centre.' She glanced across at Carole.

'Okay. I suppose we could. I'll be back there tomorrow morning so I can ask a few subtle questions and see what he has in mind, but won't he be doing it himself tomorrow? If he wants to start selling trees from Sunday, he won't leave things to the last minute, will he?'

'I think he'll probably just toss a piece of material over some MDF or something, dear. He's a very capable and talented young man but I don't think this sort of thing is really his forte. I'll rope Matilda in to help and she's got a wheelchair in her garage so that'll come in handy for me.'

***

The population of Jutsdown village may only have been

around two hundred but when all of those two hundred people seem to be talking about you, it feels like a baying mob of thousands, Carole thought as she stepped into the post office stores later in the afternoon.

'It's so good to hear that you and Sebastian have made up. Will we be hearing wedding bells for you two, after all? Although, haven't you got a fiancé already? And of course, Sebastian will have to divorce his current wife first. Still nothing can get in the way of true love, can it?' Mrs Stevens said the moment Carole opened the door.

'I could have sworn I saw her open the door to Nick last night, and this morning I saw him leave before it was even light and it looked as if he'd had a nose bleed or something!' Miss Grimshaw was saying to Mrs Edwards, the doctor's wife. 'You get those from physical exertion, don't you? I thought she was a nice girl but it seems like she's a bit of a man eater – and he's such a nice young man too. Poor Nick.'

Carole wasn't sure whether to laugh or cry and when she spotted Sebastian coming towards her on her way out, she did her best to avoid him.

'Carole!' he yelled. 'Wait up, angel.'

She stopped in her tracks at his use of the word 'angel'; she could feel her temper rising.

'Sebastian, I'm in a hurry and I really don't think you should be calling me 'angel' in the middle of the village.'

'Sorry, angel ... I mean, Carole. Old habits die hard. I always called you 'angel'.'

'Yes. Ten years ago. Have you heard what everyone's saying about us? We're the talk of the village.'

'I know but so what? You never cared what they said in the old days.'

'That was different. A lot has happened since then, not least that you're a married man and I'm practically engaged. I told you I'll call you next week. I don't think we should be seen together for a while.'

'Ooh! That sounds like we're having an affair. I rather like that.'

'Well I don't, so stop it. I mean it!'

'Okay! I suppose asking you to come to the pub with me on Saturday night is out of the question then? They still run the end of the month pub quiz. Can you believe that?'

'Yes it is, and yes, I know. I'm busy on Saturday anyway, so I can't.'

'Oh? Who with? I'm not the only person being linked with you, you know. Nick's name's been mentioned quite a few times within my earshot.'

'And mine. And I'm even less happy about it than you seem to be, so don't start, Seb. I'm really not in the mood. I'll see you next week.' She turned and dashed down the road before he could say anything more.

Her mind was a whirl and she wondered how she had got herself into such a mess. It was a good thing that Dominic wasn't coming down this weekend. How on earth was she going to be able to explain all this to him? Would he understand? Could she save their relationship? Did she want to, now that Sebastian was back?

She ran across the road without looking and only heard the screech of brakes seconds before she saw the Land Rover swerve. How it missed her, she had no idea. Unfortunately, it didn't miss the tree that was in the way of the only path the vehicle could take to avoid hitting her.

The sound of a vehicle compacting and an engine exploding was something she'd never heard before and she was frozen to the spot for what seemed like an eternity. She heard groaning metal, like a poor sound effect from a horror film when the ancient castle door opens, and she watched in stunned silence as a blood-soaked Nick staggered towards her.

This time she had killed him, she thought, as the terrifying realisation that he couldn't be covered in that much blood, and live, sank in.

'Nick!' she shrieked, finally pulling herself together and running to him as she grabbed her mobile and dialled for an ambulance.

'Are you okay?' Nick asked in a voice that sounded shocked but very much alive. 'What were you thinking? I could have killed you?'

'Killed me? Nick! You're ... you're covered in blood! I've killed you! I mean ... No! You'll live. You've got to live! I'm calling an ambulance. Why won't they answer?'

Nick grabbed the phone and pressed the end call button.

'I don't need an ambulance – I need a mechanic and the only thing dying around here may very well be that tree – and possibly my Land Rover. Thank God I didn't have Nicodemus with me.'

'But ... you're covered in blood, Nick! Don't try and be brave for my sake. You need an ambulance!'

His head and shoulders were almost completely covered in the bright red, thick liquid and she couldn't understand why he wasn't in agony.

He smirked. 'Despite your repeated attempts to end my life, I can assure you, I'm fine. I was wearing my seat belt, and my Land Rover and the tree took the brunt of it. This,' he said, wiping his forehead with a completely red hand, 'is red paint.' He yanked a handkerchief from his pocket and wiped his face. 'I had a large tub of it on the seat behind me and I obviously didn't secure the lid properly. I now seem to be wearing most of it, which is a shame, because I'd planned to use it to paint the arch for my Christmas Tree Land.'

'I ... I ... thought I'd ... killed you!' she stuttered, choking back her tears.

'Better luck next time,' he quipped. 'If I didn't know better, I'd say you were the one with the dastardly plan to do away with me and obtain total control of the garden centre for you and Mitsy. Don't worry though, I'm sure you'll think up lots more ways to achieve your goal.'

'That's not funny!' she shrieked as she threw herself on to his paint-covered chest and sobbed.

'Oh!' he exclaimed before he wrapped his equally paint-covered arms tightly around her.

It took her several minutes to realise what she was doing and regain her composure. When she finally eased herself away from Nick's embrace, she felt more than embarrassed by the exhibition she'd made of herself.

'I think I can safely say, I need a new coat,' was all she could utter. 'First it's covered in compost and now it's red paint.' She couldn't meet his eyes.

'I'm afraid you've got paint in your hair too. Oh, and on your face.'

He reached out to rub her cheek but she moved away and rubbed it herself. She needed to put some distance between them.

'Is there anything I can do to help with the Land Rover?' she asked. 'Will your insurance cover it? I'll pay for the damage if not, because it was my fault. I hope it's not a complete write-off.'

'You'll do no such thing and it'll be okay. They're pretty sturdy vehicles.'

'I thought I heard the engine explode.'

'I suspect that was the tub of paint when it hit the back of my seat. It was plastic and it hit with considerable force. Why don't you get back to Mitsy's and get yourself cleaned up if you're feeling up to the walk? I'll drop by later, if that's okay?'

'Of course. Thanks Nick. I really am so very sorry ... about everything. I'm ... I'm so relieved you're not hurt.'

She turned and walked away from him as fast as her shaking legs would carry her.

CHAPTER TEN

Carole sat in the study at her gran's about an hour later and tried to concentrate on one of her commissions. Unfortunately, it was a book cover for a romance novel and that was far too close for comfort in her present state of mind.

Ever since the accident, her mind had felt as if it were a three-lane motorway leading her in several different directions but none of them reaching a destination. It had been bad enough before when she realised she still had feelings for Sebastian, but now...

Mitsy stirred and opened her eyes. She'd been fast asleep when Carole returned.

'Hello sweetheart. I must have dozed off for a few minutes. When did you get back?'

Carole smiled. 'Not that long ago. How are you feeling? Would you like a cup of tea?'

Mitsy gave her a worried look. 'Is everything all right, dear? You look ... upset. Have you been crying? What's happened, sweetheart? What's wrong?'

Mitsy held out her arms and Carole rushed into them. For the second time today, she needed to feel the comforting hold of someone's arms around her.

'I'm so confused, Gran. Now I really do need to talk.'

'Well then dear, let's open a bottle of something, shall we and you can tell me all about it?'

Carole got up, retrieved a bottle of wine and a sherry for her gran and headed back into the study. She briefly glanced at the clock and noticed it was a little after six; she couldn't stop herself from wondering what Nick was doing now.

She poured the drinks and took several gulps of wine before telling her gran what had happened that afternoon, including the comments in the post office stores, the meeting with Sebastian and the accident. She also told her everything that had happened since she arrived on Wednesday night, less than two short but action-packed days ago.

'And finally,' she said, 'I lied to you about this weekend and Dominic. He's not away on business, he's going to Manchester to see his favourite band with some of his friends. I didn't tell you the truth because I knew what you'd say.'

'I think we both need a top-up,' Mitsy said, 'before we tackle these problems.'

'I don't know how I've got myself into this mess, Gran. On Wednesday, all I could think of was whether Dominic was going to propose and now look at me. Now I think I'm very possibly in love with three different men and I have no idea what I'm going to do about it. Worse still, my best friend is also in love with one of them and if I try to start anything with him, she'll never speak to me again. Not that I'm sure he'd want to start anything with me so that may not be an issue anyway. And why would he when I've accused him of such dreadful things and then tried to kill him several times and wrecked his Land Rover and–'

'Let's just take one thing at a time shall we, dear?' Mitsy said reassuringly. 'Do you still love Dominic? Think about it for a moment before you answer.'

Carole sipped her wine and pictured Dominic. 'Yes,' she said, 'I definitely do.'

'Enough to spend the rest of your life with him?'

'I ... I think so.'

'But you're not absolutely certain?'

Carole shook her head. 'No. I ... I thought I was but now...'

'And Sebastian. Are you sure your feelings for him are real and not just a memory of what you once had?'

Carole nodded. 'Yes. When I saw him I ... well, it was as

if none of the last ten years had happened. I even forgot about Dom for a while there.'

'And yet you're not throwing yourself in his arms and when he kissed you this morning, you pulled away.'

'Yes, but that was because of Dominic. I felt guilty. Despite what Nick thinks of me I'm not the sort of girl who cheats on her boyfriend – at least, I didn't think I was. I'm not. No. That was what stopped me kissing Seb back. I can't restart my relationship with him until I end my relationship with Dom. If that's really what I want to do and that's what I have no idea about.'

'And that brings us to Nick. You say you feel things for him that you don't feel with either Dominic or Sebastian.'

'Yes. Mainly anger,' Carole said with a sardonic laugh. 'I feel as if I would like to hit him sometimes and I've never felt like that about anyone. That's definitely not a good sign and yet, when I thought he was dying this afternoon, I would have done anything to save him, absolutely anything. And when I threw myself in his arms and felt him holding me, I ...' she shrugged. 'I don't know what I felt. I just know I didn't want to let him go.'

'That could have just been shock sweetheart, and relief because he wasn't injured. Don't confuse that with love because they are different things entirely. Out of the three men, I can say with all honesty that I prefer Nick but this isn't about me, it's about you. Love is love and it's often blind so only you can decide which one you really want. And then you must decide whether they're worth it and whether you can cope with all the baggage that inevitably comes with any relationship. Mmm, I'm not sure that was much help.'

Carole grinned. 'Possibly not but it was lovely to talk like this with you. We haven't done this for such a long time and that's my fault I know. One thing I promise, whatever comes of all this and whether I end up with one of them ... or none of them, I am definitely going to make sure

I come and see you on a very regular basis.'

'I'll drink to that!' Mitsy said, holding her glass out for a refill.

'And so will I,' Carole added, filling both of their glasses up to the brim.

***

Carole spent the morning trying to avoid Nick just as she had last night. She told her gran she couldn't face him, so Mitsy had called and asked him to let himself in as Carole was having a relaxing bath and an early night.

She still felt embarrassed by her display of concern after the accident and she needed to keep a bit of distance between them. The garden centre was fairly busy, as she assumed it probably was every Saturday morning, so that wasn't too difficult until just before lunchtime when she popped into the kitchen to make all the staff a cup of tea.

'I get the feeling you're avoiding me,' Nick said, closing the kitchen door behind him.

Carole nearly dropped the kettle. 'No. I've just been busy.' She avoided eye contact and continued to make the tea.

'Really? This hasn't got anything to do with yesterday then?'

She gave him a sideways glance. 'No. Why should it have?'

'It shouldn't, but I thought you may be feeling embarrassed because ... because you were ... in my arms yesterday. There's no need to. I know it was just the shock and you needed comforting, that's all.'

'Thank you. Yes. It was the shock. How's the Land Rover? I meant to ask earlier but ... it's been busy today.'

'It's a bit like you. In a state of shock but it'll get better with some love and affection.'

She stiffened, wondering if he meant she would also

recover with some love and affection – and whether he was offering either, or both.

'It's at the garage so I've got a hired one for the next few days.'

'I'll pay–'

'No you won't,' he interrupted, 'We had this conversation yesterday. The insurance company will, and it's not a problem so forget it. I'm just glad you weren't hurt. I could never have forgiven myself if any harm had come to you.'

She met his eyes. 'Same here,' she said.

He stepped towards her and she quickly moved away, grabbing a spoon from the drawer and picking up four mugs by their handles.

'I'd better get this tea out to them and then be off,' she said. 'Gran's expecting me home for lunch.'

'Carole?' he said, barring her escape. 'I ... I'm going to the pub tonight for the quiz and I wondered if ... if you'd like to join me ... as a friend of course, nothing more. I know you have a boyfriend, of course. I ... well I just thought it might be fun.'

'Oh. Um. I would have liked that but ... unfortunately I've made other plans for this evening.'

She saw him stiffen and a strange glint appeared in his dark eyes. 'Oh. Another time perhaps?'

He stepped aside so that she could pass. She could guess what he was thinking.

'Yes. That would be good,' she said. 'Sorry about tonight but I've promised Gran and Josie I'll spend the evening with them ... at Gran's obviously.'

He visibly relaxed. 'That's good,' he said.

'Yes. I think we're going to have a very ... exciting night. Oh, and there's no need to come round and take gran upstairs. We're having a ... sleepover party and we'll all be spending the night in the study. The sofa bed is fine for Gran for one night and Josie and I will just curl up with

Arkenarten on some cushions on the floor. Have a good time tonight, Nick. I'll see you in the morning. Your tea's over there,' she said, nodding her head to the sole remaining mug on the worktop.

She carried the other mugs out to the staff, feeling happier than she had all morning.

CHAPTER ELEVEN

Carole drew back the curtains in the study and stared out at a pristine blanket of white. It was not yet light and the glow of the street lamp opposite cast a pathway of sparkling snow crystals in the direction of the cottage. Small snowflakes were still falling and they danced before her eyes, twirling round and round in the gentle breeze.

She felt like a child again as she watched the flakes land, slowly building up a layer of snow like a *Lego* version of a winter wonderland. She smiled; she couldn't wait to see Nick's face when he opened the centre this morning and saw what she, her gran, Josie and Matilda had created last night. Christmas Tree Land might not look amazing exactly, but it did look rather pretty and it would be even more magical now that there was snow outside.

Mitsy stirred and opened her eyes, which grew wide when they spotted the snow.

'Oh Good heavens!' she exclaimed. 'It's snowing, sweetheart!'

Carole giggled. 'It looks so pretty, Gran and what perfect timing? The first day of December and the opening of Nick's Christmas Tree Land. It couldn't be better. I'll go and put the kettle on. He should be here soon.'

She kissed Mitsy on the cheek and skipped into the kitchen, chuckling as she did so. She had no idea why she felt so light-hearted, so carefree, especially as nothing much had changed since yesterday. She was still possibly in love with three different men and she still had no idea what to do about it.

One thing she did know though. After just a few short days, she'd gone from being annoyed by Nick's constant 'popping in' to actually looking forward to it. She wasn't sure whether that was a step forward or back, given her current predicament.

She thought about Dom. He would still be in Manchester, no doubt nursing a hangover after his night at *Rob The Rich*'s concert and the subsequent drinking session she knew he and his friends would have gone on. Not that he would be awake yet, of course. Dom definitely wasn't a morning person; he was a night owl.

She sighed at that thought. Despite lying to Nick on that first morning by telling him she wasn't a morning person, she definitely was, although not quite as early a morning person as he.

Sebastian was a morning person too, she remembered. When they were dating he'd often called her at six-thirty just to say, 'Good morning', and on the rare occasions they had been able to spend the night together, when they were on holiday, he had woken her with urgent kisses and passionate caresses almost as soon as the sun was up.

She could remember it so clearly; picture it so vividly, the feel of his hands on her body, his lips on hers, his–

The shrill ring of the doorbell brought her sharply back from her daydreams and she was both startled and annoyed. She realised she still wanted Sebastian, still longed for his touch and if that had been him at the door right now and not Nick, whom she knew it was, she thought she would have had a difficult job stopping herself from tearing Seb's clothes off and making love to him on the kitchen table.

She splashed cold water on her face and dashed to the door to let Nick in. To her utter astonishment, it wasn't Nick. It was Sebastian and she nearly passed out on the doorstep.

'I know you probably don't want me here,' he said, 'but Nick told me what happened yesterday and I had to come and see for myself that you were all right. Good God, Carole, you might have been killed!'

Carole was stuck on the first part of that sentence, thinking how wrong someone could be and trying very hard not to show him just how wrong that was.

'Carole!'

'What? Sorry Seb, I was ... what did you say?'

His eyes creased into tiny slits. 'Are you okay, Carole? You're not suffering from the after effects of yesterday, are you? You seem ... miles away.'

'Yesterday? Oh! The accident. No, no. I'm absolutely fine. Did ... did you say that Nick told you?'

'Yes. Last night in the pub. He said that you were crossing the road and that he almost knocked you down because he hadn't seen you but he managed to swerve and avoid you.' Sebastian sniggered suddenly. 'It must have been very funny to see him covered from head to foot in red paint though.'

'Funny! Sebastian, I was terrified! I thought ... I thought I'd killed him. I don't know what he told you or why he tried to make out it was his fault because it wasn't. It was mine. I ran across the road without looking and he had to swerve to avoid me – that part is true, but he hit a tree and smashed up his Land Rover. All because I wasn't looking where I was going!'

'Oh! Sorry I ... well at least you're both unhurt, that's the important thing. I don't know what I would have done if anything had happened to you, Carole. And ... and that made me realise something. I've told you I still love you and that I want you back but not even I'd realised how much until last night. Last night, I knew that no matter what, I have to be with you.'

Carole watched, open-mouthed as Sebastian got down on one knee on the snow-covered doorstep of the cottage. He held out a ring. And not just any ring. It was her old engagement ring, the one he'd given her eleven years ago on an eerily similar morning to this one.

It had been snowing on that morning too, she remembered, although it wasn't the 1st of December; it was on Christmas Eve and it was one Christmas Eve she thought she'd never forget. It had been the happiest of her life since her father's death.

'I know I'm still married,' Sebastian was saying, 'and I know you're living with ... Dominic, but Carole Ann Singer, will you make me the happiest man on earth by saying you'll be my wife ... as soon as my divorce comes through, that is?'

She tried to form the word but couldn't. Only minutes earlier, she'd been daydreaming about being in his arms and here he was, like the granting of her very own Christmas wish, kneeling in front of her and holding her dreams in his fingers.

'You ... you kept the ring?' she asked, incredulous that he still had it after all these years.

She'd asked Josie to give it back to his parents the moment she received the note saying he was now married. Foolishly, she'd kept it until then, still worn it even, although she had moved it over from her left hand to her right. But once she knew he was married she couldn't bear to wear it, couldn't bear to see it and although she'd put it out of sight in her jewellery box, it had taunted her. Like *Gollum* and *The One Ring*, she kept taking it out and twisting it round and round in her fingers. She'd wished it had the power to turn back time and bring her love back to her.

'Mum kept it,' Sebastian said, still down on one knee with his hand raised in the air, holding out the ring to her.

'Oh Sebastian,' she said, her voice raised by the heat of the emotions running through her, 'you don't know how long I've waited for this moment!'

As Sebastian smiled triumphantly and began to struggle to his feet, after kneeling on freezing snow for several minutes, a dog barked and ran towards Carole, barging past Sebastian and into the hall.

Carole's head shot up, and over the top of Sebastian's she saw Nick, standing transfixed beneath the lamp post opposite.

A hissing, spitting Arkenarten, fur raised, back arched, came bounding out of the front door, yowling in shock as his black paws disappeared beneath the snow. He'd been sauntering happily towards Carole as if to see what he was missing when Nicodemus had spotted him and assumed he'd want to play.

Nicodemus followed him out into the snow. Arkenarten lashed out and then leapt onto Sebastian's bent back, claws still out, in an attempt to avoid the hound's wet muzzle.

'Arrgh!' Sebastian yelled as Arkenarten's claws dug deeper, piercing the layer of coat and jumper to gain a firmer grip. He clung onto Sebastian's wildly gyrating back for one of his nine lives.

Carole watched as if in slow motion as the ring shot out of Sebastian's hand, up into the air, made a perfect arc and landed in the soft snow, sending tiny fragments of frozen water rocketing upwards like pieces of Carole's shattering heart.

She reached out for it but Nicodemus trampled the snow where the ring had fallen and a spinning Sebastian stomped on it further as he attempted to grab hold of Arkenarten and remove the cat from his back.

And all the while Nick stood motionless beneath the lamp post with his hands stuffed in the pockets of his thermal jacket as if he were encased in a block of ice and couldn't move.

'What on earth is going on?' Mitsy yelled from the study.

Suddenly, Nick dashed across the road, grabbed a snarling Arkenarten with one hand and deposited him in Carole's outstretched arms, where the cat seemed to immediately feel safe because he retracted his claws. With the other hand, Nick restrained Nicodemus by the collar and instructed him to sit, which Nicodemus did instantly.

'I think you should take Arten into Mitsy,' Nick said to

Carole. 'Sebastian, are you okay? Perhaps you should let Carole take a look at your back.'

'The ring!' Carole pleaded, staring directly at Nick.

He hesitated for a moment. 'I'll look for your ring,' he replied without a trace of emotion in his voice.

'That cat ought to be classified as a lethal weapon,' Sebastian declared.

Arkenarten hissed at him and huddled closer to Carole's chest.

'What?' she said, still staring at Nick before coming to her senses. 'Oh, Sebastian, he was frightened. What do you expect?' She glanced up at him, irritated now. 'Come with me and I'll put some antiseptic on your, no doubt severe, wounds.'

'There's no need for sarcasm, Carole. It bloody well hurts. You try having several needles stuck in your back and see how you like it.'

She tutted. 'I have,' she said. 'It's called acupuncture, and I can assure you, I didn't make anywhere near the fuss you're making.'

She marched off towards the study and Sebastian followed her.

'That's totally different and you know it,' Sebastian said.

Carole deposited Arkenarten with Mitsy. 'I'll tell you all about it later, Gran. Sebastian has war wounds and I need to see to them for him. Nick's outside but he's got Nicodemus with him so I don't know if he'll be coming in.'

'Good morning, Grandma Mitsy,' Sebastian said somewhat sheepishly.

'Is it?' Mitsy said. 'This is rather early for a social call, isn't it, young man? I hope you haven't been scaring my cat.'

'It wasn't–'

Carole stopped him by grabbing his hand and dragging him down the hall.

'Leave it,' she said. 'I'll explain it to her later. Take your clothes off.'

Sebastian brightened. 'It's been a long time since I've heard you say that, angel.'

'Not now, Sebastian. I'm really not in the mood any more. You know what I meant. Take your coat and jumper off so that I can see the damage to your back.'

Sebastian did as he was told, wincing slightly as he moved. Carole watched him, aware that his body was as good as she remembered, possibly even better, and it was still tanned from the Australian sun he'd only recently left. Less than ten minutes ago, she'd have liked nothing more than to have Sebastian standing exactly where he was now, removing his clothes. Now she wondered why she had not the slightest inclination to pounce on him or assist in any way.

Probably because she knew Nick was outside, she reasoned, scrabbling in the snow looking for her engagement ring. Such irony wasn't lost on her. The entire situation seemed to be getting more bizarre by the minute.

'How bad is it?' Sebastian asked, turning so that she could examine his back.

Carole flinched as she saw the long red weals covering a substantial portion of his back. She'd been too hard on him. They probably did hurt like hell.

'You'll live,' she said, 'and there won't be any permanent scars but I'm going to have to put antiseptic on it and it's going to sting.'

She cleaned the scratches thoroughly and administered a coating of soothing ointment.

'Oh God, that feels good,' Sebastian said. He turned and smiled down at her, sliding one arm around her waist and pulling her towards him. 'I never thought my proposal would end like this. Are you going to kiss me better?'

'I ... Oh, Nick!'

'I hope I'm not interrupting anything.' Nick stopped in his tracks in the doorway. He held out the ring and it sparkled teasingly in the light from the bulb overhead.

'Wow! Thanks Nick,' Sebastian said, letting go of Carole and moving forward to take the ring from Nick's fingers. 'What a hell of a morning this has turned out to be.'

'I was just thinking the same thing,' Nick replied. 'I'm sorry about Nicodemus chasing Arten. He doesn't seem to realise that not everyone likes him. I'll just say hi to Mitsy and I'll be off. Oh, and congratulations ... I think.' He turned and marched along the hall.

***

'It really wasn't funny, Josie, so there's no need to chortle quite so loudly!' Carole said some thirty minutes later. She, Josie, Mitsy and Matilda were sitting in the study drinking hot chocolate, which seemed suitably comforting to everyone as conditions outside were now blizzard-like.

'Oh, I just wish I'd been here,' Josie said, hugging her sides as if they hurt. 'When Matilda called me and told me that Sebastian was down on one knee, I was very tempted to dash round. If only I had!'

'I'm sorry dear,' Matilda said. 'I couldn't help myself. After our little secret agent routine last night I just couldn't sleep, and this morning I was sitting beside the window watching the snow and thinking how peaceful it was ... and then I saw Sebastian. I ... I just had to tell someone and I knew Josie would be up so ... I called her.'

'And then all hell broke loose,' Carole said, grinning in spite of everything.

'So ... does this mean that you're engaged to a married man whilst living with another one? Isn't that getting very close to bigamy?' Josie asked.

Carole sneered. 'I'm not engaged. I ... I didn't actually say yes ... this time.'

'Oh! So ... are you having second thoughts about Seb then?' Josie looked almost hopeful.

Carole shook her head. 'To be totally honest, I have no idea what I'm doing at the moment. When Seb was proposing this morning, it was so much like the first time that it brought mixed memories. A dream come true on the one hand but bearing in mind the way that worked out, a potential nightmare on the other. Part of me wanted to say yes but I ... I just couldn't bring myself to say the word. And then, after everything that happened, when he asked for my answer later, in the kitchen, once Nick had found the ring, I ... I just said I needed time, and of course, there's Dominic to think of.'

'I bet he was pleased,' Josie said.

'He didn't look pleased,' Mitsy said, glancing at Carole over the rim of her mug.

'He stormed out like a bear with a sore head,' Matilda added. 'Oh, wait a minute, that was Nick. I didn't see Sebastian leave. Your house is getting to be a bit like Piccadilly Circus, Mitsy.

'Why was Nick in a bad mood? Hasn't he seen what you did last night?' Josie asked.

'What *we* did,' Carole corrected her. 'And I assume not. He usually pops in here, then takes Nicodemus for his walk, pops back in here, then goes to the garden centre. I ... I'm not sure what he did after he left here, are you Gran?'

Mitsy shook her head. 'No. He said he had some things to do before going in today but he didn't say what and I didn't think to ask. I just said that you'd planned to be there around nine as it's Sunday and he said, in a rather gruff manner now that I come to think about it, that he thought you'd probably have other things on your mind and that the garden centre would be the last place you'd be thinking of right now. That was before I knew what had been going on of course, so I had no idea what he meant at the time.'

Josie furrowed her brows and looked thoughtful. 'It sounds to me as if he may be jealous,' she said. 'Is there anything you should be telling me, Carole?' She gave her friend an accusatory glare.

'No! Well ... no. Nothing.'

'Now's the time,' Josie added.

'No I ... oh hell. Okay. I'm really sorry, Josie but I like him. I ... I think I like him rather a lot, actually.'

Josie's eyes narrowed. She smiled, albeit a little sadly. 'Of course you do. I knew it. And why not add one extra man to the pot. After all, two are never quite enough, are they?'

'Are you really annoyed?' Carole asked.

Josie shook her head. 'No. He's not interested in me anyway so it's irrelevant. Let's face it, as Grandma Mitsy said, I've done everything but sit on his lap naked. If he had any intention of asking me out, he would have done so by now.'

'Oh, my dear!' Matilda said. 'Does that mean that you can't make up your mind between three men? Goodness gracious! But you can't have them all, you know. Well, that just wouldn't be right, would it?'

'Not to mention that it would be downright greedy,' Josie said.

'And illegal,' Mitsy added. 'You can only marry one of them – unless you're thinking of setting up three little love nests and flitting between each one – which I really do *not* recommend, sweetheart. Apart from anything else, you'd be exhausted!'

'I have no intention of doing that, Gran so don't worry. As for marrying one of them, well, let's not forget that Nick hasn't even said he likes me, Dom seems very reluctant to ask me and the only one who has proposed, is married to someone else.

'Life can be such a bitch sometimes!' Josie said with considerable feeling.

CHAPTER TWELVE

Carole trudged towards Four Seasons Gardens in ankle-deep snow, not knowing what to expect when she got there.

Her mind was whirling almost as much as the snow around her. It was still snowing heavily and she began to wonder if Nick would even bother to go to the garden centre in this weather. Would anyone actually be out buying plants, or compost or even Christmas trees in conditions like these?

All the way there she wondered what Nick must have thought seeing Sebastian propose. He knew she had a boyfriend and he'd already told her that he didn't realise she was "that sort of girl" after he'd seen Seb kiss her, so now... But would he even care? Other than thinking she was some sort of wayward trollop or something, did it matter one way or the other to him what she did in her love life? She needed to know but she wasn't quite sure how to find out. She couldn't exactly ask him, could she?

She arrived around nine thirty, unsure whether she was pleased to see Nick's hired Land Rover parked in one of the snow-covered bays. She smiled almost fondly at the line of human footprints – Nick's footprints, and the line of Nicodemus' paw prints running closely alongside. They led from the Land Rover to the door and despite having to make a slight detour in order to do so, she had an overwhelming urge to make her own imprint beside Nick's and his hound's.

She was so busy matching footprint for footprint that it wasn't until she was just a few footsteps away that she saw Nick standing at the door watching her. She saw his boots first as she had her head bent and she slowly raised her eyes up the full length of his body until she met his dark, questioning ones.

'Oh!' she said. 'I was ...' She half turned, about to point at the trail of footprints behind her before realising how silly that would make her seem, so she straightened her body and pulled the collar of her compost and paint-stained coat up around her chin instead. 'It's freezing out here. May I come in or were you just leaving?'

'Um ... I was just coming round to see you actually. To say thank you. I'm assuming you're the one I owe for making Christmas Tree Land so ... Christmassy?'

She wasn't sure if he were pleased or not. He didn't sound that happy.

'Don't ... don't you like it?' she asked, shivering, and not just from the cold. 'I ... that is we, we thought you'd be pleased. I can take it down if you don't. It's–'

'We?' he interrupted, his dark eyes narrowing.

'Gran, Josie, Matilda and me. We did it last night when you were in the pub. It was Gran's idea.'

He brightened visibly but by the look on his face, he still had questions. 'But why?'

'Could we do the interrogation inside, please? I'm rapidly turning from my usual drama queen persona into an ice queen!'

'Sorry! Of course. Come in.'

He stepped aside and closed the door, shutting out the blizzard and making the garden centre seem eerily quiet. Nicodemus was clearly relieved not to have to venture out and he bounded towards his bed in Nick's office.

'I'll make coffee,' Nick said, heading towards the kitchen. 'Did you walk here?'

'No, I drove my invisible car. It's my vehicle of choice in a snow storm.'

He turned and furrowed his brows before a loud chuckle burst from him and his handsome face softened considerably.

'Ask a stupid question ...'

She grinned. 'Do you think you'll get much business

today? I wasn't sure you'd be here.'

'Oddly enough, yes. The kids will want to buy sleds, which I just happen to have and the adults will want grit for their driveways, which–'

'You just happen to have, too,' she added. 'I can see why you called the place Four Seasons Gardens now. You're a man of all seasons.'

He smiled. 'Actually it's from Vivaldi's *Four Seasons*. The concertos were my grandmother's favourite piece of music.'

'You have a grandmother?'

'Had. She died a few years ago. This place is a sort of tribute to her. She was a keen horticulturist. I get my love of plants from her.'

'Oh, I'm sorry.'

'Thanks. Why do you always seem so surprised to learn I have relatives – or had in Gran's case?'

Carole hesitated. 'I honestly don't know,' she said, giggling.

He handed her the coffee he'd made and grinned. 'I've washed the mugs thoroughly, you'll be pleased to hear although as the kitchen was spotless when I arrived this morning, it wasn't strictly necessary. I thought I'd had little elves in overnight but now I realise it was you.'

She glanced around the kitchen. It was just as she'd left it and she couldn't help but notice that Nick had even wiped the dribble of milk he'd spilt when he'd made the coffee.

'I have a bit of a thing about cleanliness,' she confessed.

He raised his eyebrows in mock surprise. 'Really? I hadn't noticed. Anyway I really want to thank you for what you did. Even Nicodemus was impressed.'

She smiled. 'He said that, did he?'

Nick grinned. 'He was going to pee on the lamp post you drew because he thought it was real. That's praise indeed. Don't worry, I stopped him. I can't believe you did all that in just one night though. What time did you leave? I drove past on my way home and I didn't notice any lights on.'

'No idea. Around ten-thirty I guess but we got here at six-thirty and there were four of us. Matilda's got a wheelchair so Gran came too.'

'It's so beautiful,' he said, staring directly into her eyes.

She could feel herself blushing even though he wasn't talking about her but her artwork.

'Well, it is what I do for a living so I'm very glad you think so.'

'I do. More than you could possibly imagine and far more than I can find words to say. And I'm not the only one. You may have made a rod for your own back, I'm afraid. Bert Threadgold was here earlier and he saw it. You know of course that he organises the Christmas musical at the village hall every year? Well, he saw the castle turrets, the shop window and the trees and he's decided he must find a way to persuade you to do some stage scenery for this year's production.'

'Rats!' Carol said.

'Surely you mean *Cats*?' he said, chuckling into his mug.

'Don't be facetious. You know exactly what I meant and you're very lucky that's all I said! What is it this year anyway? I forgot to ask Gran and Josie. You're helping out I hear.'

'It's one of Dickens' classics, that old chestnut, *A Christmas Carol*. Although to be honest, it's one of my favourites. Oh! Are you okay, Carole, you look as if you've seen a ghost!'

Her heart felt heavy but she managed a smile. 'That was my dad's favourite. He read it to me every Christmas Eve until the year he died. Partly because my name is Carole but mainly because we both loved it.'

'God! I'm so sorry, Carole. I can be such an idiot sometimes.'

'No. It's fine. Well, there's no way I can refuse to help

with that then, is there? It looks like it's going to be a rather hectic December what with looking after Gran, completing my work commissions, helping out here and now, the Christmas musical. It's a good thing I like to be busy!'

He leant back in his chair and stared at her for several seconds as they drank their coffee in silence. She heard the garden centre doors open and several people from the village piled in, all moaning about the weather and the cold.

'Not to mention juggling your boyfriend and, it now appears, your fiancé,' Nick said, getting to his feet and marching out to meet the babbling throng without a backward glance in her direction.

Carole banged her mug down on the desk, startling Nicodemus who was curled up in his bed.

'Sorry boy,' she said, 'but how do you live with that man? He makes me so cross!'

Nicodemus let out a tiny whimper, yawned, licked his lips and went back to sleep.

Carole knew Nick would have to mention it, of course. She'd been expecting it and if she were honest, she'd have to say that she was surprised it had taken him so long. But why did he always say something controversial and then walk away? Was it because he didn't want to hear her reply?

Oh well. It was pretty obvious he wasn't interested in her romantically anyway, so at least she could strike him off her Christmas list, metaphorically speaking.

She sighed for the umpteenth time, stood up, took off her coat and headed out to help Nick serve the increasing number of customers streaming in. To her complete amazement, bad weather and garden centres did seem to go together. Well, well, she thought, who would have guessed?

***

Christmas Tree Land was a roaring success from the very

first moment. Nick said it was because of Carole's superb artwork and the layout of that entire area. She, Josie, Matilda and even Mitsy had placed strips of artificial grass between the trees and then covered everything with a light dusting of spray snow. Ornamental robins were pinned amongst the branches of some of the trees, and fairies and elves were peeping out from various spots along the way. They'd wrapped empty boxes in shiny Christmas wrapping paper, attached giant bows and ribbons and positioned them under several trees that were for sale.

An archway featured multi-coloured twinkling lights; large painted red ribbons encircled the two castle turrets on either side and warm golden lanterns hung in the painted windows. There was a toyshop window, open where the glass would have been, revealing several of the carved toys, books and stuffed animals which were also for sale, together with handmade Christmas stockings and ornaments of all shapes, sizes and colours.

At the end of the winding pathway through this magical forest was a large, plump ornamental Santa sitting beside a small red felt sack, decorated with silver ribbon and full of single sweets in silver wrappings that Carole had bought as a treat for the children.

Carole said that she thought the day's success had more to do with Nick and his straight-forward yet clever sales technique: 'I'm not going to sell you anything you're not one hundred per cent happy with.'

In Nick's mind that clearly meant not being pushy; to the customers it meant spending more money than anticipated as Nick would ask: 'Are you really sure this is the tree you want?' Or 'Do you think you have enough decorations for a tree this size?' This resulted in people deciding the tree they'd picked wasn't big enough and that they needed to buy more decorations for their larger tree.

When Carole finally left at two o'clock having called Matilda at noon and asked her if she could stay with Mitsy,

Nick had taken orders for more trees than he had in stock and there were several empty shelves which only that morning, had been full of boxes of lights and decorations. Not to mention the numerous sales of books, cards, toys and gifts; Christmas shopping madness it seemed, had firmly taken hold in Jutsdown and whether it was because of Carole's artwork, Nick's sales patter or the snowy, Christmassy weather, Carole and Nick neither knew, nor cared.

***

Nick was right about Bert Threadgold. When she got back to her gran's cottage, she discovered he'd popped in to see Mitsy and asked her to 'encourage' Carole to help with the scenery.

'I told him you were very busy, sweetheart but you know Bert. That man only hears what he wants to hear and if it isn't a yes, then he keeps asking until he gets one.'

'It's okay, Gran. They're doing *A Christmas Carol* this year so I've got to help. Dad would want me to and I'm sure I'll find the time although Nick did rather *gallantly* remind me that I also have a boyfriend and a fiancé to juggle!'

Mitsy nearly choked on her mouthful of tea. 'Nick said that? Really? Did he sound annoyed when he said it?'

'No. Just sarcastic. I'm not sure he has a very high opinion of me, to be honest but he did seem very pleased with what we did to Christmas Tree Land, so at least he likes my artwork.'

'He'd have to be blind not to, sweetheart, and as for him not having a very high opinion of you, I'm not so sure about that. Are you going to the village hall this evening?'

'Yes, if Matilda will come round and sit with you.'

'Don't worry about me, dear. You'll only be a couple of hours. You can bring Nick back here with you and tell me all about it before he takes me up to bed.'

'Okay. I'm going to get on with my commissions now. Then I must call Dom and see if he's made it back safely from Manchester or whether he's leaving it until tomorrow. I can't believe where today has gone or that it's the 1st of December. Just think, Gran, it's only three weeks and a few days until Christmas Day. Oh, that reminds me, I must call Mum and tell her we won't be going up there for the holidays. That'll please her.'

'Not as much as it'll please her to hear that Sebastian's back and he's asked you to marry him – again. That'll really be the icing on the cake. It's probably a good thing Sarah did move all the way to Scotland. If she were within driving distance of that young man, he wouldn't live to see next week, let alone Christmas Day.'

***

The scheduled 'planning and rehearsal meeting' for *A Christmas Carol* went ahead in spite of the weather. Once the blizzard had stopped, the villagers seemed to go about their business as usual, unhampered by the deep snow. Not that the blizzard had actually stopped them – in fact, far from it.

Carole and Josie arrived at the village hall just as Nick pulled up in his Land Rover.

'Hi Josie,' he said, smiling at Carole, 'I owe you a drink or something at the very least. I hear you helped make Christmas Tree Land the magical vision that it is.'

'I did indeed,' Josie replied. 'I cut up the fake grass and covered it in fake snow. I wrapped up the fake presents ... and I made the tea. Carole, of course, just sat and doodled. You don't owe me a thing. Call it repayment for the many hours of your time I've wasted, trying to find out how *not* to kill plants.'

'Have you succeeded?'

'No. Carole tells me today was a virtual sell-out. Will you be getting more trees in?'

'It was. Thanks to all of you and yes, I shall. I've got a couple of hundred coming in that I'm supplying to my sister and brother-in-law's TV production company and a few hundred more that I was planning to grow on but we'll see.'

'I didn't know you had a sister,' Josie remarked.

'No. It seems to come as a surprise to everyone,' he said, opening the door and letting them pass. 'I'm beginning to get a bit paranoid about it.'

'Perhaps if you weren't so secretive about yourself, people wouldn't be surprised,' Josie added.

'I'm not secretive, Josie. I'm an open book. You get what you see and you see what you get.'

'Apart from your surname!' Carole could not resist reminding him.

Nick's eyes met hers briefly. 'Apart from that. Oh look, your fiancé's here. I must go and congratulate him–'

'No!' Carole interrupted but Nick was already heading towards Sebastian.

'Didn't you tell him that you haven't said yes?' Josie asked.

Carole sighed. 'There didn't seem to be much point. He clearly couldn't care less.'

'Oh well. I guess Seb will tell him. I suppose we'd better get stuck in to this musical. God, I really hope they don't expect me to sing.'

'I think they know better than that, Josie. And they won't be asking me either!'

***

Whether Sebastian told Nick or not, Carole didn't find out. After the meeting to discuss allocation of roles and who was doing what, Nick disappeared, saying simply that he assumed Sebastian's dad would be giving her a lift in his Range Rover and that he'd pop round later to help with Mitsy.

She was even more disappointed to find that, after having to go out and rescue Arkenarten from Miss Peabody's garden shed where he'd managed to get himself locked in, by the time she got back, Nick had been and gone and Mitsy was fast asleep in her own bed.

Carole was more than a little annoyed when she snuggled into bed some time later with Arkenarten curled up safely on her bed, not just because she hadn't got a chance to talk to Nick but also because Miss Peabody had flatly refused to open her garden shed and let Arkenarten out unless Carole came to get him. 'There was no way' the old battleaxe had said that she was going to 'let that wild thing out and be clawed to shreds as poor, dear Sebastian had been'.

Carole was sorely tempted to tear Miss Peabody to shreds herself – verbally, but she knew that would also end up being twisted and elaborated upon. There was quite enough gossip about her doing the rounds of the village as it was.

CHAPTER THIRTEEN

'I can't believe it's Friday already!' Carole said, grabbing her bag from the floor and a slice of toast from the plate of several slices she'd brought into the study for her gran's breakfast.

'You should sit down and have a proper breakfast,' Mitsy said, tutting.

'I don't have time, Gran. I'm late again and I promised Josie I'd pop in on my way to the station. Don't forget, I'm going straight to the garden centre after my meeting and then on to the village hall. I'll try to pop back at some stage today but it's pretty hectic so I may not be able to.'

That was an understatement, Carole thought. She had no idea where the week had gone and what with her work, the garden centre and the Christmas musical, she was spending less and less time with her gran. Something had to give.

And today was going to be the worst day of all. She had a meeting with a client in Tunbridge Wells and although that was only about a half hour away by train, the snow from last Sunday's blizzard had still not completely cleared and services were severely delayed. Only in England could it take five days to clear one lot of snowfall.

'I'm really sorry about this, Gran. Next week will be better, I promise. Are you sure you'll be okay?'

'I'll be fine, it's you I'm worried about. You seem to be racing around all over the place. You'll wear yourself out.'

'It's just been one of those weeks. I'll be okay and I'll take it easy this weekend when Dom's here. You have remembered he's coming down today, haven't you?'

'How could I forget, sweetheart?'

Carole detected the hint of coolness in her gran's voice but she didn't have time to defend Dominic now.

'He'll be here around eight-thirty. If I'm not back from

the village hall by then, ask Matilda to let him in please. I've made the blue bedroom up for him. Right, I'm off. I'll see you tonight. Have a good day with Matilda.'

Carole dashed out of the cottage and almost knocked Nick flying.

'Where are you off to in such a hurry?' he asked.

'I told you yesterday. I've got a meeting with a client in Tunbridge Wells. I'll see you later. I can't stop. I'm late. Sorry.' She raced past him and ran towards Josie's.

'Have a good day,' he yelled.

She waved a hand in the air without looking back and cursed herself for oversleeping. If she'd got up at six as she'd planned, she wouldn't have been in the shower when Nick had come round earlier and carried Mitsy downstairs. She'd hardly had five minutes alone with him all week and she was wondering if she were subconsciously trying to avoid him or if he were avoiding her – subconsciously or otherwise.

The last time they'd spoken properly was on Sunday night at the village hall, just before he'd gone to congratulate Sebastian. Since then, despite them often being in the same place at the same time, they'd been like ships in the night. On the few occasions they had started to have a conversation, someone or something had interrupted them and if they weren't avoiding one another, then perhaps the universe was conspiring to keep them apart.

It was just as well really, Carole decided as she rang Josie's doorbell a few minutes later. The less she saw of him, the less she had to deal with the very definite effect he had on her psyche. It was bad enough trying to sort out her feelings for Dom and Sebastian without adding unrequited love to the mix. And she was very sure that her love for him – if that was indeed what it was and not just lust – was definitely unrequited.

'I'm running late, Josie so I've only got ten minutes, unless you want to walk to the station with me and wait for my train.'

'I'll do that,' Josie replied, grabbing her coat and shoving Carole away from the door. 'You'll need to sit down for what I've got to tell you and I can help you get on your train if the shock is too much for you.'

'Oh my God, Josie! What the hell is it?'

'Walk,' Josie commanded, linking arms and propelling Carole forward. 'I'll tell you when we get to the station. We can grab a coffee because you'll definitely need it.'

Carole tried to keep up with Josie's frantic pace. 'What's it about? Are ... are you ill? You're scaring me!'

'It's not about me. Well, I suppose it is in a way but it's mainly about Sebastian's dad.'

'Sebastian's dad? You mean Mr Jarvis?'

Josie stopped for just one second, gave Carole a look as if she were mad and then dashed onwards. 'Of course I mean Mr Jarvis. How many dads do you think the man has?'

The station was in sight and the Platform Coffee Pot was empty.

'Sit down,' Josie said. 'I'll buy.' She returned with two cappuccinos and sat opposite Carole. 'Now, I don't want you to tell anyone else about this. Okay? Except your gran, of course. She can keep a secret but on no account is Matilda to hear of it.'

Carole tutted. 'As if I'd tell Matilda. Come on. What is it?'

'He made a pass at me.'

Carole stared blankly at her friend. 'Who made a pass at you?'

'Carole! I've just told you. Sebastian's dad.'

'Mr Jarvis?' Carole said in disbelief.

'Oh for Heaven's sake, Carole! Yes! Mr Bloody Jarvis.'

Carole burst out laughing. 'When? You must have imagined it?'

'Of course I didn't imagine it! And why are you

121

laughing?'

'Because it must be a joke. Mr Jarvis wouldn't do that.'

'Well he did! He pinned me up against the piano and he asked if I'd like – and I quote, "me to tickle your ivories," that is, *him* to tickle *my* ivories, if you see what I mean. And he certainly didn't mean that he wanted to play the piano – the dirty old bugger!'

'He was joking, Josie! He ... he must have been joking.'

'He wasn't, believe me. I should have guessed, I suppose. There's always been a sort of harmless banter between us but on one or two occasions in the past he's made a really lascivious remark. I just ignored them, thinking he's got a weird sense of humour. How wrong was I!'

'When ... when did this happen? Was it at the village hall? Last night, you mean.'

'Yes and yes. You, Nick and Seb had gone and I stayed to work on that last song, the big finale, remember? Anyway, I thought I was the only one there so I had a little dance around and suddenly I heard clapping. It frightened the life out of me. I thought it was a serial killer or something.'

'In Jutsdown? Really? You're getting as bad as me.'

'Serial killers live in villages too! That's beside the point. I said I'd scream and he laughed and said he liked a woman who screamed. When I saw it was him, I relaxed ... although even then I think I knew something wasn't quite right.'

'So what happened?'

'I packed away my music and said I'd got to go and he asked me what the rush was and then he came over and said that stupid line about tickling my ivories.'

'And he definitely meant it in a revoltingly lecherous way.'

'Hmm! I think one hand grabbing my boob and the other lifting up my skirt is pretty lecherous and it was certainly bloody revolting!'

'Oh my God! What did you do?'

'What do you think? I kneed him in the groin, stomped on his foot and got the hell out of there.'

'Why didn't you come to me last night?' Carole was finding this difficult to take in.

'I did, but I saw Sebastian's car was still outside and I was hardly going to stroll in and say, "Oh, hi Seb, your dad's just tried to molest me," was I?'

'Wh … what are you going to do?'

Josie shook her head. 'I'm not absolutely sure. He put this note through my door last night.'

She handed Carole a small scrap of paper. It read:

Dear Josie,

I'm sorry about our little misunderstanding. I'm a happily married man.

Regards,

Justin Jarvis. JP

'That's short and sweet,' Carole said.

'Short notes seem to run in the family. Sorry, I shouldn't have said that.'

'What's the JP?' Carole asked, ignoring the obvious dig at Sebastian's notes.

'Justice of the Peace. He became a magistrate a few years ago, remember? He made a big thing about it.'

'Vaguely. I've tried to avoid all contact with that family if possible.'

Josie raised her eyebrows. 'Yes. So Sebastian having his tongue down your throat and proposing on your gran's doorstep is avoidance, is it?'

'Fine. I meant until this week.'

'He's such a git. Not Sebastian – his dad … although, like father like son …'

Carole frowned. 'That's not nice, Josie. Just because his dad did something stupid, and because they both seem to prefer brevity in their correspondence, doesn't mean

Sebastian would ever do anything so ... awful.'

'The thing is,' Josie said, 'it may have been a genuine misjudgement on his part. He may have actually thought I fancied him or something. We do have that sort of pseudosexual banter sometimes as I said, and I've always thought he just had a weird sense of humour. But what if it's more? What if he ... well you know ... preys on women?'

'I think we would have known about it before now if he did. He definitely fancies himself though. I've always thought that but he's never made any sort of move towards me or anyone else that I know of. Perhaps ... perhaps it's just you he fancies.'

'Lucky me,' Josie said. 'I think I'll tell him that if he ever comes near me or touches me again, I'll call the police.'

'Oh Josie, I really don't know what to say. I'm sure he would have stopped if you're told him to anyway. I'm sure he didn't mean any harm. I think he's just a middle-aged man who made a really bad mistake.'

'And mistakes are another thing that seem to run in that family, if Sebastian is to be believed. Sod it, I'm taking the morning off and coming to Tunbridge Wells. I could do with some retail therapy while you're at your meeting. I'll call in sick – and believe me the thought of Justin Jarvis lusting after me is making me feel very sick indeed.'

***

Carole couldn't believe what Josie had told her. She knew her friend wasn't lying, of course; they'd known each other since primary school and they'd always told one another the truth, even when that truth had been painful. Best friends did that.

But the thought of Mr Jarvis trying it on with someone young enough to be his daughter, and someone who was a friend of his son what's more, well, that was just too

124

difficult to comprehend. He was Sebastian's dad. Only dirty old men seduced young women. Dads didn't.

She realised how ridiculous that premise was though. Thousands of young women had affairs with much older men; some even married them and lived perfectly happily together for the rest of their lives, but this was Sebastian's dad for heaven's sake. And no matter how much she thought about it – and she thought about it a great deal all day long, she just couldn't get it to sink in.

What she really needed to do was to talk to her gran about it but once she and Josie had returned to Jutsdown after her meeting, she'd gone directly to the garden centre. Thanks to yet more delays and train cancellations, she was now running even later.

'Are you okay? You seem ... preoccupied,' Nick asked.

'What? Oh. Um. No. I mean, yes, I'm fine, it's just ...'

'Just ...?'

'It's not something I can talk to you about.'

Nick gave her a serious look. 'You can talk to me about anything, Carole. Is ... is it about Sebastian and Dominic? I hear your boyfriend's coming down this weekend. That's going to be difficult to–'

'You see! That's it, right there. We just can't have a conversation without you making some sarcastic remark about my boyfriend and my fiancé!'

Nick seemed surprised.

'Do I? I can't even remember the last time we had a conversation, well not one that lasted for more than two minutes anyway, and I certainly don't recall mentioning either your boyfriend or your fiancé when we did. Although I'd heard that he isn't your fiancé ... yet.

'Well, that just shows how much attention you really pay when we do have one! And he isn't my fiancé. At least the village gossips have got that bit right.'

'Okay. Look, I apologise if you think I'm always being sarcastic but you must admit, it's a pretty odd situation. I suppose it's a good thing only one of them lives here. You'd never be able to have a relationship with two people if they lived in the same village, especially such a small one as this. Are you worrying how you're going to keep Dominic from finding out about–?'

'You're doing it again!'

'No, I'm not. That's not sarcasm, that's a genuine question. Or does he know about Sebastian?'

'Of course he knows about Sebastian! Well ... he doesn't know he's back in the village. I haven't had a chance to tell him that yet. And he doesn't know that Sebastian proposed either.'

'So that's pretty much a 'No' then? This weekend should be fun. You could always spend the entire time ensconced in Mitsy's cottage and ...'

'And what? Go on. Have a good laugh about it. You clearly find the whole thing terribly amusing.'

'Actually,' Nick said, 'I don't.'

He sounded almost sad and that annoyed her even more.

'Oh, of course, I forgot. You don't approve of such behaviour, do you? I remember you telling me how disgusted you were by the whole thing and how disappointing it was to discover that I am 'that sort of girl'. Well, Mr High and Mighty, Holier than thou, I'm not the only one you know. You'd be surprised by how much this sort of thing happens – even in a small village like this!'

She stormed into the office to get her coat. Yet again, Nick had made her so mad that she really felt as if she wanted to hit him. She had never been the type of girl to even raise her hand and give someone a friendly slap, let alone a punch in the face as she so very much wanted to give him. The man definitely brought out the worst in her; there was absolutely no doubt about that.

She hadn't heard Nick follow behind her so when he closed the door and stood in front of it barring her exit, she very nearly did punch him in the face.

'Excuse me,' she said as calmly as her mounting temper would allow.

'No! Not until you tell me what's going on. What did you mean by that remark just now? About me being surprised how much this sort of thing happens. Has Sebastian been seeing someone else, too? Is that why you're so upset?'

She couldn't believe her ears. 'What? Sebastian! Don't be so ridiculous. He...'

'He ... what?'

'Nothing,' she said, putting on her coat and giving him a look which she hoped said, "If you don't let me out of here, you're going to regret it." Clearly he misread it.

'Sit down,' he said, 'I'll make some hot chocolate and you can tell me all about it.'

'I don't want hot chocolate. And there's nothing to tell,' she said, folding her arms and hanging her head. 'Don't you have a garden centre to run?'

'Yes, you do and yes, there obviously is. And the garden centre can wait. You're more important than this garden centre.'

Her head shot up at that and her eyes met his. He looked flustered.

'I mean ... as Mitsy's granddaughter, that is. Well ... you're a sort of stand-in for my business partner, aren't you? And ... and you're a friend. At least I'd like to think you are. And I care about my friends ... and my work colleagues.'

The spark of hope he'd ignited by his remark died and Carole slumped onto a chair, feeling thoroughly dejected.

'I'll make the hot chocolate,' he said, 'and then you had better start talking because I'm not letting you out of here until you tell me exactly what's wrong with you today.'

'It's Sebastian's dad,' she said without even realising she'd said it.

Nick had only just put the milk in the microwave but he

127

came back into the office and sat down opposite her, looking her directly in the eye.

'What about Sebastian's dad?'

Carole could detect the note of apprehension in his voice and she noticed the muscles at the side of his mouth seemed to twitch, but not in a good way. She saw his lips form a hard, tight line as if he were trying to hold something back and she wondered why he should be so concerned for Sebastian's dad.

Nick sucked in a breath. 'Carole? Has he ...? Has he tried ...? Has he done something he shouldn't have?'

Carole just nodded. She could feel tears pricking at her eyes and wasn't sure she could hold them back. She was so tired. So confused. So ... disappointed.

Nick jumped to his feet. 'The bastard! I'll kill him.' He dropped back down onto the chair and took Carole's hands in his. 'Did he hurt you? Tell me, Carole. What did he do to you?'

Carole blinked several times and little teardrops fell off her lashes like ticking time bombs. She shook her head in astonishment.

'N ...nothing! He ... he didn't do anything to me! It was Josie. He tried to grope Josie!'

Nick let out a long sigh as if he'd been holding his breath. 'Thank God for that. For one terrible minute there I thought he'd done something serious.'

He still held her hands but she snatched them away.

'He has! It is serious!'

'Are you saying he molested her? Or ... or worse? Has she been to the police? Is she okay?'

'What? No. I mean, yes, she's fine. She kneed him where it hurt and stomped on his foot so I don't think he'll be trying it again but that's not the point.'

'What is the point then exactly? You're losing me.'

'The point is he's a dirty old man. Sebastian's dad is a dirty old man!'

'Tell me something I don't know,' Nick said drily, flopping against the back of the chair.

Carole stared at him in disbelief.

'Y ... you knew? How did you know?'

'Josie isn't the only woman half his age he's hit on. From what I've seen I would say she's one of many.'

'What? No way! That ... that can't be true.'

'I assure you it is. I've seen it with my own eyes. And he tries to touch up Jenny every chance he gets. Mind you, she doesn't seem to mind and I'm not sure which is worse, the fact that he does it or the fact that she lets him.'

Nick shook his head as if he found the whole thing too distasteful to dwell on.

'Who ...who's Jenny?' Carole asked, wondering if she was about to find out that Nick fancied someone and her name was Jenny.

'The barmaid in the village pub. Don't you know her?'

'No, I rarely go to the pub.' Not someone he fancied then. She could tell by the disinterested way in which he'd made that statement.

'Of course not. You prefer to drink at home.'

'What's that supposed to mean?' Carole snapped.

'Nothing. Just that you prefer to have a glass of wine at home, that's all. What on earth is wrong with you? You seem to fly off the handle every time I open my mouth.'

'It's the way you say things. You make it sound as if you think I've got a drink problem or something. And don't forget, I've just had a very nasty shock!'

He burst out laughing. 'Good God, Carole. You really can be a drama queen sometimes you know. I don't think anything of the sort, I can assure you. As for the nasty shock, I can see why Josie would be very upset but if he hasn't tried to grope you, why has it affected you so badly? Oh, silly me. Because he's your ... sorry, he's the father of one of the two men you're thinking of marrying. Yes, I can see that would be a little unpleasant.'

'Unpleasant! I may be a drama queen sometimes but you're the king of understatement. It's horrendous! I'll never feel safe to be alone with the man again.' She shivered for dramatic effect.

Nick smirked. 'Actually, now that I think about it, I'm sure you'll be perfectly safe with him. I don't think he finds you attractive.'

Her mouth fell open and she felt her temper rising again.

'Thank you very much! Just because you don't think I'm attractive, that doesn't mean that no one else will either. Some men find me very attractive indeed.'

He raised his eyebrows. 'Of course they do. And I don't remember ever saying that I don't find you attractive. This isn't really about you, Carole, it's about him. I just don't think you're his type. In fact, I'm certain you're not. All the women I've seen him come on to have been blondes and you, Carole are definitely not a blonde.'

'Oh. I see what you mean. Josie's blonde. I assume Jenny is then, and Penelope, Sebastian's mum is. Yuk!

Nick glanced over his shoulder as someone called his name from somewhere in the garden centre. 'Just a minute,' he called back. He smiled at Carole. 'I'll have to get on. Are you okay?'

She saw the concern in his eyes and smiled back. 'Yeah. I'll be fine, thanks. I ...I'm sorry I'm such a drama queen, Nick.'

She stood up and he opened the door for her.

'You're not always a drama queen,' he replied. 'Sometimes you're really very nice. I never did make that hot chocolate for you, did I?'

She gave him a sideways glance. 'Another time perhaps. Thanks for listening.'

'Any time.'

She stopped and looked up at him. 'You know ... he is just like a serial killer, isn't he? Mr Jarvis, I mean. He only goes after a certain type.'

'But thankfully he doesn't try to kill any of them,' Nick added, grinning.

'He tries to kiss them and grope them.' Carole hunched her shoulders and shook them for even greater effect. 'And believe me, from where I'm standing, that's almost as bad.'

CHAPTER FOURTEEN

Carole and Josie arrived at the village hall around six p.m. for the ongoing rehearsal of *A Christmas Carol. To Music. Being a Ghost Story of Christmas. As Performed by The Jutsdown Village Players.* This new title for the Christmas musical had been agreed and adopted just the evening before.

Oddly enough, the new title was the suggestion of Mr Jarvis who had insisted it should be as close to Dickens' original as it could possibly be. Carole, Josie and Nick had opted out of the ensuing long and heated debate, preferring to make tea instead. In the end, Mr Jarvis got his way.

It therefore came as quite a surprise to everyone except Carole and Josie when Sebastian announced that, unfortunately, his dad had pulled out of the event for health reasons.

'Yes,' Josie said as she and Carole walked into the cloakroom to hang up their coats, 'he probably knew I was thinking of repeating my performance of last night, just to make sure he'd received *my* message.'

'It seems he got it loud and clear the first time around,' Carole added. 'I wonder if Sebastian knows the truth. Nick said that it was obvious that ... oh, hello Nick.'

Nick stepped into the tiny cloakroom area and grinned. 'Talking about me?'

'No,' Josie said. 'About Justin Jarvis, JP ... and jerk. I can't think of any other words to describe him. Well, not beginning with a 'j' anyway. Carole told me you know all about it.'

Nick smirked. 'I do. Are you okay?'

'Yeah. I was hoping he'd be here tonight so that I could ... have another word with him but Sebastian's just announced his dear dad has health problems.' She grinned broadly. 'Perhaps his wife's found out about it – Justin's wife that is, not Sebastian's. Oh, you know what I mean.'

'I was rather hoping to have a word with him myself,' Nick said. 'I don't like to see my friends upset. Another time perhaps. So ... who's taking over from Justin then? For the musical I mean.'

'Sebastian, I expect,' Josie replied.

'You're quiet, Carole,' Nick remarked. 'Everything okay?'

Carole simply nodded.

'Don't worry about her,' Josie said, linking her arm through Carole's. She's still sulking because she's not Justin's type.'

Nick grinned. 'I'd think she'd be glad about that.'

'Actually,' Carole said, 'I was just thinking how awful it would be to discover your own father is a lech. Poor Sebastian.'

Josie huffed. 'Yeah, especially when he's such a saint himself. Dear Saint Sebastian who can do no wrong in your eyes.'

'Josie! Sometimes you can be really mean, you know. And Sebastian hasn't done anything wrong.'

Carole felt a little uncomfortable defending Sebastian within Nick's earshot but she thought it was necessary.

'Unless you count proposing to a woman who is dating another man, when you're still married to someone else, as wrong,' Nick said. 'Which clearly you don't.'

'And let's not forget emptying that woman's bank account and running off on your wedding day. Then marrying someone else,' Josie added.

'That's enough!' Carole interjected. 'You've made it perfectly clear, Nick, that you find the way I conduct my love life distasteful but it's *my* love life and I'll thank you to remember that, and as for you Josie, well ... I'm beginning to think it's Mr Jarvis who had the lucky escape!'

Carole untwined Josie's arm and stormed off towards the makeshift stage at the back of the hall. She was absolutely furious. How dare they both gang up on Sebastian? What had he ever done to them?

And why did Nick think it was okay to constantly criticise her? Well, perhaps not constantly, she reasoned. He had been a godsend this afternoon when he'd listened to her ramblings about Mr Jarvis and he'd been so eager to avenge her. Why was that? Probably because that was just the sort of self-righteous person he was. Protector and champion of damsels in distress, be they young or old.

She squeezed herself between the stage and around the stacks of chairs, piled one on top of another, in order to get to the very back of the hall. This was where various sized slabs of MDF and hardboard were waiting for her to turn them into Scrooge's bedroom or his office or his nephew, Fred's, house, or some other backdrop from the story.

So far, she'd finished three but there were still the Cratchit house, the Fezziwig's Christmas party and a London street to do, together with a few other bits and bobs she had up her sleeve. Several of the backdrops could double up for other scenes by adding curtains or various pieces of material here and there and some scenes would be brought to life by adding stage props.

But this wasn't the West End of London so the more she could bring the story to life with her artwork, the happier she would be. Tonight though, as she was feeling far from happy, she decided to work on the graveyard scene.

Her mobile rang and she pulled it out of the pocket of the pair of old trousers she was wearing; one of the pairs that Nick had lent her, belonging to his sister. Dominic's smiling face greeted her.

'Hi babe. How's things?'

'Hi Dom. Fine thanks. Where are you? I can hear really loud music.'

'Yeah. I'm still in the City, hun. I'm not going to be able

to get down there tonight, I'm afraid. One of the partners insisted my department stay and work through the night to finish a big merger we're working on. A few of us have just popped out for a beer and a bite to eat. Then it's back to the grindstone, unfortunately. I'm so sorry, hun. I did try to call you earlier but it's been manic here.'

'You're joking?' Carole said even though she knew he wasn't.

Dom often had to work through the night; that's what young lawyers in the City did if they wanted to rise up the career ladder. Those who didn't went home to their families.

'I'll definitely be down tomorrow though. I'll nip home first thing and grab a shower and then I'll be on my way. I should be there by nine at the latest. I can't wait to see you, babe. I ... I've really missed you.'

Carole wondered why that seemed to surprise him so much but then she realised, hearing him saying it, it had surprised her.

'I've missed you too, Dom although it has been so busy here I haven't really had a minute to myself.'

'I've missed having sex more than I ever thought I would. We are going to be sharing a room, aren't we, babe? You have got the old ... your gran to agree to that, haven't you?'

'Er ... let's discuss that when you get here, shall we? We haven't finalised the sleeping arrangements yet.'

'Well, we'd better be or I'll be sneaking into your room in the middle of the night, regardless. I haven't had sex since you left and that was nine days ago! It's weird, isn't it? When you've got it on tap, it doesn't seem to matter but as soon as it's gone, well, let's just say you'd better get a good night's sleep tonight because you won't be getting much over the weekend. Sleep that is. Sex, you'll be getting plenty of!'

'Oh! Well I have to say, I'm not sure I like the idea of

135

being referred to as 'sex on tap' and if you're working all night tonight, sex will be the last thing on your mind tomorrow anyway. It'll be you who'll need a good night's sleep and there is no way we're having sex in gran's house during the day. That's one thing I *can* assure you!'

She turned to see where she had put the black paint she'd need for the graveyard scene and was mortified to see Bert Threadgold and his wife, Ivy, together with Nick, standing just a few feet away. From the horrified expressions on Bert and Ivy's faces they'd heard every word of that last comment, and clearly so had Nick, although as he turned and walked away, it was difficult to see what he thought.

'Not even a quickie?' Dom was asking.

'I ... I've got to go. We'll discuss it tomorrow.'

'But–'

Carole pressed the end call button and smiled sheepishly at Bert and his wife. 'That ... that was my boyfriend,' she said.

'Really, dear?' Ivy asked, giving her a curious look. 'Which one?'

Carole opened her mouth to reply but thought better of it. There really wasn't any point. Instead, she smiled back and continued her search for the tin of black paint whilst Ivy Threadgold regaled her with reminiscences of her own 'wild' days and Bert went off, he said, to see where young Nick had got to.

***

'Peace offering,' Josie announced an hour later, holding out a cup of tea and two chocolate digestives.

Carole smiled. 'Get me two more choccie biccies and you're forgiven.'

'Consider it done. I'd offer to buy you a drink in the pub but I know you've got to get back for Dom so maybe one day next week instead.'

'Sure. I can't remember the last time I went to the pub. It'd be fun even if only to see your competition.'

'My competition? Oh! Jenny, the barmaid, I assume you mean.'

Carole grinned and bit into one of the biscuits. 'And Dom's not coming down tonight,' she said through a mouthful of crumbs.

'Why not?'

'He's working.'

'Did I just hear you say your boyfriend won't be down, after all?' Sebastian asked as he squeezed past the pile of chairs. 'Working again? He was away on business last weekend, wasn't he? I hate to say this, Carole but are you sure he's telling you the truth?'

'He ...' She was about to say that he wasn't working last weekend and that it was she who had lied about it, not Dom, but she realised that by saying he'd gone to see a band without her was probably just as bad in Sebastian's mind. 'Yes, Sebastian, I am. He works really long hours. All City lawyers do. It goes with the territory.'

'Well, I know where I'd rather be, given a choice between you and a stuffy old office, and it wouldn't be the office.'

'And I'm sure Dom would rather be with me too, Seb, but if you want to get on and make a real career for yourself, you've got to put in the time. And Dom does want to make a career for himself. He's hoping to be offered a salaried partner position in the next year or so and after that, if he can keep up his billable hours and bring in new clients, he may be offered an equity partnership.'

'It sounds like hard labour to me,' Sebastian said. 'Anyway I came to say that Bert has decided he wants to add a Christmas carol to the list of songs – and I mean an actual Christmas carol as opposed to the book. He's looking for you, Josie.'

'Oh joy! Perhaps I'll suggest *Silent Night*,' Josie

quipped. 'Let's face it, by the time we get round to singing a carol, that's what everyone will be praying for – a very, very, silent night. See you in a mo.'

'So,' Sebastian said, moving closer to Carole after Josie had gone, 'do you fancy doing something tonight?'

'Like what?'

'Like ... anything you fancy. I know what I fancy.' He reached out and ran a finger down the row of buttons on her blouse.

'Sebastian!' Carole backed away. 'Dom may not be coming down tonight but he will be here tomorrow. I can't do this. Not now. Not ... not until I get things straight in my own mind. Despite what some people in this village may think I'm not the sort of girl who cheats on her boyfriend.'

She saw the look of disappointment in his eyes.

'What do you mean by "get things straight" in your mind? Are you ... are you saying that there's a chance you may not ... that you may decide to stay with him?'

'Well ... yes. Yes there is. Of course, there is. Come on, Sebastian. I haven't seen you for ten years. Ten whole years and the last time I did, I thought we were getting married ... until you ran off. I've been with Dom for three years now and despite what you say, he won't run off and leave me, I'm fairly sure of that. He may take his time to actually propose but I honestly think he'll be around for the foreseeable future. Can I say the same about you, I wonder?'

'Yes! Of course you can. Look Carole, I made a mistake. People make mistakes. All I want is a chance to make it up to you. To show you how much you mean to me. I'll marry you next week if that's what it'll take. Tomorrow even. I'll prove to you that you can rely on me. I mean it, Carole. I want you to be my wife. That's why I proposed!'

'Er ... aren't you forgetting one teensy-weensy thing?' Josie chipped in from the other side of the pile of chairs. 'Sorry, Bert's gone walkabout so I was bringing more biscuits to Carole and I couldn't help but overhear. I hate to be a fly in the ointment, Sebastian, but don't you have to get divorced first? I don't know how long it takes to get divorced in Oz but over here you may recall, it takes a while.'

'Semantics,' Sebastian said, scowling at Josie.

'I don't care what religion you are,' Josie said, giggling at her own joke, 'it still takes a while.'

Sebastian sneered and stood his ground. Josie shuffled past the pile of chairs, grabbed one off the top and sat down.

'Well, I'll leave you to think about it then, Carole. I don't want to rush you. You obviously need time to come to the right decision and I'm not going anywhere so that's okay with me. I'll see you later.'

He turned and gave Carole a lingering kiss on her cheek before smiling broadly at them both. They watched in silence as he marched off.

'I thought he just said he wasn't going anywhere,' Josie joked as she bit into one of the biscuits.

'And I thought you said those biscuits were for me.'

'Oops! It seems you can't trust anyone these days.' Josie stuffed the rest of the biscuit in her mouth and smiled as broadly as Sebastian had just done.

CHAPTER FIFTEEN

Carole heard the shrill ring of the doorbell and realised she'd overslept again. She didn't know what the matter was with her lately; she just seemed so tired all the time. She tried to get up but her head was swimming and when she suddenly sneezed, a piercing pain shot through her throat and chest. She'd got a cold – and a bad one.

She reached out for her mobile and called Nick.

'You'll have to let yourself in,' she managed to say, 'I've got a really bad cold and I can't get out of bed.'

He didn't reply and she ended the call when she heard the front door open.

'I'll bring you up some honey and lemon,' he called up the stairs. 'Stay put.'

She thought that was a rather futile comment as she had just told him that she couldn't get up anyway.

Moments later, he popped his head around the door and strolled in.

'Don't bother to knock.'

'I see your sarcasm is alive and well.'

'Yep. Just me who's dying.'

'Drama queen.'

She opened her mouth to retaliate but couldn't think of anything suitable to say. Another sneeze took her totally by surprise.

Nick jumped back and crossed his index fingers in the shape of a cross, grinning as he did so.

'It's not funny,' she snapped. 'It hurts.'

'Sorry. I've put the kettle on and I'll make you a hot honey and lemon drink but I thought I'd check to see if you want anything else. What time is your boyfriend arriving?'

'Bugger, I'd forgotten he was coming today. Oh God, I'd better try and get up.' She lifted her head off the pillow and twisted onto one elbow.

'That's far enough,' he said, placing a cold hand on her shoulder and easing her back down.

'Your hand's cold,' she said.

'And you're hot,' he replied.

'So I've been told – although Mr Jarvis doesn't seem to think so.'

Nick smirked. 'And your humour is hanging on by a thread. We may be able to save you yet.'

'It's too late for me. Save yourself.'

'I don't get colds.'

'Nor do I. This isn't a cold. It's bubonic plague or ... or stage fever. I got it from that draughty village hall. Atchoo! Atchoo!'

'It's a pity we're not doing *Cinderella*. You could play the part of Sneezy.'

'Wrong production. That was *Snow White and the* ... A... tchoo!'

'Hmm. That's a new one on me. Just as well it's not *Sleeping Beauty*.'

Her watery eyes shot open. 'Thanks very much. You certainly know how to make a girl feel better!'

He grinned. 'I meant because you keep sneezing, not that you aren't beautiful. You have looked better though, if I'm going to be honest.'

'Thanks. You say the nicest things. Atchoo!'

'I'll make the drink.' He headed towards the door, stopped and looked back. 'It's none of my business of course, but why don't you phone your boyfriend and tell him not to come down this weekend?'

'Why?' Carole asked, wondering for just one moment if...

'Well, I get the distinct impression that he and Mitsy don't quite see eye to eye. There's no point in him being here kicking his heels if you're going to be spending the weekend in bed, is there? Although ... having said that, isn't that precisely what he was hoping for?'

'Very funny. I'm not going to be spending the weekend in bed. I'll just stay here for a few hours and then I'll get up.'

'I don't think so. You really do look dreadful.'

'Go away,' Carole mumbled, turning over and burying her head in the pillow.

He had a point though, she thought. It would be silly for Dominic to drive all the way here and then find he'd have to play nursemaid to both her and her gran. None of them would enjoy that. Damn it! Nick was right.

She reached out for her phone again and called Dom. It took him a while to answer.

'Have you left yet?' she asked.

'Sorry babe,' he said sleepily. 'I didn't get in until five and I just crashed out for a few minutes. I'm leaving now.'

'No!' Carole said. 'I've got a really bad cold, Dom and I can't get out of bed. That's why I'm calling. I think it's best if you don't come down this weekend. I won't be able to do anything and you'll just be sitting here twiddling your thumbs. Besides, I don't want to give you my germs.'

'But hun, I miss you. I've been looking forward to this weekend all week.'

'Me too, Dom but I can't do anything, and I do mean, anything. I can't even get out of bed yet because I feel so bad. Come down next weekend instead.'

He didn't answer for several seconds. 'Okay,' he finally said, followed by a lengthy sigh.

He sounded like a little boy who'd just been told he can't go out to play, Carole thought.

'I'm sorry, Dom,' she said. 'But it is only a week.'

'Yeah, but it feels as if you've been away forever already. I suppose you're right though. And that'll give you time to talk to your gran and make sure we're in the same room because if I've got to go without sex for another week, by next weekend I'll be ready to rip your clothes off

142

on the doorstep.'

For some reason that didn't sound quite as appealing as it should have. She must be ill, she thought.

'Okay. I'll see you next weekend.'

'I love you babe. Get better soon.'

'Thanks, Dom. I love you too.'

She ended the call and dropped the phone onto the bed. Her head was thumping and her nose was running; her eyes were streaming and her throat was sore but she suddenly realised that, although she did love Dom and she did want to see him, she was actually rather pleased that he wouldn't be coming down for the weekend – she just wasn't sure why.

***

Carole spent all of Saturday in bed, not because she wanted to but because Nick insisted on it.

'But I need to look after Gran,' she argued.

'And give her your cold. That's a brilliant idea. Matilda's coming round to be with Mitsy, so you can stay put. I've made you this flask of honey, lemon and hot water,' Nick said, putting a giant-sized flask on her bedside table, 'and here's some of my homemade remedy to help soothe your throat even more.'

'What's in it?' Carole asked warily.

'You probably don't want to know but it's good for you and it works, so do as you're told and take it.'

'Don't be bossy. I'm ill!'

'Which is why I'm being bossy. Stay in bed, get plenty of sleep and I'll see you this evening. Call me if you need me.'

'Dom's not coming down,' Carole said, hugging the duvet around her for comfort. 'You were right, so I called him and told him not to.'

'And he agreed?' Nick seemed surprised.

'Of course he agreed. Why wouldn't he agree?'

Nick shrugged his shoulders. 'No reason.'

'What? You might as well just say it. There's clearly something on your mind.'

He fixed his gaze on her. 'If it were me, I'd still come down.'

Her mouth fell open in astonishment. 'That's just silly! You said yourself that he and Gran don't get on. And why risk getting a stinking cold just to see me?'

'Love?'

'Atchoo! Are ... are you suggesting he doesn't love me?'

'I'm not suggesting anything. I'm merely saying what I would do.'

'But you were the one who told me to tell him not to come!'

'Yes.'

'Why do that if you thought he should be here?'

He shrugged again. 'I ... thought it was for the best.'

'What does that mean?'

She thought she saw something in his eyes but as hers were so watery, she couldn't be sure.

'Does it matter?'

'Yes it matters! What are you playing at, Nick?'

'I'm not playing at anything. It was the sensible thing to do. And as you said yourself, why risk getting a cold?'

'So ... now you're saying he's doing the right thing by not coming? A ... tchoo!'

'I'm not saying it's right or wrong. We all do what we want to do. We all make our own choices.'

'So ... you're saying that you think he does love me. He just makes different choices?'

'It doesn't matter what I think, does it?' He turned and walked towards the door, stopping briefly at the threshold and glancing back at her. 'All I'm saying is that Love isn't sensible.'

***

When Carole awoke on Sunday morning, she heard three things.

The first was the sound of Nick's deep, throaty, infectious laughter.

The second was a loud, gravelly Scottish accent.

The third was her mother's unmistakeable voice.

She was dreaming, obviously. She must be dreaming. Please, dear God, let me be dreaming!

The footsteps on the stairs weren't Nick's. The person humming *God Rest Ye Merry Gentlemen* wasn't Nick. The long, wavy but elegantly tied back, titian hair definitely wasn't Nick's.

'Morning darling!' Sarah Singer said as she positively bounced into her daughter's bedroom.

Carole's head shot up from the pillow as if she were seeing *The Ghost of Christmas Past*. Her mother was carrying a tray, bearing a mug of tea and a plate of her special scrambled eggs.

It was as if the clocks had been turned back and Carole was a child again, living in a happy and loving home where her mother dressed like a mum and not like mutton dressed as lamb, and brought her tea and curried scrambled eggs, which were Sarah Singer's remedy for curing all ills.

'Mum?' She wondered if she were suffering from a fever causing her to hallucinate. 'Is ... is that really you?'

'Of course it's me, cherub. Who else do you think it is?'

'I'm really not sure. You ... you look so different. So much like ...'

'Like I used to when I was a mum and not a raving lunatic, you mean?'

Carole's eyebrows shot up in surprise. 'No, I ... well ...'

Sarah placed the tray on the bedside table and sat on the edge of Carole's bed. She took her daughter's hands in hers and squeezed them.

'It's okay, cherub. I know I haven't been the best of mums over the years and for that I'm truly sorry but I'm going to make it up to you, I promise. To you and to Mum. I ... I put you both through hell sometimes after ... well ... after your father died, I realise that, but it's taken me until now to see it.'

'And ... and what's brought about this ... Epiphany?'

'Jamie. Purely and simply, Jamie. He's made me see what I was doing. Where I was going wrong. How much ... I've been hurting you and Mum. I can't say I've completely and utterly transformed or reverted to the way I was before, but I'm getting there. It'll take time but with his love and understanding and with your help and Mum's, I think I can finally say goodbye to crazy, depressed Sarah Singer, single, widowed mother out of control, and hello to rational and happy, homely Mum. Now eat your scrambled eggs. We need to get you well.'

'Wow!' was all Carole could say. She really couldn't think of anything else.

With her mum's help, she sat up and bolted down the scrambled eggs. She hadn't realised how hungry she was but as she hadn't eaten anything all day yesterday, in spite of both Matilda and Nick trying to make her, she wasn't really that surprised.

Sarah sat on the bed and watched her eat, taking the plate from her when she had finished.

'Is that Jamie I can hear downstairs?' Carole asked, leaning back against the pillow and feeling much better already.

Sarah smiled and Carole could see the love in her eyes, in her smile, in fact, everywhere. It was as if her mum were surrounded by an aura of love.

'Yes. He wanted to come with me.'

'But ... but why are you here, Mum? I mean ... how did you get here?'

Sarah chuckled. 'Well, I should give you a telling off

about that. Imagine not telling me that my own mother had broken her leg and that you were coming to look after her. But I suppose I can't really blame you, can I? I'm here now and that's all that matters. I called you at home on the landline and Dominic told me you were here, looking after Mum but that you were ill. I told Jamie I had to come and see you, both of you, and the next thing I know he's booked our flights and here we are.'

'Wow!' Carole said again. She had never been so surprised in her entire life, as far as she could recall.

'And it'll be a good opportunity for you and Mum to really get to know Jamie. That's why we wanted you all to come up to us for Christmas. So that we could be together. Be a ... family. Now we'll be spending Christmas here instead.'

Carole's eyes were watering and it wasn't from her cold.

'But ... what about your business? What about his job?'

'I can run my little bath product business from anywhere and Jamie can do the same with the websites he designs and builds. We don't need to be in Scotland to do that. In fact, cherub, we were discussing it on the way here and ... well, nothing's certain yet but with Mum getting on, and Scotland being so far away from you both, we may be thinking of moving down to Sussex – permanently.'

Carole was astonished. 'But ... you've only just moved up to Scotland to be with Jamie. Would he want to come down here?'

'He says he'll be happy to. He wants to be with me so if I decide I need to be here, he'll come here. I went to Scotland to be with him but there's no reason we have to stay there. I hadn't really thought about how far it was from you, and he says he can live anywhere as long as we're together.'

'Wow!' Carole said yet again. Words failed her completely.

147

CHAPTER SIXTEEN

Nick wasn't quite sure how he felt.

On the one hand, he was really pleased to have finally met Carole's mum. He'd heard so much about her from Mitsy and snippets here and there from Carole, but when he saw her in the flesh she was nothing like he'd imagined.

Mind you, he clearly wasn't the only one surprised by Sarah Singer. Mitsy was evidently astonished, not just to see her daughter whom she hadn't laid eyes on since Sarah had moved to Scotland in the summer, but also that apparently, Sarah had metamorphosed into the person she had been, many, many years ago.

Carole had been almost overwhelmed, it seemed. On the insistence of her mother, she had remained in bed and Nick had only seen her for a few brief seconds when he'd popped his head around the door to say hello, but as Sarah was sitting on the bed and brushing Carole's hair, he hadn't stayed.

Despite Mitsy saying he was welcome to come back for Sunday lunch which Sarah had insisted she would be cooking, or to pop back later for tea, he'd felt it wasn't his place. They were a family reconnecting and Nick didn't belong there. He wasn't a relative and nor was he ever likely to be and somehow that took some of the pleasure out of the evident joy both Mitsy and Carole were experiencing. He wanted them both to be happy; he just hadn't realised their happiness would come at such a cost to him.

'I'm a fool, Nicodemus,' he said to his hound as they sat in his office on Sunday evening. 'Nothing but a bloody stupid fool.'

Nicodemus didn't comment but merely let out a long, doggy kind of sigh and went back to sleep.

His phone rang and Nick felt an even bigger fool when he answered it.

'Hi, it's Carole. I just wanted to check that you were okay. You haven't been round since this morning, Gran tells me.'

'I'm fine, thanks. Just busy that's all. How are you feeling?'

'So much better, thanks. I'm not sure if it was your homemade remedy, Mum's special scrambled eggs, or just the unbelievable shock of seeing her, and not just seeing her but seeing her so happy and so much like the mum she used to be. Perhaps it's a mixture of all three.'

'Possibly. It was clearly a wonderful surprise for you and for Mitsy. I'm so pleased for you both.'

'Thanks Nick. And you have no idea just how much of a surprise it was, believe me. When Dad died, Mum really lost it. And I do mean *really* lost it. I can understand why, of course. Dad was, well, the most wonderful man anyone is ever likely to meet and he and Mum were so happy, so completely in love. It was the kind of stuff in fairy tales, and then suddenly, he was gone. She literally fell apart. Shattered before our eyes, and each little fragment dashed off in different directions. I honestly never believed for one single second that they would ever all come back together again and I would get my mum back. Sorry, I'm rambling. You don't want to hear this.'

He sat up in his chair. 'I do, Carole. I do want to hear it. I just wish you were here with me, instead of telling me over the phone.'

'Oh! ... I ... Um ... well ... Gran was wondering where you were so ... why don't you pop in for a cup of tea later ... or ... hot chocolate?'

He realised he'd been stupid, said the wrong thing and now she felt she had to be polite.

'I can't, I'm afraid,' he lied. 'There's lots to do and with you not being here for the last two days, things have started to pile up.'

'Oh! Of course. And I'm really sorry about that. I'll ... I'll be in tomorrow. The cold has almost completely gone. It must have been one of those twenty-four hour things so don't worry about catching any of my germs. And Mum says she is going to be staying, so as she'll be able to look after Gran, I can put in more hours at the garden centre if you like, especially as it'll be Christmas in less than three weeks now.'

'Really? I'd have thought you'd want to take the opportunity to go and see your boyfriend for a couple of days. I can manage here perfectly well without you, so there's no need to worry about that.'

He knew that was a mistake as soon as he'd said it but it was too late to explain that he hadn't meant it to sound quite the way it had.

'Oh! Fine. I may just do that. At least he'll be pleased to see me. Thanks again for the remedy and stuff. Oh, and don't worry about coming round to help put Gran to bed or get her up in the morning. Jamie's more than capable and he and Gran are getting on like a house on fire. That's one burden off your shoulders, at least. Bye Nick, and thanks for all your help. I'll see you in a few days.'

'Carole I ...'

She had rung off.

He slammed the phone down on his desk, startling Nicodemus who whimpered.

'Sorry boy,' Nick said. 'I told you I was a bloody fool, didn't I?'

Nicodemus stood up, stretched his long graceful legs in front of him and strutted over to Nick. He plopped his head on Nick's knee and stared up at him with huge brown, sympathetic eyes.

Nick smiled and stroked Nicodemus' sleek golden fur. 'At least someone loves me,' he whispered, 'even if it is just you.'

Sebastian was beginning to have doubts.

Surely if Carole really loved him, she should have made a decision by now? How much more would it take to convince her that he loved her and that they should be together?

When he'd bumped into her that day in the village, he'd been overjoyed. He'd often thought about her over the years and wondered if he'd made the biggest mistake of his life. He'd wondered what she looked like, whether she had changed. He'd wondered if she was happy, or whether she still longed for him as much as he sometimes longed for her.

When he saw her in the flesh and she looked even more beautiful than he remembered, he'd been more certain than ever that his decision to return to Jutsdown had been the right one, even if perhaps, it hadn't been for the right reasons.

He felt as if fate were giving him another chance – giving them both another chance, at finding happiness.

Now he wasn't so sure.

He knew that Carole was devastated when he left. He knew it had taken her years to get over him; that much he'd heard from his mother and father via the Jutsdown grapevine. He knew that she was still running her own business, the business she'd started in the study at her gran's house, and that it was doing well. He also that knew she was living with someone and he'd felt an odd sort of heartache when that news reached him – almost as if a door that he had thought would be permanently open, had slammed shut in his face.

He hadn't really known what to expect when he returned to Jutsdown. Things had changed and people had moved on but somehow it was still the same as it had always been and as he walked through the village, he began to feel as if he'd never left.

Seeing Carole and the look in her eyes had reinforced that. It was clear she wasn't completely over him; that she still had feelings for him, and a trickle of hope ran through his veins. Perhaps they could pick up where they left off? Perhaps it could be as it once was? Sex had always been good between them and they had so much in common that he was sure it would only take a few words, a few looks, a few kisses and she'd be back in his arms. She'd be his again and he could forget the last few years and put Australia and his life there, very firmly behind him.

But he'd been giving her the looks, the words, the kisses – or at least he'd tried to, and she seemed oddly reluctant to commit. She seemed to doubt him, doubt his love. Even when he'd got down on one knee in the snow and proposed, just like he had all those years ago, she didn't seem sure.

Perhaps her feelings for her new boyfriend were stronger that he'd thought. Perhaps it would need more time. She hadn't said 'No', after all. She'd only said she needed to think about it, to sort her feelings out. All he needed to do was be there, tell her he loved her, remind her of the sex they had, show her what she was missing, make her realise that she wanted to be with him; needed to be with him.

He and Carole were meant to be together – he just had to convince her of that fact. It seemed though that this was proving more difficult than he had ever expected.

***

Dominic had made a decision.

Now that he had, he wondered why it had taken him so long to get there.

He thought he was happy with things the way they were; thought he and Carole would just go on living together for the foreseeable future and that nothing much would change. He now realised he was wrong.

Change was good. Things needed to change. Change meant moving forward, planning a future, laying firm foundations. Change was a positive step in the right direction. But would Carole think so too?

He opened a bottle of wine, poured himself a large glass and went over the three years of his relationship with Carole as if he were reading a client file and separating the positives from the negatives. He analysed what each of them brought to the relationship; debated the merits of a permanent merger. He'd done something similar before of course, just a little over a year ago when he suggested she move in with him. And that had been a wise move – a good decision and a beneficial relationship for both of them.

He worked very long hours and his career was important to him so having Carole work from home was a positive on so many levels. She made breakfast for him; she kept the house immaculate, perhaps a little too immaculate but what the hell – we're all allowed our little foibles. She had a meal waiting for him when he got home and she was good in bed.

Not that that part had mattered to him very much. He liked sex – didn't every man? But there were other things far more important than sex in a lasting relationship. And Carole ticked all those boxes and then some.

Oddly enough, since being with Carole he'd started to enjoy sex more. He hadn't realised quite how much until these last few days, in fact. He was getting to the stage where he was thinking of little else, even at work, and that really wasn't a good thing. He was finding it increasingly difficult to concentrate and if he didn't get some soon, he was sure his work would suffer and the partners would notice.

Damn his luck, he thought. Why did she have to go and get a cold this weekend? Now he'd have to wait another five days and he wasn't sure if he could do that. How could this have happened? How could he, Dominic Smith, one of the brightest young lawyers in the square mile with a razor-sharp mind and negotiating skills par excellence, suddenly be ruled by his dick?

And not just by his dick, but by his heart. He had assumed that he and Carole would get married one day; he'd taken that for granted but since she'd been away he'd realised that he had a problem. He did take her for granted and he was beginning to get the strangest feeling that she was slipping away, or possibly even, being courted elsewhere like one of his top clients being wooed by a rival firm. He had to seal the deal and he had to do it soon. Perhaps he'd do it next weekend. He'd go down to Jutsdown village. He'd face the barely hidden disapproval from her gran and he'd make Carole an offer he hoped she couldn't refuse. He'd ask her to become his wife, Mrs Carole Ann Smith. And ... he even liked the way that sounded.

CHAPTER SEVENTEEN

Carole sat on the floor of the study, curled up at her mum's feet and leaning her elbow on Sarah's knees whilst Sarah stroked Carole's hair just as she had so many years ago.

Arkenarten was sprawled on his back, legs stretched out, on the cushions of the window seat, purring contentedly and no doubt dreaming of mice. Mitsy was resting comfortably on the sofa bed listening to Jamie who was reading her the latest of her favourite author's murder mysteries, which he had downloaded just that evening to his iPad.

Carole watched his face as he acted out the part of each character with some relish and she wondered how it was that a person's life could change so dramatically in the space of just a few short hours.

If *The Ghost of Christmas Yet to Come* had shown her this vision, she wouldn't have believed it and she would have suggested very firmly that the ghost needed to seek alternative employment because foretelling the future clearly wasn't his forte.

For almost twenty years she'd watched her mother become a virtual stranger; one whom she saw less and less of over the years until it had got to the point of meeting only on rare occasions such as Christmas and birthdays. A woman who was so disinterested in anything very much except an almost deranged pursuit of finding another man who would take care of her and then running off from him as soon as she did. A woman who had once been jolly and loving and carefree to a woman who had become depressed, detached and turned everything into a bit of a drama.

She had never been as obsessed with cleanliness as Carole was – in fact far from it. Carole's childhood home had been filled with treasures and mementos, books and toys, her mother's collections of this and that but it had never been dirty or untidy. It was a sort of organised chaos. Everywhere they had lived since had become progressively worse to the extent now that visitors were tempted to wear biohazard clothing before entering.

Both Carole and Mitsy had tried to convince Sarah to seek professional help to combat her grief and depression but she had dismissed the idea, assuring them that she could cope and that they should worry about themselves, not her. And she had coped, but for almost twenty years, she had been desperately unhappy. Until now.

'I'll go and make some hot chocolate,' Sarah announced. 'It's ten o'clock and I don't know about the rest of you but I'm ready for bed.' She smiled lovingly at Carole. 'And you need to get a good night's rest, cherub. You're not completely over this cold and you need your sleep.'

'I'll help,' Carole said, rising to her feet and stretching just as Arkenarten would.

Sarah took her daughter's arm, linked it through hers and they wandered towards the kitchen in a comfortable silence.

'So are you going to tell me what's wrong or do we have some way to go before we're back to a mother and daughter sharing confidences kind of relationship?' Sarah asked as she put the saucepan of milk on the gas hob.

Carole grinned. 'To be honest Mum, this is all a bit surreal. Wonderful, but weird nevertheless.'

Sarah nodded. 'I can understand that and things won't get back to the way they were or even close to an average mother and daughter relationship for some time, I suppose. There are a lot of bridges to build and for me, a lot of bad habits to break but I want to try, cherub. I really want that with all my heart.'

'Me too, Mum and today has been ... magical. Jamie is a wonderful man and it's been great to spend more time with him. I'm not sure if I should say this but–'

'He reminds you of your dad,' Sarah interrupted. 'I think that was what drew me to him. They're not exactly the same, of course. That would be too weird but they both have that something, a sort of quiet strength. And a kindness and tenderness that you only find in men with truly good hearts. And they are few and far between, cherub, let me tell you.'

'I ... I feel as if I've known him for years, Mum, and not that I've only met him a few times before. I feel really at ease with him. Comfortable.'

'That's exactly how I felt the moment I met him. You know what I was like with men. I shudder now to think of the way I behaved, mainly because of the unhappiness I caused you, but with Jamie, it was different. I am truly sorry for all that my darling. I hope one day you can forgive–'

'Forget it, Mum. There's nothing to forgive. That's one thing we can put in the past. I'm a big girl now and believe me, I know how confusing emotions can be. You were grief-stricken over Dad. I get it, really I do. I'm just so pleased to see you so happy now. It really is incredible though.'

'I know. But Love is a gift. Your dad always used to say that. And it comes to you in the most unexpected ways and in the most unexpected packages. It wasn't love at first sight with Jamie but I felt something from the very first moment I saw him and I knew my life was going to change. I just didn't know it was going to turn into something so wonderful. But that's enough about me. Let's get back to what's going on with you. I may not have been around much and I may have chosen to ignore the signs but I can still tell when something is troubling you.'

'I think I'm in love with three very different men,' Carole said, surprising herself by her openness.

'Well,' Sarah replied, 'let me just take this hot chocolate in to Mum and Jamie and then you and I can sit and have a good talk.'

'But I thought you wanted to go to bed?'

'Carole, my darling, some things are far more important than sleep but you do need your rest so I'll tell you what, why don't you go upstairs and get ready for bed and I'll come up and we'll snuggle under the duvet, just like we used to. The last time we did that was when you had that crush on Bradley Dawes after your fourteenth birthday party.'

'God Mum, I can't believe you still remember that!'

'I remember everything, cherub. I just forgot it all for a while there.'

Carole followed her mum into the study, said goodnight to her gran and Jamie and took her hot chocolate upstairs. Part of her wondered if her mum would do what she said and she was a little surprised when Sarah tapped on her door and came in, followed by Arkenarten.

'Jamie and Mum are having a brandy with their hot chocolate so I thought we may as well,' she said, holding out two brandy glasses. She snuggled under the duvet and took one of Carole's hands in hers. 'So,' she said, 'you're in love with three men. Dominic is obviously one of them. Am I right in thinking Nick is one and I already know who the third one is. I heard that Sebastian's back.'

Carole almost choked on the mouthful of brandy she'd just swallowed.

'What makes you think one of them is Nick?' she asked in astonishment.

'Well, for one thing I met him this morning and I have to say, I'd have fallen in love with him myself if I were twenty years younger and for another, it's the way you look when you mention his name.'

'The way I look? What do you mean? How do I look?'

'Like a woman in love. Your eyes light up and your cheeks glow and he makes you cross and he makes you laugh and you hardly talked about anyone else all evening.'

'Oh! Well ... that's because he has been so good to Gran and to me too, although he does have a way of making me so cross that I want to hit him. But I ... I don't think I talk about him *that* much ... do I?'

'Yes dear, you do. And Sebastian?'

Carole nodded. 'I know it's crazy and I know I shouldn't – especially as he's still married, but I just can't help it, Mum. The minute I saw him again, it was as if time had turned back. I felt just the same as I did the day he left.'

'Oddly enough cherub, so do I.'

Carole tilted her head round to look at Sarah's face. 'But you wanted to kill him!'

'I know I did darling, and I feel exactly the same as I did that day. So does your gran. But it doesn't matter what we think. It's what you think and feel that's important. If you decide he's the man for you, then Mum and I will welcome him with open arms and so will Jamie.'

Carole sighed. 'I just don't know, Mum. I've been hoping for the last few months that Dom would propose, but he hasn't. Sebastian has. I expect Gran told you that, didn't she?'

'Yes she did, dear. But you haven't said 'Yes', Mum told me.'

'No, I haven't. Did she tell you what happened? It was all rather funny, although I didn't think so at the time.'

Sarah chuckled. 'Yes, she told me about Nick's dog, and about Arkenarten, and the ring getting lost in the snow and Nick finding it. That was nice of him.'

'He's a nice man ... sometimes.'

'And what about him? Does he know how you feel?'

'Good God, no! He already thinks I'm some kind of ... slapper or something because I'm living with Dom and *encouraging* Seb. If I told him I loved him too, he'd probably ban me from going to the garden centre ... ever again.'

'I don't think he would, dear. What makes you think

that?'

'Because he has made it very clear that he was disappointed that I am, and I quote, "that sort of woman". He's not interested in me in that way at all. I think he ... likes me ... as a friend or work colleague but that's it.'

'Are you sure, cherub?'

'Absolutely.'

'Hmm. That surprises me.'

'Why?'

'Because of the way he talked about you this morning when we met. He had nothing but good things to say.'

Carole sipped her hot chocolate, having finished her brandy. 'Really? Well I suppose he couldn't very well stand in front of you, Gran and Jamie and say that he thinks I'm a harlot, could he?'

'I suppose not, darling, but it was more than that. I wouldn't rule him out, but you shouldn't make a decision based on whether someone does or doesn't like you. You need to decide which one of the three you want to spend the rest of your life with and once you know that, you just follow your heart.'

'That's what Dad used to say, didn't he?'

'He did, cherub, and when it came to Love, your father really knew what he was talking about.'

***

Carole heard the knock on the door and half expected, half hoped that it would be Nick. She could see little cracks of light creeping over the top of the curtains so it must be early morning.

'Are you lovely ladies decent?' Jamie asked.

Carole glanced to her side and saw her Mum still snuggled up beside her.

'Yes,' Carole said. 'Come in, Jamie.'

'Oh. Good morning, cherub. Good morning, darling,'

Sarah said, sitting up. 'Did you sleep well?'

'Like a log,' Jamie replied, turning on the light and smiling broadly. He was carrying a tray with a small teapot, a coffee pot, two mugs, milk and sugar. 'I've made tea and coffee because I wasn't sure which you prefer in the morning, Carole, my dear.'

'I prefer coffee but either is fine, thanks,' she said.

'Coffee it is in future then. I'll remember that. It's a lovely day out there, or it will be when the sun comes up. It's a bit like you two sleepy heads this morning. Not quite awake yet but lovely, nonetheless.'

He leant forward and gave Sarah a quick kiss on the lips.

'You can see why I love him, can't you, cherub?' Sarah said.

'I certainly can,' Carole replied. And she could.

'I went for a wee stroll just now,' Jamie said, 'and I bumped into Nick. I hope you don't mind but I thought I'd maybe pop into the garden centre and see if there's anything I can give him a hand with. Mitsy was telling me last night that he's a bit short-staffed and I thought it would give you an extra day, Carole, to take it easy or maybe catch up on your work commissions and chat with your mum.'

'I think that's a lovely idea, don't you, cherub?'

Carole smiled and nodded. 'Yes. That ... that would be great. Thanks Jamie.'

'It's my pleasure dear. Nick seemed to think you would be heading back to London for a few days to see your young man so if you want me to, I can stand in for you until you get back, if that's okay with you and Mitsy, sweetheart.'

'That's fine with me,' Sarah said. 'Are you going up to London, cherub?'

'Well ... I haven't decided yet,' Carole said, 'and there's the Christmas musical. I've got to get on with the scenery for that ... and Dom will be busy at work so ...'

161

'You decide whatever you want to do, dear, and we'll fit in with you, won't we, sweetheart?'

'We will,' Sarah said, smiling at Carole.

'Actually, Dom's coming down next weekend so ...' She trailed off and drank her coffee.

It wasn't as good as Nick's but she knew she'd just have to get used to the fact that Nick wouldn't be bringing her coffee in bed any more.

***

Carole hardly saw Nick all week. She knew that he popped round to see Mitsy several times because her gran told her so. Apparently, Mitsy had told Nick in no uncertain terms that just because *the prodigal daughter* had returned, Mitsy's relationship with him hadn't changed and that he should consider himself welcome at any time.

On each of his visits so far though, Carole had been out either with her mum, or Josie, or at meetings with her clients, three of whom had suddenly decided that they simply must get things rolling on new projects they were planning for the following year. It was just as well her mum had come to stay because there was no way that Carole could have managed otherwise.

She'd only been able to spend a few hours at the garden centre and that was on Wednesday, the one day that Nick had been called out to do some emergency work on a tree which was dangerously overhanging Mr Purefoy's fishpond. By the time he got back, she was just leaving.

'I thought you were going back to London for a few days,' he said when they met in the doorway.

'It's good to see you too,' she said sarcastically, 'and I don't know what gave you that idea. Dom's working all week so there really isn't much point.'

He held the door open for her. 'Does he work all day and all night, seven days a week then?'

'No, but he's very busy and so am I and ... anyway, he's coming down this weekend.'

'You'd better take care not to catch anything then, hadn't you?'

She stopped in the doorway. 'What on earth do you mean by "catch anything"? How dare you suggest that—'

He grinned down at her. 'I meant like another cold or something. What did you think I meant?'

'Oh, I thought ... it doesn't matter.'

Carole pulled on her gloves and wrapped her scarf tighter around her neck. She was trying to think of a reason to go back inside, some excuse to stay and talk for a few minutes longer but she couldn't think of one and it was freezing standing in the doorway.

'Are you going or are you coming back in?' he asked, as if reading her mind. 'You're letting all the hot air out.'

She glanced up at him. 'I'm tempted to say, perhaps you should keep your mouth closed then, but I won't.'

Nick's brows furrowed momentarily and he burst out laughing. She stood mesmerised. She loved hearing the sound of his laughter; she loved the way his dark eyes seemed to glint with amusement; she loved the tiny lines which appeared at the sides of them; she loved ...

'Are you going to rehearsals tonight,' he said, still chuckling, 'I've missed seeing you.'

'I've missed you too,' she said, blushing when she realised the implication of her words. 'I ... I've had a lot of new work with very tight deadlines so I haven't been able to get there, but I will be there tonight. Perhaps ... perhaps we could go for a drink afterwards? ... All of us I mean not ... not just ...' She thought she'd better stop. She was digging a hole for herself and she was about to fall into it.

'I know what you mean,' he said, giving her an odd look. 'I'll see you tonight then.'

But he didn't.

Carole kept the door of the village hall within sight all

evening whilst she worked on the scenery, but Nick was a no-show.

It wasn't until she was leaving and she asked Bert Threadgold as casually as she could, where Nick was this evening that she discovered he had been called out on yet another tree 'emergency'.

'What is it with bloody trees, today?' she cursed.

'Oh dear, Carole!' Mr Threadgold said. 'I really have no idea. But Nick said exactly the same thing. And now that I think of it, he did ask me to mention it to you but I told him I didn't think you would be here this evening. I was sure I heard Sebastian say you were having dinner with him.'

Carole's mouth fell open. 'And ... and did you tell Nick that? About me having dinner with Sebastian, I mean.'

'Of course I did, my dear. There are few secrets in a village, as you well know.'

Carole considered calling Nick on some lame excuse but she thought better of it. What was she going to say? That Bert had got it all wrong and that she wasn't seeing Sebastian for dinner that night. That much was true, at least. The problem was that she'd have to say that she was seeing Sebastian for dinner on the following night and that would sort of take the shine off her denial.

Damn him, she thought, and damn Sebastian too. The only reason she'd agreed to meet Sebastian on Thursday was because he'd seemed so hurt when she refused. He told her that he was beginning to doubt whether she really cared for him at all.

She also realised, after discussing it with her mum – a circumstance she was getting used to surprisingly quickly – that as Dominic would be down on the Friday, it might actually help her to reach a decision regarding her feelings for him.

'Tell Sebastian you'll see him on Thursday instead,' Sarah had suggested on Wednesday afternoon. 'That way, you can see Nick tonight at the rehearsals and in the pub you can try and gauge what you really feel. Whether it's lust or love. Meet Sebastian tomorrow and have a serious talk about exactly why he felt he had to run away the first time. And on Friday, you'll be seeing Dominic. By then you should have a much clearer idea of which one of them really makes your heart skip a beat. And that's what it all comes down to, cherub. It's the one your heart wants.'

'But what if my heart isn't sure, or worse still, what if it wants all three?' Carole asked.

'It won't, darling. Hearts aren't greedy. They only want their one true love and they always tell you who that is. Some people just don't listen to them, and others use their heads or their subconscious to rule them, and that's not always a good thing where love is concerned. You follow your heart, cherub. It'll lead you in the right direction.'

Walking home towards the cottage, Carole wasn't so sure about that. She was beginning to get the feeling that her heart was leading her in completely the wrong direction and there seemed to be less and less that she could do about it.

'Hold up!' Josie yelled after her. 'I thought we were going to the pub?'

'Sorry Josie,' Carole said, 'I'm not sure I can face it. I'm tired and it's freezing. I just want to get home.'

'Don't be such a grouch. I need a drink and so do you by the sound of it. We're going.'

CHAPTER EIGHTEEN

'Come on then,' Josie asked impatiently, 'tell me what's wrong. I thought you'd be blissfully happy now that your mum is almost back to her old self. You seem to be getting on great and Jamie's really lovely, isn't he? So what's up?'

'Nothing,' Carole replied, fiddling with the stem of her wine glass.

'Yeah right! You're staring into that glass as if you'd like to dive into it head first and drown yourself. Come on. Spill. And I don't mean the wine.'

Carole smirked. 'It's just ... why does life have to be so complicated? Just a few weeks ago, I was happy and content with my life with Dom and now ...'

Josie looked thoughtful. 'Perhaps that means you weren't. Happy and content I mean. After all, if you really, truly were and if you really, truly loved Dom, you wouldn't be thinking of leaving him, would you? Let's face it. It's better to find out now that you still have feelings for Sebastian or even that you may have feelings for someone else, than to find out ten years down the line that you've made a huge mistake.'

'Like Sebastian, you mean?'

Josie shrugged. 'Yeah. Or anyone. Lots of people do it. They get married for totally the wrong reasons and then regret it. I know you love Dom but it seems to me that the real reason you wanted to get married was just so that you could change your name from Carole Singer to Carole Smith – and frankly, I'm not convinced that's a great improvement. Carole Singer sounds jolly and light and carefree, like the Carole I know and love. Carole Smith sounds ... well, sensible and ... boring.'

'Hmm. Jolly, light and carefree? I think you have me confused with someone else, Josie.'

'Rubbish! I'm sorry to stir up painful memories but before your dad died, you were the life and soul of the party. I know you went through a terrible time and then all the stuff with your mum and Sebastian but you came through it all and even at your lowest moments, your dad's death and Seb leaving you, you managed to retain some humour. I'm sure that's what got you through it all. And you get that from your dad. And let's be honest, if you really hate your surname so much, why not change it by deed poll?'

Carole stared at her friend. 'Because it's my dad's! I ... I couldn't do that. I'd ... I'd feel as if I were betraying his memory somehow. I know it sounds stupid but changing it by getting married is different. That ... that seems okay because that's the natural course of things.'

'Hmm,' Josie said. 'I forgot mad. Jolly, light, carefree and as mad as they come. You could have changed the Carole part. No, don't tell me. That was the name your dad gave you.'

'Well it was!'

'Fine. Anyway, I'm just saying, perhaps instead of trying to decide whether you love Dom or Sebastian or ... you know who, who just happens to be walking in the door right now, perhaps you should try to decide *why* you love them. Hi Nick. We missed you at rehearsals tonight.'

Carole's back was to the door but she could feel Nick's eyes on her as if an archer had loosed a quiver of arrows at her.

'Hi,' he replied, walking over and standing beside their table with Nicodemus following and sitting at his feet. 'I had an emergency call out. Couldn't make it.' His eyes seem to scan the bar. 'Where's Sebastian?'

'No idea,' Josie said.

'Oh! I'd heard you were–'

'You heard wrong,' Carole interrupted, seeing him direct his comment to her and knowing what he was going to say.

She stroked Nicodemus' head and tickled him under his chin. He leant towards her, resting his body against her legs and his head on her knee.

'Oh,' Nick said, giving Nicodemus an odd look as if to say 'traitor'.

'But I am tomorrow,' Carole added as an afterthought. He'd no doubt find out anyway so she may as well get it over with. She waited for the sarcastic barb but there was none.

'Oh. Can I get you a drink? Wine is it for both of you?'

'Yes please,' Josie said.

Nick headed to the bar whilst Nicodemus stayed where he was. Carole couldn't help but notice that the hound's eyes were watching Nick's every movement and she suddenly realised that hers were too. Eventually, Josie leant in towards her.

'Shall I make an excuse and leave you and Nick to it?'

'Don't you dare!' Carole exclaimed. 'I mean it, Josie. No.'

'Coward.'

'I'm not a coward. I ...'

'So ... how was the tree?' Josie asked as Nick returned.

'Not as bad as I thought it was going to be,' he remarked, handing them their wine. 'It's difficult working at night and even with emergency lights and a generator, you can't see as clearly. Shadows can deceive you so you have to be doubly careful but this one went very smoothly. How were rehearsals?'

'Good,' Josie said. 'Astonishingly, it all seems to be coming together and with Carole's scenery and the costumes I'm helping with, which even with my abysmal sewing skills, aren't half bad, I think we'll have a pretty impressive production. For a tiny hall in a small village, you understand.'

Nick grinned. 'I saw some of the costumes the other night. They really are very good, Josie. Perhaps you should give sewing lessons as well as music lessons.'

'I could have 'sew while you sing' evenings ... or should that be 'sing while you sew'? Anyway, I can picture it now, all sitting round a roaring fire with our sewing baskets to one side, mop caps on our heads, me playing the piano, struggling to breathe in my whalebone corset. Oh sorry, I was forgetting which century we're in.'

'I can picture it too,' Nick said with a serious look on his face as if he were doing just that. 'A group of women wearing only mop caps and whalebone corsets ...'

Josie gave him a playful slap on his arm. 'Talking of women, Nick, is there anyone in the village who takes your fancy?'

Carole thought she saw Nick spill some of his beer but as she was trying not to choke on her mouthful of wine, she couldn't be sure.

'Well,' he said, giving Josie a sideways glance, 'if Mitsy were only a few years younger.' He let out a long, dramatic sigh and grinned before gulping down several mouthfuls of beer.

Carole gave Josie a look, which she hoped said, 'Stop it now,' but Josie grinned at her, so she prepared herself for the next remark.

'Carole looks remarkably like Mitsy did when she was Carole's age.'

Carole hoped the gasp she made didn't sound as loud to Nick as it had to her.

'I know.' Nick was giving nothing away in his tone. 'I've seen the photos. And what about you, madam? Who've you got your eye on ... now that we know it's not Justin Jarvis?'

'Oh, I'm just waiting for Carole to make up her mind, then I'll have one of her cast-offs.'

'Josie!' Carole shrieked, glaring at her friend.

'And what if Carole decides to keep them both?' Nick cut in, grinning, although there wasn't a trace of humour in his voice.

'Nah. She's not the type, Nick. She's a one man kind of woman deep down. She–'

'Would you mind not discussing me as if I'm not here, please?' Carole snapped.

Nick ignored her and leant forward. 'She ...?'

'Oh. She believes in *the one true love*. Don't you, Carole?'

Carole saw Nick look at her but he quickly looked away.

'So what if I do! What's wrong with that?'

'There's nothing wrong with that,' Nick said, 'I happen to be a believer myself.'

'She just can't decide which one of the three is her true love though. Ah!' Josie shot a look at Carole and clearly realised her mistake. 'Two! I meant, which one of the two.'

Nick glanced from Josie to Carole.

'I think that's quite enough about me, thank you very much, and I also think it's time I went home. I've got a really busy day tomorrow.'

'It must be very difficult for you then,' Nick said, staring her straight in the eye. 'Being in love with two different men and not being able to decide.'

Carole swallowed and tried to avoid his gaze. She looked down at Nicodemus and stroked his head.

'Dad used to say you should listen to your heart,' she said. 'So that's what I intend to do.'

'Your dad was right,' Nick agreed.

'And in the meantime she's just got to figure out a way to keep them apart,' Josie said. 'Sorry! But it's true.'

'You could always try telling them how you feel,' Nick said. 'Being honest with them both might be a good place to start.'

Carole's head shot up. 'Is this going to be another lecture on my morals? Because if it is, I'm not sure I want to hear it.'

Nick shook his head and got to his feet. 'Nope. No

lecture. It's none of my business anyway. And it's time I took Nicodemus for his walk. I'll say goodnight, ladies.'

Nicodemus was already on his feet at the mention of his walk and both man and hound were gone before Josie and Carole had finished saying goodnight.

'What the hell was all that about?' Carole demanded when she was sure Nick was out of earshot.

'I wanted to see what he'd say,' Josie said, grinning.

'Why? What good did it do?'

Josie furrowed her brow. 'Didn't you see him? Didn't you see the way he looked at you?'

'Yes. He looked at me as if I'm a trollop. 'Be honest with them. Tell them how you feel'. How am I supposed to tell Dom that not only do I think I'm still in love with my ex-fiancé but there is a very strong possibility that I may also have fallen in love with a total stranger? And the worst thing about it, the absolutely infuriatingly sickening part of it is, he's right. Nick is absolutely right. I should tell them the truth. And do you know what? I shall! Sebastian knows about Dom of course, but I'll tell Dom about Sebastian on Friday.'

'That should go down well. And Nick? Are you telling either of them about Nick?'

Carole shook her head. 'There's no point because nothing's going to happen between me and Nick. I've just got to decide if I want to be with Sebastian or with Dom or ... with neither of them.'

'That's good. Because I have been wondering how on earth you planned to keep Dom from finding out, especially as everyone in the village knows that Sebastian proposed to you ... again. And I think you may be wrong about Nick. I wouldn't be at all surprised if something happened between you two. Not surprised at all.'

***

Carole was beginning to wish she'd insisted on meeting Sebastian for just a drink and hadn't agreed to dinner. It had been a very long Thursday, or at least it seemed as if it had and all she really wanted to do was curl up in front of the fire with a glass of wine and a good book.

She knew it was going to be a difficult evening when Sebastian texted her telling her to 'dress up' and she was tempted to send a text back saying, 'No', but she didn't. It got worse when she went downstairs to ask her mum to zip up the dress she was wearing.

'Mum, can you zip this up for me. I can't ... Oh! Nick. Hi.'

Nick was chatting to Mitsy but he glanced round at the sound of Carole's voice. And he did a double take. Even Mitsy saw it, Carole was sure.

'Wow!' he said, looking her up and down.

It felt to Carole as if the red crepe crossover bodice had suddenly constricted and she couldn't breathe and that if it were possible for a dress to spring to life and flirt, then the A-line skirt seemed to be doing just that. It clung to her hips, swung around her thighs and danced just above her knees. If it had worn a talking banner saying 'Look at me' it couldn't have got any more attention. And it certainly had Nick's undivided attention.

'Wow!' he repeated when his eyes had scanned every inch of her. 'You look ... incredible!'

Embarrassed and more than a little flustered by the strange look in his dark eyes she said, 'You sound surprised. But thank you ... I think.'

'I am surprised,' he said. 'Sebastian is a very lucky man. You wanted help with the zip, I believe.'

'No! I mean, Mum can help me.'

'She can't, I'm afraid, sweetheart, Mitsy said. 'She and Jamie have popped out to get fish and chips from the village. They'll be at least ten minutes. And you do look gorgeous, dear. Come here and give me a twirl.'

'Gran. I ... I'd rather not. And I can wait until Mum gets back.'

'Don't be silly,' Nick said, walking towards her. 'I'm perfectly capable of zipping up a dress.' He took her gently by the arms and twisted her around.

'Oh!' she said, shocked by the feel of his hands on her bare arms.

'And it's not the first time I've had to do this you know.'

She felt her backbone stiffen. 'I don't suppose so,' she replied which sounded somewhat snippy even to her ears. But when his fingers brushed her skin, ran over the hooks of her bra and trailed up her skin again, she had to close her eyes and bite her lip to stop a little moan of pleasure from escaping.

He slid his hands across her shoulders and turned her around to face him and they were just inches apart. He looked into her eyes and a slow grin formed on his mouth.

'Mary was always asking me to zip her up when she was dating Harry,' he said, letting his hands slide slowly down her arms before he turned and resumed his seat opposite Mitsy.

Carole knew the floor couldn't be swaying but she felt as if it were. He did that on purpose she thought and it made her madder than she had been all day.

'Well' she said, 'as you won't be here by the time I get back and Mum and Jamie will no doubt be fast asleep in bed, I'll have to get Seb to help me unzip it.'

She wasn't sure which of them looked more shocked and annoyed – Nick, or her gran, but as the doorbell rang at just that second, she was saved from their responses. She quickly slipped her arms into her matching red, fluffy shrug, grabbed her coat and dashed towards the door.

'Have fun you two,' she called out but neither Nick nor Mitsy answered. She wasn't sure whether she should be pleased or disappointed.

'Bloody Hell!' Sebastian exclaimed when Carole opened

the door.

She wasn't sure if Nick and Mitsy had heard it but they must have heard the loud and rather long, wolf whistle he made. After her comment just now about him unzipping her dress later, she felt this might be pushing things a bit too far. She quickly shut the door and ushered him away from the cottage.

'Where are we going for dinner?' she asked.

'I've booked a table at The Manor Court Hotel. And with you in that dress, I'm really hoping you'll say I can book us a room too.'

'What? I'm afraid there is no chance of that, Sebastian. You seem to keep forgetting that I'm living with someone.'

'I assure you I can't forget that. But so what? I'm married. The point is, Carole if we love one another, nothing else matters. And we do love one another, don't we? I know that I love you and I'm pretty sure, after tonight, you'll realise you love me too.'

'We'll see,' she said. 'But I'm still not spending the night with you. Not until I've finished things with Dom, if that's what I decide to do.'

'We'll see.' He held the door open for her whilst she got into his car.

To Carole's ears, that sounded almost like a challenge.

***

Carole was surprised by how well the evening went. They talked about old times, about people they used to know. About all the things they had in common and found they still had. He told her a bit about his life in Australia although not as much as she would have liked and what he did say was rather vague. But by the time he walked her to the door of the cottage, she was beginning to feel that she could be happy with him. That she could still have the life she'd thought she'd have all those years ago.

'I understand why you want to know about Julia,' he said when they stood at the door, 'and I promise I'll tell you all about her one day but I made a mistake and although we both tried to make it work, it's over. We both knew it a long time ago. She'll let me have a divorce because we both want to move on.'

'So it's an amicable split then? You both just fell out of love, is that what you're saying?'

'I think she knew that I never stopped loving you, deep down. We just drifted apart. I decided I wanted to come home and she agreed that was for the best. That's it really.'

'So ... what I don't understand, Seb is why, if you loved me so much, you ran off and left me the day before our wedding without even talking to me about it? And that note. It was so ... cold.'

He shook his head and took her hands in his. 'I really don't know, angel. I wanted to marry you, truly I did but ... I got frightened I guess. I saw myself turning into my dad and spending my entire life in this village and suddenly, I just had to get out. I knew you wouldn't go so I booked a flight and that was it. I ... I wasn't thinking straight but one thing I did know was that if I spoke to you, if I saw you, I wouldn't be able to go. And I had to go. I just had to.'

'I'm not sure I understand completely but I do know how the mind can make you go a little crazy and do things you wouldn't normally do. But ... why marry someone else then? If ... if you really loved me I mean, and you just needed to get away for a while?'

He shook his head again. 'Mum and Dad told me how upset you were, how upset everyone was and ... well, I didn't think you'd ever want to see me again. I hadn't thought it all through until then and when it seemed that I'd lost you ... I was so lonely and sad. I was working for her dad at his marina, selling boats and he offered me a permanent job. Next he offered me a senior position, and I think perhaps I married Julia because it didn't matter who I married if I couldn't have you. That sounds dramatic I know but that's really how I felt. At least I had a career even if I didn't have the one woman I really loved.'

Carole couldn't help but think this was all a little far-fetched and yet somehow, she desperately wanted to believe it.

'But why didn't you just call me? Or write to me? Why just assume you'd lost me and not try to find out how I felt?'

'I don't know, angel. I really don't know. But over the years, I realised that I had to come back and try and find you. Try to see if there was some hope for us, or if I had come to my senses far too late and that I'd lost you for good. You don't know how happy I was to see you that day. It was like a sign. Like a miracle or something. And I could see it in your eyes the moment you saw me. You still loved me too.'

'That much is true,' she admitted. 'I do still love you. I don't think I ever stopped loving you. But I love Dom too. Not in quite the same way but I do love him.'

'I know you say you don't want to and you wouldn't let me book a room tonight but I really think that if we made love ... like we used to ... you'd know. You'd remember how good it was, how good we were, and you'd know. Is ... is sex as good with him?'

Carole was feeling flustered again but this time she was feeling under pressure. She could remember what it had been like with Seb and just thinking about it was making her want him.

Sex with Dom was nothing like sex with Sebastian. That, she also had to admit – but not to Seb. That wouldn't be fair to Dom. Some men are simply better lovers than others. That was a fact of life and Sebastian was definitely a good lover. Not that she had had many. Just Andrew at uni, Sebastian and now Dom, but out of the three, Seb was definitely the most memorable.

'It's different,' she said. 'And believe me, Seb, I can still remember how good it was with us but I can't spend the night with you. Not now. Not yet. You need to give me time. I just need a little more time.'

He wrapped his arms around her and pulled her to him.

'You can't blame me for trying,' he said. 'I can't help it, angel. I just want to show you how much I love you.'

He tipped her head back and kissed her. Although she felt guilty she let him, and she began to kiss him back. She knew it was wrong though and she eased herself away from him.

'I'm sorry, Seb,' she said. 'I can't. I really can't. I've got to go. We'll talk soon. Thanks for dinner. Goodnight.'

She dashed inside and closed the door. She thought she heard Seb say something but she couldn't make out what it was and she had no intention of opening the door to ask him.

CHAPTER NINETEEN

Carole wasn't superstitious but Friday December 13th was clearly going to be one of those days. She knew it the moment she realised she'd overslept – yet again.

She dashed downstairs to find that Nick had arrived with a large and very beautiful, six foot Christmas tree to go in Mitsy's sitting room and a small one about two feet high for the study.

'Look what Nick's brought us, sweetheart,' Mitsy said as Carole popped into the study to say good morning. 'Have you seen the one in the sitting room? It's gorgeous. You must come round after rehearsals tonight Nick, and help us decorate them.'

'I wouldn't want to be in the way,' Nick replied, casting a meaningful look in Carole's direction.

'As if you could ever be in the way,' Mitsy said. 'Now don't argue with me. You're coming and that's that.'

'Gran, you can't force people to do things they don't want to,' Carole said. 'Besides, Nick might have plans for tonight, and aren't you forgetting that Dominic will be here?'

'No, I hadn't forgotten that. Sarah's making up the spare front bedroom for him.'

Carole saw Nick's raised eyebrows and the huge grin on his face. Again, she had an almost overwhelming urge to slap him, but she didn't.

'But what's that got to do with anything?' Mitsy continued. 'He can help too if he wants but he never has before, so I don't see why this year should be any different.'

'I'm looking forward to meeting him,' Nick said. He smiled at Mitsy. 'Everyone's talking about this weekend. It should be good–'

'I don't care what everyone's talking about,' Carole butted in, 'and for your information, I plan to tell Dominic everything so the gossip mongers won't have as much fun as they expect to.'

Nick gave her a curious look and furrowed his brows. 'Er ... I think we have our wires crossed. Everyone is talking about the lighting of the tree outside the village hall. I'm erecting it today remember, and there's going to be a little ceremony tomorrow evening with carols, mulled wine and mince pies. Your mum's making several batches today and tomorrow. I thought she said you were helping but perhaps you'll be too busy with ... other things.'

'Oh,' Carole said. She had forgotten, although she had no idea why. She'd told Dom about it when he'd phoned only yesterday – just before she'd gone out to dinner with Sebastian.

'Did you have a good time last night?' Nick asked.

Carole raised her head and stuck her chin out. 'Very good, thank you. It was just like old times.'

Nick frowned. 'Oh dear.'

'What's that supposed to mean?'

'I'm sure you can figure that one out. I'll see you tonight then, Mitsy. Bye Sarah. See you later Jamie. You should get some rest, Carole. You look tired and you don't want your other boyfriend to see you like that, do you?'

Carole's mouth fell open but he was gone before she could reply.

Two minutes later, a yowling noise came from the sitting room, accompanied by a resounding crash. Jamie and Sarah ran to see what had happened, followed by Carole who was nursing a mug of coffee she'd just poured. Arkenarten had decided to investigate the Christmas tree it seemed.

'That's my fault,' Jamie said, standing the tree upright and picking up fragments of a shattered ceramic fruit bowl. 'I asked Nick to leave the tree propped up against the wall and I'd fix it in a stand in a wee while. Sorry about the bowl. Was it valuable?'

'Priceless,' Sarah replied, grinning and giving him a quick kiss. 'At least that's what Mum often called it, but I don't think she meant it in a good way. I gave it to her for Christmas a few years ago. It was atrocious and I have no idea why I bought it. I think you and Arkenarten have done us all a favour.'

Arkenarten didn't look quite as pleased. He dashed towards the safety of the study, making Carole stumble as she tried to avoid tripping over him. She spilt her coffee down the front of her favourite blouse and that didn't make her happy.

'I knew it was going to be one of those days,' she grumbled as Sarah took the mug from her.

'Well, it's Friday the 13th,' Sarah said, 'so I expect it probably will be.'

Carole raced up the stairs as quickly as she could to get changed. She had a lot of work to do today. She needed to finish an illustration for a romance novel. She'd promised Josie that she'd meet her for lunch to tell her about last night, and it was true that she'd said she'd help her mum with the mince pies. She was actually looking forward to that. It would be just like old times.

Just like old times. Hmm. Nick had made an obtuse comment about that. What had he meant?

'Ooh!' she shrieked as it suddenly clicked. He'd meant that Seb might run off again if it were just like old times. 'Sometimes,' she hissed through gritted teeth as she stared at her reflection in the mirror, 'I really do hate that man.'

And now she hated him even more. He was right. She did look tired.

'I hope that Christmas tree bloody well falls on him today,' she cursed, grabbing her cardigan and heading back downstairs.

***

Carole was feeling much happier by four o'clock in the afternoon although she was surprised that she hadn't heard from Dominic. She assumed he must be stuck in meetings and he hadn't had a chance to call. She was sure there was no need for concern. He'd probably call any minute now.

She put the finishing touch to the book cover by adding the title, *My Heart's Desire* and sat back to study the final result. The novel was a rather racy Regency romp according to the synopsis from which she'd worked, and the publishers had given her a virtual carte blanche on the design, the only proviso being that the hero and heroine must appear as described.

She tilted her head from side to side and studied the cover from all angles. Yes, she was happy with the image. She typed an email, attached the jpeg and sent it off for approval. At least something had gone well today she thought and as she heard her phone ring and saw Dom's smiling face on the screen, she heaved a sigh of relief.

'I was wondering when you'd call,' she said happily. 'I've been a little worried but I know you must be busy. What time are you getting here?'

'I'm not,' Dom replied, sounding utterly miserable.

Carole sat bolt upright. 'What ... what do you mean, you're not? Has something happened? Are you okay? Has someone ...' Her voice trailed off. Surely, no one would have phoned him and told him about Sebastian? Of course, they wouldn't. Who would have his number? She was being silly.

'I've got chickenpox!'

Carole blinked in stunned silence before bursting out laughing. 'Oh Dom! You really had me going there. I thought you were being serious. Now stop messing about. What time will you be here?'

'I won't!' he said angrily. 'I'm not messing about. I have got chickenpox! The senior partner's wife brought their grandson into the office on Wednesday and he had it, although she didn't know that then. Godwin told us all last night. When I woke up this morning, I was covered in sodding spots. Well, not covered exactly, although it feels like I am, they itch so bloody much. The doctor's been and he thinks I've just got a mild case. He's given me some antiviral drugs which he says should lessen the symptoms, and Mum's getting me some cream or something to ease the itching. I've got to stay off work though and obviously, away from people for several days. Carole? Are you listening? Are you still there?'

'Yes. Yes, I'm here. I ... I just can't believe it, Dom, that's all. I thought you'd had chickenpox.'

'Well, I haven't. Mum said she was sure I'd had them too but I don't ever remember itching like this and I certainly have never had spots before in my entire life. Ever!' he complained, sounding like a five-year-old.

'Well ... I'd better come up then,' Carole said, feeling almost as dejected as Dom sounded.

'What for? You don't want to get covered in spots. It's not a pretty sight, let me tell you.'

'I've had chickenpox and although you can get it again, it's rare, so I'm sure I'll be fine. You need someone to look after you.'

'Oh! Mum's offered to do that. She's on her way over now. I called her first because I needed her to get this cream for me. There's no point in you both being here. And if you were here, I'd want to have sex and I can't. Apart from feeling absolutely awful, I've even got a spot on my dick! Can you believe that?'

Carole almost laughed but she stopped herself. This was no time for spotted dick jokes she realised. She was surprised though. For someone who had never seemed that interested in sex, over the last two weeks, Dom seemed to talk of little else.

Every time he called now, he told her how much he

missed it and only last night he'd told her in some detail what he was going to do to her over the weekend. Apart from wondering if he'd been reading up on it on various sex sites on the internet, she hadn't had the heart to tell him that her gran had relegated him to the spare room, so activities would be somewhat curtailed. Not to mention the fact that after she'd told him how she felt, sex may not even be on the table. Well, it definitely wouldn't have been on the table, not at her gran's cottage. But it may not have been on the bed either.

'Oh you poor darling,' she said. 'When do you think you will be able to come down then? Will it be before Christmas?'

'God knows,' Dom replied. 'The doctor thinks the spots will take a week or so to crust over, dry up and drop off. So that takes us to the 20th. Possibly a day or so after that. Maybe not until Christmas Eve and I'm telling you now babe, if your gran puts me in the spare room, we're checking into a sodding hotel because by Christmas Eve I'll be absolutely gagging for it.'

The thought of Dom's spotted appendage had been enough to turn Carole off albeit in a vaguely amusing way, but this was just too much.

'I know you're not feeling well, Dom, and I'm very sorry, but that isn't terribly romantic, you know. "Gagging for it" doesn't exactly make me want to throw myself in your arms. But anyway, let's just hope it's only the spots that crust over, dry up and drop off or you may find yourself in some difficulty.'

'What? Oh! Trust you to make a joke of it. It isn't funny, Carole. It hurts. And as for romance, well I can be just as romantic as the next man. I've got to go. Mum's at the door.'

***

Carole saw Nick, balancing rather precariously she thought, at the top of a ladder, which was resting against the branches of a gloriously full Norway Spruce. The Christmas tree was at least twenty feet high and Nick was attaching a huge gold star to the top of it. He'd clearly just finished erecting it, and it was secured by ropes and pegs on the green outside of the village hall.

Josie and several others from the village stood at the foot of the tree, holding boxes full of decorations and coloured lights, which they were placing on the tree and handing up to Nick so that he could decorate the higher branches. A mini generator rumbled on the grass and two huge commercial spotlights that Carole knew belonged to Nick, pointed upwards, illuminating the proceedings sufficiently for everyone to see what they were doing.

It was around five-thirty p.m. and the sun had long since set, having been chased across a previously clear blue sky by a bright, waxing, gibbous moon which now hung in the rapidly fading silver of the final twenty minutes or so of twilight.

The air was crisp and cold and even though there hadn't been any more snow since that first heavy fall thirteen days ago, as Carole approached the tree she felt it was really beginning to feel like Christmas at last.

'Mind you don't fall,' she called up to Nick as she reached Josie's side.

Her voice seemed to startle him and he very nearly did. He had to grab a branch to steady him. He glanced down at her and grinned.

'Thanks for that,' he yelled down. 'I almost landed on top of you!'

She blushed and looked away as a picture of him on top of her popped into her head. Good grief, she thought, now she was the one who seemed to be gagging for it. She blamed it on her conversation with Dom, and the fact that she'd been working on that romance cover for most of the day.

At least that was one piece of good news she'd had. The publishers loved the cover, so much so in fact, that they'd asked her to do the rest in what was going to be an ongoing series of titles based on desire. And desire was something she seemed to be experiencing rather frequently these days; almost every time she looked at Nick, in fact – apart from the times she'd wanted to slap him, of course.

'Here,' Josie said, handing Carole a box of decorations, 'don't just stand there like a love-sick cow. Make yourself useful!'

'Thanks so much for the analogy, Josie. And I'm not lovesick ... or a cow, come to that, although Dom probably thinks I am.'

Josie's head whipped round. 'Have you told him? Is he here?'

Carole shook her head. 'No. He's not coming. In fact, I won't be seeing him until possibly sometime around Christmas Eve. And you'll never believe this – he's got chickenpox.'

Josie's mouth fell open and her eyes grew as wide as the Christmas bauble she was about to hang on the tree. 'You have got to be kidding me,' she said. 'Dom's got the Pox! Oh that's a classic!'

'Who's got the Pox?' Sebastian asked rather loudly, making both of them jump as he came up behind them.

A stunned silence fell amongst the villagers as all heads turned in Carole's direction. Even the generator spluttered and coughed.

Nick slid down from his perch by placing his feet either side of the ladder and he landed at Carole's feet, so close that she could smell the scent of pine from several little needles caught in his fleece.

'What's this,' he said, looking serious. 'Has someone in the village caught chickenpox? I assume that's what you meant. I hear there's a lot of it going around.'

'Carole's boyfriend, Dominic,' Josie said. 'He's got it and he won't be down until Christmas.'

Nick looked at Carole but she avoided his eyes and waited for the sarcastic comment.

'I'm really sorry to hear that,' he said, sounding genuinely sympathetic. 'I know chickenpox isn't that serious but it can cause complications. I hope he recovers quickly. Are ... are you going up to take care of him? Have you had it?'

Carole met his eyes. 'Yes, I've had it and no, I'm not going up. And not because I don't love him, before you say anything but because he doesn't want me to. And yes, I still would but his mum's there already and she and I get on even worse than Dom and my gran do. Besides, she was a nurse, so he's in better hands than mine.'

Nick's lips twitched a fraction. 'I wasn't going to say anything but now that you mention it, I know whose hands I'd rather be in. Not that I'm suggesting you go. Far from it. I think he's right to tell you not to. That much I do agree with him about.'

'Me too!' Sebastian announced, apparently only now comprehending the implications of this news and moving closer to Carole. 'And this means I'll have you all to myself for at least another week or so. I wasn't happy with the thought of him being alone in that cottage with you, even if Grandma Mitsy dumped him in the spare room. I know that wouldn't stop me and–'

'Sebastian!' Carole exclaimed, extricating herself from the arm he'd wrapped around her waist. 'That's enough, thank you.'

She noticed Nick step closer but he seemed to check himself and she wondered what he'd been thinking.

'We'd better get to rehearsals,' Josie said. 'It's almost six o'clock.' She linked arms with Carole and led her towards the village hall. 'I hate to say this, Carole seeing as you think you still love him and everything, but sometimes

Sebastian can be such a prat, and worse still, he often reminds me of his father.

Carole glowered at her.

'What? I'm just saying. That's the sort of remark the venerable Justin Jarvis JP would make. Or should that be ... venereal?'

Even Carole sniggered at that.

CHAPTER TWENTY

'Do you like meteor showers?' Nick asked Carole and Josie as they were about to leave the village hall after rehearsals had ended.

'I like any shower if it's hot,' Josie replied, 'especially if I can share it with a man who's even hotter.'

'Don't be silly,' Carole said, grinning. 'Can't you see the man's being serious? Are these the ones advertised on TV? Faster than a power shower but only available in heavy water areas?'

Nick grinned as Carole and Josie giggled like schoolgirls.

'Sorry,' Carole said. 'You were saying?'

'I was saying ... that if you do, you should be in for a treat tonight although having said that, the moon is too bright to get really good sightings. You'd see more once the moon has set. Between then and dawn it should be spectacular.'

'See more what?' Josie asked. 'Sorry, I'm still thinking of hot men in hot showers.'

'Meteors,' Carole said. 'Shooting stars, as we still call them. The kind we'd make a wish on. There's a meteor shower tonight then?'

Nick nodded. 'Yes. And tomorrow night. It's the Geminids and they should be visible from early evening, around the time we came in here actually, until dawn. They radiate from a region near the stars, Castor and Pollux in the constellation of Gemini. It's one of the best meteor showers on earth. Well, not on earth – in the heavens, but you know what I mean. There'll be between fifty to one hundred meteors per hour at the height of the shower.'

'Wow!' Carole and Josie exclaimed simultaneously.

'What are we waiting for? Let's get out there,' Carole

suggested.

'There won't be that many yet,' Nick said, 'as it's only seven-thirty but after we've decorated the trees, it might be worth taking a look.'

'I thought we'd finished the tree,' Josie said. 'I've got a piano lesson tonight so I can't stick around.'

'Nick means our tree,' Carole said. 'Well not *our* tree – Gran's tree. Trees actually. There're two of them.'

Nick shot her a look but didn't say anything.

'Oh,' Josie said. 'I thought they came in trees. Get it? Trees. Threes. My talent is wasted in this village.'

Carole grinned. 'It's a bit late for a piano lesson, isn't it? Or is that just a euphemism?'

Josie giggled. 'I wish it were. I'm making an exception for this guy actually. He's the dad of one of my pupils, and talk about hot men. Wow! I'm melting, just thinking about him.'

'Is this the guy you told me about at lunch today?' Carole asked. 'The one whose wife ran off with someone she met on one of the social networking sites?'

'Yep. She left him and his son. They're divorced now and Jason, he's the son, goes to his grandparents every other weekend. Aidan, he's the hot dad, drives him there and stays for supper. That's why he can't get to me until nine.'

'And you're hoping he'll stay for more than just one piano lesson, I take it?' Nick asked.

'I hope so. I'd like to find a way to get him to stay all weekend, to be honest. I'm telling you, that man can tickle my ivories – to borrow a phrase from Justin Jarvis – any time he likes, and not just my ivories but my ovaries too.'

'Josie!' Carole gasped. She was blushing although she had no idea why.

Nick burst out laughing. 'Just tell him that, Josie. That should do the trick.'

Carole shot him a look and their eyes met briefly before

she looked away.

'It might scare him off,' Josie said. 'The mention of ovaries does that to some men. They hear the words babies and fatherhood and they're off like ... a meteor.'

Nick grinned and nodded in agreement.

'What about you, Nick?' Josie asked. 'Would you be off like a meteor if a girl said that to you? Not me I mean but ... a girl?'

'It depends on the girl,' Nick replied, still grinning. 'If I really liked her, then no. Not ovaries or anything else for that matter would make me run off.'

'That's good to know, isn't it, Carole?'

Carole didn't answer.

'How long have you known this Aidan guy, Josie?' Nick asked. 'You said he's the father of one of your pupils.'

Josie nodded. 'Yeah. I've known him for about two months. Jason comes to me once a week on Thursday afternoons and Aidan goes for a walk during the lesson but he always stops and chats for a few minutes afterwards. It was only yesterday that he asked if he could have lessons and if he could start tonight.'

'Then it sounds to me like it is your ivories he wants to tinkle, Josie. No guy is that desperate to learn to play the piano, I can assure you.'

'Really?' Josie visibly brightened. 'So ... you think this is may be a preamble to ... to him perhaps asking me out or something?'

'Definitely,' Nick said.

'How can you say that?' Carole asked. 'Perhaps he just wants to learn the piano because his son is, and perhaps Friday night is the only night he has free? He may not be interested in Josie at all. No offence, Josie and I think the guy's mad if he isn't interested in you, but I'd hate you to get your hopes up and ... and do something you may regret. Flirt or something and get rejected.'

Nick's brows furrowed. 'For a woman who's dating two

men at the same time, Carole, forgive me, but you don't seem to know much about men.'

Carole glared at him.

'Don't look at me like that,' he said, grinning. 'I'm sorry but it's true. No man. And I do mean *no* man, would have a piano lesson at nine o'clock on a Friday night just to learn the piano. And before you say, "But he's got his son all week," – so what? He could get a baby sitter or he could have a lesson over the weekend. Saturday morning, for example. Nope. He's interested in you, Josie. I'd stake my life on it.'

Carole had to grudgingly admit Nick was probably right. 'I suppose so. Just be careful,' she added as they reached Mitsy's cottage.

'Should I wait for him to make the first move then, Nick?' Josie asked. 'Or should I make a move on him? Some men don't like forward women, do they?'

Nick chuckled. 'I never thought I'd be giving relationship advice to you, Josie. If it's taken him this long to get this far, I'd say you may need to move things forward. He's probably worried you may not feel the same and then it'd be embarrassing for you both given that you teach his son. Don't throw yourself at him exactly but make it obvious you're interested. Then let him take the lead.'

'What lead? I'm not a dog, you know. Seriously though, I'm not sure what you mean. You mean by flirting and stuff and then waiting to see if he reacts?'

'Well yes, but more direct. Tell him there's a meteor shower you were going to watch and if he's not busy, would he like to stay for a glass of wine and watch it with you. If he says no, there's no real harm done. You can say some friends are popping round and you thought he might like to join in rather than be at a loose end on a Friday night. That's just being friendly. If he says yes ... well.' Nick grinned broadly.

'Ooh! Thanks Nick. I like that.'

'What if he says no and then when Josie mentions other friends he says, "Oh. Okay"? What will she say when no one else turns up?' Carole asked.

Nick gave her a questioning look. 'Do you always think things through to such an extent?'

Carole nodded. 'Always.'

'Okay. Then Josie can call us and we'll go round. But I really don't think he will. Good luck, Josie,' Nick said.

'Yes. Good luck. And call me and let me know what happens,' Carole said.

'I will,' Josie replied as she turned and headed home, 'but hopefully that won't be until tomorrow ... or if things go really well and I'm very lucky, not until Sunday night. Hey!' She stopped and turned back to look at Carole and Nick. 'I just saw a shooting star! I'm sure I did. One of those meteors.'

Carole and Nick both stared up into the sky but saw nothing.

'Knowing my luck it was a flying pig. One that glows in the dark! See you.'

Carole let out a long meaningful sigh. 'At least someone has the possibility of having sex this weekend,' she remarked, not realising she'd actually said it out loud.

'You could always call Sebastian,' Nick suggested just as Sarah opened the door.

'Come in you two. We're waiting to decorate the trees. Mum's opened the Baileys, I've made mince pies. Jamie's given Arkenarten the 'Cats Don't Climb Christmas trees' speech, but I'm not sure that's done much good. Anyway, I think we're all set, so don't stand out here on the doorstep.'

'We were looking for shooting stars,' Carole explained, 'and saying goodbye to Josie.'

'Oh,' Sarah said. 'Is this the meteor shower you told Jamie about today, Nick? He's decided we need to go for a walk at some ungodly hour to go and look at it.' She smiled fondly at Nick. 'Thanks for that.'

Nick chuckled. 'Sorry Sarah. It is worth seeing though, if you like such things of course.'

'I'll forgive you, but Carole may not. The two of you are coming with us.'

Carole and Nick exchanged glances.

'Why?' Carole asked.

'Because if I'm going stargazing at four o'clock in the morning, then so are you. And don't even think of saying no, Nick!' Sarah gave him a mock threatening look.

'I had no intention of doing so,' he said sheepishly.

'Good. We've got both trees in the sitting room because there's more space, and either you or Jamie can carry the smaller one to the study when it's done, Nick.'

Nick and Carole followed Sarah in and as Carole took off her coat, she stopped in her tracks. Something caught in her throat, bringing tears to her eyes.

'What's wrong, cherub?' Sarah asked, turning round and noticing the look on Carole's face.

Carole shook her head. 'Nothing. It's ... it's just so ... Christmassy in here. It reminded me of ... well, you know.'

'I know, cherub.' Sarah handed her a large glass of Baileys. 'And I hope this is okay, please tell me if it's not. I asked Jamie to go into the loft and bring the old decorations down. The ones we had in our old house. The ones ... you and your father used to decorate the tree with. I think it's time they saw the light of day again, don't you?' She slipped her arm through Carole's and led her to a large box with the words, 'Xmas Decs' written on it.

Carole stared at the box and a hundred memories came flooding back. It was her dad's handwriting and she ran one hand over the words as if caressing them. She bit her lip and tried to stem the tears but she couldn't.

'I'm so sorry, darling.' Sarah's voice was breaking with emotion. 'I was wrong. Jamie? Take them–'

'No!' Carole said in a strangled sob. 'You were right. It is time and ... Dad would want this. He ... he would want to see us all together like this. A family decorating the tree as we used to. I ... I just need a few minutes, that's all.'

She turned and left the room. She threw her coat around her shoulders and opening the front door, stepped outside. The air was still and the waxing moon sat like a single bauble in a bed of black tissue paper sprinkled with little silver stars.

Her dad had loved nights like this and he'd taught her the famous nursery rhyme, *Star Light, Star Bright* and told her she should recite it on seeing the first star of the night, or on seeing a shooting star.

She stared up at the sky for several minutes. It was too late to wish on the first star of the night as she'd seen several already but she stood looking upwards, hoping, wondering. She smiled a little sadly and was about to look away and go inside when she saw it. There, right before her eyes was a shooting star. Quickly, she recited the words she remembered so well:

Star light, star bright,
Shooting star I see tonight,
I wish I may, I wish I might,
Have the wish I wish tonight.

Then she closed her eyes and made a wish.

Seconds later the front door opened and Nick stood in the doorway.

'Oh!' He was clearly surprised to see her there. 'I thought you'd ... actually, I'm not sure what I thought but I didn't expect you to be out here. It's freezing!'

'I just saw a shooting star, Nick,' she said, feeling like a little girl again.

'One of many, I should think,' he replied.

'Yes, but it's the first that counts. It's the first you have to wish on.'

'And did you? Wish on it.'

'Of course!'

'What did you wish for?'

'I can't tell you that! Wishes don't come true if you tell people.'

'No.' He sighed deeply. 'I don't suppose they do.'

'Where are you off to anyway?'

'Home.'

'Why? I thought you were helping with the trees.'

He shook his head. 'I shouldn't be here. I know Mitsy says that's silly but I'm not part of the family and you said it yourself, this is a family thing. Your dad would want it to be.'

'Oh! But ... No. No, you're coming back inside. If I've got to go and watch stars at four o'clock in the morning, then you've got to stay and help decorate the trees. So don't argue.'

She put her hands on his arms and pushed him back in through the doorway. She removed her coat, rubbed her hands together, took a deep breath, pulled her shoulders back and marched into the sitting room with Nick following behind.

'Right,' she announced. 'Let's get started. And don't we need some Christmas music in the background? Where's Arkenarten? I think he needs a little red Christmas bow.'

'That'll please him!' Mitsy teased.

'Rather you than me,' Jamie added, chuckling. 'I heard in the village that he's really a puma, a wee dwarf-sized one but a puma nonetheless.'

'He definitely gives Nicodemus what for,' Nick added, 'although Arten does usually keep out of Nicodemus' way, discretion being the better part of valour in Arten's mind.'

'It's always better to avoid a fight if possible,' Carole said.

'Not always,' Mitsy said, looking directly at Nick. 'Sometimes we have to fight for what we want. Feint heart never won fair maid. Now where did I put my sherry glass? Get me a refill would you please, Nick? The bottle's on the sideboard. None of this Baileys stuff for me.'

195

Carole found the Christmas CDs and picked one by Michael Bublé. He was one of her mum's and her gran's favourite singers, not to mention she was rather partial to him herself. Jamie and Nick sang along and Carole was surprised to hear that Nick had a very melodious voice.

'Why aren't you singing in the Christmas musical?' she asked. 'You've got a lovely voice.'

He raised his eyebrows in surprise. 'I think that's the nicest thing you've ever said to me.'

Carole grinned. 'It's possibly the only nice thing I've ever said to you. Don't get used to it.'

'I won't. I'm sure you'll be trying to kill me again before too long. Why aren't you singing?'

'Believe me, Nick you don't want to hear me sing. You'd actually want me to kill you.'

But within the time it took to decorate two trees, Carole was singing, albeit very quietly. She saw Nick smile at her and stopped but he prodded her in the ribcage and called her a coward so she hummed along to the music instead.

Without realising it, she was singing again as Nick and Jamie hung several metres of both indoor and outdoor coloured lights, and attached rows of silver bells around the doorframes both indoors and out. Every so often, they nipped back into the warmth of the sitting room and stretched out on one of the wing chairs either side of the fireplace with a mince pie and a glass of whisky.

Once or twice, Carole found herself wishing she could decide which one of three men she really loved. She could have this every year, and the possibility of a family Christmas with either Dom or Seb. She couldn't have it with Nick but she could have a wonderful friendship with him – until he fell in love with someone and wanted to be with her instead.

No. She wouldn't think about that. She wouldn't ruin tonight. She stepped over Nick's outstretched legs and stood in front of the fire with its glowing coals and crackling logs to dress the mantelpiece with pine twigs, snow-covered cones, red candles in little robin-shaped candle holders, and sprigs of holly. Another CD started playing, telling them all *It Was Beginning to Look a Lot Like Christmas.*

Stepping back to admire her handiwork she forgot about Nick's legs and stumbled, landing half on his lap, half on the arm of the chair. He reached out to catch her and his arms wrapped awkwardly around her. For a few seconds they just stared at one another before she jumped to her feet, blushing.

'I'm not sure who was trying to kill whom there,' she joked. 'Well, I think we're done, don't you, Mum? Mum?'

Sarah came in shivering with cold. 'Sorry cherub, I just popped out to see if there are any more shooting stars yet. It's really cold out there but I did see one and yes, I made a wish.'

'Well,' Nick said, getting to his feet. 'I'd better go and take Nicodemus for a walk before he thinks I've deserted him for good. Are you really planning on going to see the meteors later?'

'Yes,' Jamie said, grinning.

'Okay. I'll pop back around four-ish then. Make sure you wrap up warm. It's going to be a very cold night.'

'We'll come to the door with you,' Sarah said, grabbing Carole's hand.

Jamie was wheeling Mitsy towards the study in the wheelchair Matilda had lent them on a semi-permanent basis, and Carole and Sarah stood in the hall.

'Are you all making sure I leave?' Nick joked as he put on his coat.

Sarah smiled. 'We've just come to admire the view.'

He turned and stepped outside and the cold night air hit him like a wall of ice.

'Goodnight then,' he said, standing on the doorstep as if he were reluctant to leave.

'Er ... Nick?' Sarah said, shoving Carole forwards so that both she and Nick stood face to face on the doorstep.

Sarah pointed her finger upwards and Carole and Nick looked up to see a large bunch of mistletoe hanging above their heads. They seemed as shocked as each other.

'Mum!' Carole snapped, feeling furious and embarrassed as she looked everywhere but at Nick's face.

'Kiss her, Nick,' Jamie insisted, grinning broadly.

'This is ridiculous,' Carole said, stepping back.

Sarah stood in her way. 'It's bad luck not to,' she said, 'and what with it being Friday the 13th too, are you sure you want to risk any more bad luck?'

Nick sighed as if all the cares of the world had landed squarely on his shoulders.

'We may as well get it over with,' he said.

Carole's head shot up and she frowned. 'I apologise for my mother forcing you to do this.'

He leant forward and gave her a kiss on the cheek and even she was surprised. She thought he'd at least give her a quick kiss on the lips if only to conform to tradition.

'Auch man!' Jamie chided. 'That's ne'er a kiss!'

Carole tutted. 'That was good enough for me. 'I've got a boyfriend, don't forget.'

'That didn't stop Sebastian,' Mitsy chipped in.

'You've got two at the last count,' Nick mumbled.

Sarah held Carole's shoulders, pinning her to the spot. 'It's got to be a real kiss or you'll still get bad luck.'

'I don't want a real–'

'Oh for heaven's sake!' Nick interjected.

He grabbed Carol's wrist and pulled her, a little roughly she thought, into his arms. Her head fell back in surprise and her mouth fell open. She saw a sudden grin appear on his lips and then his mouth was on hers in a kiss that was nothing like she'd been expecting. From the way he'd grabbed her, she'd expected the sort of kiss Sebastian had given her. A possessive, passionate kiss.

This kiss was gentle, slow and teasingly tender. Carole completely forgot they were on the doorstep being watched by her mum, her gran and Jamie. All she saw was him. She closed her eyes and kissed him back.

Without even realising she was doing so, her hands which had been pushing against his arms, slid around him and his arms tightened about her waist. He eased her towards him and she went, willingly.

His mouth moved on hers with growing longing and as the kiss deepened, she felt herself matching his yearning. Her hands gripped his coat and she clung to him, never wanting to let go.

'Carole?'

She recognised Sebastian's voice; immediately, the spell was broken. Nick clearly heard it too because he let her go so abruptly that she almost tripped but he reached out and steadied her.

'Damn Sebastian,' Mitsy said.

'It's a kiss under the mistletoe,' Sarah called out to him, pointing upwards again.

'Oh!' Sebastian replied as if that made things all right.

Carole tried to pull herself together. 'Y …yes. Just a silly kiss under the mistletoe, that's all. Mum made us do it. We really didn't want to, did ... did we, Nick?'

Nick stared at her without taking his gaze from her face. 'No. We really didn't want to.'

'Well,' Sebastian said, striding towards them. 'I'd better have a kiss under the mistletoe too, hadn't I? And at least you'll want to kiss me.'

Nick's eyes narrowed momentarily. 'I've got to go. Nicodemus needs a walk. Goodnight.' He turned and walked away.

'Now that's what I call a kiss,' Jamie remarked as Nick was leaving.

'We'll see you later, Nick,' Sarah called out.

'She's all yours,' Carole heard Nick say as he passed

Sebastian, 'for now.'

Carole desperately tried to think of an excuse not to kiss Sebastian but she couldn't.

'Just a quick kiss, Sebastian,' she said, trying to smile. 'I'm beginning to feel a bit like a cow at a market.'

Jamie had the good grace to wheel Mitsy to the study and Sarah followed.

Sebastian kissed Carole as he had before and he even tried to fondle her breast but she grabbed his hand. When she finally managed to ease herself free, her lips felt bruised and sore.

'I'm going to bed,' she said. 'Goodnight, Sebastian.'

She closed the door before he could say anything and leant against it, shaking her head.

'Thanks for that,' she said sarcastically when her mum poked her head round the study door. 'I'll be glad when this day's over.'

'What was it like? With Nick, I mean. He looks like a really good kisser.

Carole let out a long, lingering sigh. 'He is. He … really, really is.'

***

She felt as if she'd only been asleep for ten minutes when she was woken up. Her mum assured her it had been at least four hours as it was three forty-five in the morning and Nick would be here any minute.

Carole dragged herself out of bed and threw on some clothes. She knew she should have made an effort but she was too tired, confused and upset. She'd hardly got a moment's sleep. She'd been tossing and turning all night with strange dreams about Dominic, Sebastian and Nick, but she couldn't remember what they were

It was still dark outside and bitterly cold. Carole was glad she'd worn two pairs of socks in addition to her fleece-lined boots. She had a T-shirt, jumper and her coat on but she still shivered as she, Sarah and Jamie walked down the path to meet Nick who was holding Nicodemus firmly by his lead in case Arkenarten should be out and about.

'Good morning, Nick,' Sarah said cheerfully. 'Did you sleep well?'

'Yes thanks. You?'

'Not bad thanks but I could have done with a few more hours. Carole got hardly any and she's feeling a little fragile this morning, aren't you cherub?'

Carole was dragging her feet and trying to avoid looking at Nick, which was proving to be harder than she thought. How could the man look so bloody gorgeous at this ungodly hour whilst she looked like a ragdoll with very tangled red hair? It struck her that she only thought of her hair as titian when it looked sleek and well styled, and just plain red when it looked like something Medusa would have envied. This morning, she felt her hair looked very red indeed – and Medusa would be seething.

'Carole?' Sarah said.

'Oh sorry, what?'

'You see,' Sarah commented, 'she's still half asleep now.'

Nick didn't say a word but Carole could feel his eyes staring at her as if they were little drills boring into her soul.

They weren't the only ones who had come out to see the meteor shower and as they approached the top of the lane and the green near the village hall, they saw several others all oohing and aahing at varying intervals.

Carole looked up to see one shooting star after another and marvelled at the majesty of it. It really did make one feel rather small and insignificant, yet somehow very special to be a part of such a diverse and magical universe; a universe where fragments of rock from outer space could enter the earth's atmosphere and become the heavens own firework display.

To think that a piece of matter could travel through space at hundreds of kilometres an hour to appear before her eyes as a streak of bright silvery light, a flash across the clear, dark sky and disappear, leaving only a memory of what it once was, seemed unimaginable.

It was only after she'd seen several that she remembered her wish from last night. She shot a sideways glance at Nick, who almost immediately looked in her direction, their eyes locking for just a moment before he looked away and up into the heavens.

CHAPTER TWENTY-ONE

Carole didn't see Nick or Sebastian all day. It wasn't until she and Josie, Sarah and Mitsy, being wheeled along by Jamie, went to the tree lighting ceremony that she saw them both, and to her surprise, they were standing side by side.

She wasn't sure whether this was a good or a bad thing but she was inclined to lean towards bad.

'Hello Nick,' Mitsy called out.

He turned and smiled warmly but the warmth seemed to fade as his eyes reached Carole. Nicodemus, who'd been sitting in front of Nick and hidden by Nick's legs, also turned, bounded towards her and gave her a much friendlier greeting by licking her hand and nuzzling against her legs. He looked delightful, if somewhat comical, in a bright red, dog coat with a white fleecy collar and a headband of tinsel. Two Christmas stars bounced around on springs at the top, adding the finishing touch.

Nick looked gorgeous and surprisingly not at all comical but rather sexy, in a Santa hat, black and red fleece and a pair of jeans. Sebastian looked good too in a pair of black trousers, a brown leather jacket and, she noticed in astonishment, a Christmassy reindeer jumper which she was certain was the one she'd knitted for him over ten years ago. Surely he hadn't kept it for all these years ... had he?'

Sebastian stepped forward and gave Carole a quick kiss on her cheek.

'I need to talk to you,' he whispered, 'but not now. I'm here with Mum so it'll have to be later. Are you free this evening? I'll call round.'

He was gone before she had a chance to answer.

Nick turned to Mitsy. 'It's quite a turnout, isn't it? Let's hope none of the bulbs are blown.'

He was right about the turnout. It looked as if the entire

village were there. In fact, the only people conspicuous by their absence were Justin Jarvis and Josie. She had no idea why Mr Jarvis wasn't there but she did know why Josie wasn't. She had called Carole first thing this morning and told her that Nick had been absolutely right about Aidan; that she'd tell her all the details later but suffice to say, she couldn't talk now. At least Josie's wish on her shooting star seemed to have come true.

Bert Threadgold, who appeared to have stepped into yet another role Justin Jarvis would normally have played, gave a speech about how grateful they all were to Nick for the tree and all his hard work and how this year was going to be a wonderful Christmas for everyone.

'And without further ado,' he announced, 'let there be light!'

And there was. Hundreds of multi-coloured bulbs lit up the tree and cast a kaleidoscope of colour onto the grass around it. The gold star glinted in the glow from the lights and as if the gods were adding their own special something to the event, the Geminid meteor shower began its repeat, and final, all night performance of the year.

Carole wiped a tear from her eye.

'It is pretty magical, isn't it?' Nick said.

She turned to look at him, not realising he was standing beside her. 'Yes, it is.'

'Have you heard from Josie? Was her night a success?'

'Yes ... it was.'

Carole wondered why she seemed to be having difficulty saying anything else.

'Speak of the devil!' Nick exclaimed, grinning broadly. 'Here she is now. I take it that's Aidan and his son with her?'

'Yes it–'

She stopped as Nick gave her a look of irritation. 'Fine. You obviously don't want to have a conversation with me,' he said, marching off in Jamie's direction.

Carole tutted but she really couldn't think of anything to say to him. Well, nothing he'd want to hear anyway.

'Hi ya!' Josie said, smiling like the cat that had not only got the cream but also the cow that produces it and the farmer who makes it. 'I'd like you all to meet Aidan and his son, Jason. This is my best friend Carole, her mum Sarah, Sarah's partner Jamie, Carole's gran Mitsy and her ... this is Nick, a friend of ours.'

Everyone greeted Aidan and Jason enthusiastically and Carole could see why Josie was so happy. Aidan, apart from being good-looking in a comfortable, homely way, with his light brown hair, gentle facial features, and glasses, was clearly besotted with her. Even Jason seemed at ease with both Josie and the fact that his dad had his arms wrapped tightly around her. If Carole didn't know otherwise, she would have thought that the three of them were a family.

'I thought Jason was with his grandparents for the weekend,' Carole said as Nick took Aidan and Jason over to where the hot drinks and mince pies were being served.

'He was,' Josie replied, 'but when I told Aidan about the tree lighting and the meteor display, which we missed last night – although I saw a few shooting stars of my own if you get my drift – he said that it was a shame Jason couldn't see it. He called him this afternoon and here we are.'

Carole smiled. 'You look like a ready-made family. You seem to ... belong.'

'I know! It's weird, isn't it? Good weird obviously, not bad weird. I'm so unbelievably happy. Who'd have thought that one evening can possibly change your life forever?'

'I'm so pleased for you Josie, and you deserve it.'

'Thanks Carole. And so do you. Are you any nearer making a decision yet?'

Carole sighed deeply. 'Not really but I've got something to tell you. Nick and I ...' She trailed off as Nick returned with Aidan, Jason and a tray bearing glasses of mulled wine and a plate of mince pies.

'Okay. Tell me later,' Josie said.

They looked around the happy throng as Bert waved his hand and the village choir, which consisted of most of the actors in the Christmas musical, burst into song. Aidan, Jason, Nick, and Carole's family joined in but Carole and Josie sipped their mulled wine.

'Aren't you singing?' Aidan asked, taking Josie's hand in his and smiling lovingly at her.

'No. This is a happy event. Carole and I don't want to ruin it.'

He leant across, kissed her on the cheek and resumed singing, rather well in fact, along to *Silent Night*.

'Speaking of weird,' Josie continued, 'where's Justin Jarvis tonight? I can see Sebastian and his mum but no sign of JJ.'

Carole shook her head. 'No idea. I haven't seen him since the night he ... well, you know. Perhaps he really does have health problems.'

'Either that or Sebastian and his mum have locked him up somewhere. I hope it's somewhere very dark and very unpleasant. That would match his hidden personality. It's odd isn't it that we think we know someone and they turn out to be completely the opposite of what we'd believed?'

Glancing between Nick and Sebastian, who seemed to be avoiding her this evening, Carole couldn't have agreed more.

***

'Let's all go back to the cottage,' Mitsy suggested after several more carols had been sung.

Carole was only too pleased to leave, having endured the inevitable, "For someone called Carole Singer, you don't seem to do much of it," and similar comments, all made in good fun, she was assured but getting more tiresome by the minute. She was less pleased to find that Nick was included in the 'all' as the atmosphere had been rather frosty between them since their 'conversation' about Josie. She was very glad however, to discover that Josie, Aidan and Jason were also invited.

'But what about Arkenarten?' Carole asked. 'He doesn't like Nicodemus and–'

'Well, he's going to have to start getting used to him,' Mitsy said. 'It is the season of goodwill after all, and if he doesn't, he can always find a quiet spot or go to his usual place in the study. Nick can make sure Nicodemus behaves himself, can't you, Nick?'

'I can, but I think Carole's right and–'

'Nonsense!' Mitsy said. 'Nicodemus, you behave yourself, you hear.'

To Carole's amazement, the hound actually nodded, although as it was followed by a sneeze, it may just have been a coincidence.

They walked towards the cottage and as Nick was talking to Aidan, Josie hung back to speak to Carole.

'Well,' she said. 'You and Nick did what exactly?'

'Oh! Um ... we kissed. But not like that, so don't get excited. Mum set it up. She hung mistletoe outside the cottage and then when Nick was leaving, she pushed – and I do mean pushed, me outside so that we were both standing beneath it.'

'And ...?'

'He really didn't want to kiss me, Josie. I was so embarrassed. He kissed me on the cheek but Mum and Jamie insisted he give me a real kiss. He seemed very reluctant and then he said, "Oh for heaven's sake," as if it was a chore. He yanked me into his arms and ... and he gave me one of the best kisses I think I've ever had.'

'Wow!'

'Double wow, Josie! It was ... incredible. So much so

that ... that I kissed him back and I actually forgot everyone was watching us!'

'Triple wow! Then what?'

'Then Sebastian appeared and he said he wanted a kiss under the mistletoe too. Nick let go of me, like a handful of hot coals and told Sebastian he was welcome to me. Well, he said, "She's all yours, for now," or words to that effect. Then he left.'

'Hmm. What did he mean by "for now" do you think?' Josie asked, looking thoughtful.

Carole sighed heavily. 'I assume he meant, until Dom comes down at Christmas.'

'It looks like your mum is planning a repeat performance,' Josie commented as they neared the cottage and saw Sarah point at the bunch of mistletoe.

'I'll pop back in a minute,' Nick said, backing away from the door. 'I ... I'd better make sure Nicodemus has a pee first.'

Without as much as a glance in Carole's direction, he set off down the lane as quickly as he could.

Carole was feeling more annoyed than relieved. I see! That makes things perfectly clear, doesn't it? He found kissing me so distasteful that he'd prefer to watch Nicodemus pee!'

Josie was right about Sarah and the mistletoe. It took at least five minutes for the men to line up and give the women a quick kiss on the cheek, or a longer one in some cases. Jason was included, much to his evident distaste; he pulled a face and wiped his mouth with the back of his hand several times after each kiss.

'I made some mulled wine earlier and left it to simmer,' Sarah said. 'I'll go and see to it and organise some nibbles.'

'You go and sit down, Mum. Josie and I'll do that.'

'Thank you, cherub.'

Josie gave Aidan a reassuring wink but Carole noticed he seemed perfectly at home in the company, so she grabbed Josie by the hand and dragged her towards the kitchen.'

'I know it's true love and everything,' Carole teased, 'but could you manage to keep your hands off the man for two minutes and come and help me?'

Josie grinned. 'At least I've only got my hands on one man, not three different ones!'

'I'm going to have to sort that out soon, aren't I?'

'You're not kidding! And not just because the village is starting to think of you as some sort of Jezebel. Do you know, in the old days they'd probably have stoned you, dragged you through the streets, then burnt you at the stake or something. Lucky for you times have changed. Now all they do is talk about you behind your back.'

'And not just behind my back! They say it to my face now. Someone asked me the other day how my two boyfriends were and how did I have the energy to cope with two when she found it difficult to cope with one. And I have no idea who she was.'

'Just as well no one saw you and Nick kissing then, especially as you clearly enjoyed it. Actually, Carole, surely that tells you something?'

'Other than that he hated every minute of it and was just putting on an act, you mean?'

'No! That you really enjoyed it. How did it make you feel? What was it like compared to Sebastian and Dominic's kisses? Better? Worse? Undecided and need to do it again to be sure?'

Josie pulled out a chair and sat down as if she expected this to take some time. Carole did likewise.

'I'd ... I'd like to do it again, Josie. And not just kissing either. If it hadn't been for Sebastian, I might ... we might ... well, let's just say, you might not have been the only one to have a good Friday night.'

'But ... I thought you said he wasn't interested. Are you saying that you think you might have ended up doing the dirty deed on the doorstep? That would have really given the village something to talk about. That would have made the local paper!'

'And not just the village. My family were standing on the doorstep watching, let's not forget.'

Josie chuckled and leant back in her chair. 'So who's best then? Nick, Seb or Dom?'

'At kissing? Obviously, I can only comment on that because ... Nick and I haven't ... well. Okay, don't look at me like that ... Nick. Without a doubt, Nick. Dom is second and Seb, oddly enough, is last. Don't get me wrong, Seb is a good kisser – or he used to be, but each time he's kissed me recently he's been ... well, it seems to be more about taking than giving, if you know what I mean, whereas Nick.' She let out a sigh. 'Well, need I say more?'

'Nope. So do you reckon he'd be best in bed too? What's Dom like on that score? You said he wasn't that interested in sex.' Josie sat upright again and leant forward. 'Come on. Tell all.'

Carole shook her head. 'You know you're going to have to tell me all about you and Aidan afterwards, don't you?'

Josie nodded enthusiastically. 'Yep!'

'Okay. Well, as I said ... out of Dom, Seb and Nick, Nick is definitely the best kisser and ... Oh!'

Carole's mouth fell open in horror as she saw Nick stop in his tracks at the kitchen door, an expression on his face somewhere between confusion and pleasant surprise.

Josie turned her head round, saw Nick and smirked, rather too loudly in Carole's opinion. No one said a word for at least ten seconds.

'So,' Nick said, leaning leisurely against the kitchen doorframe, 'despite it being "just a silly kiss under the mistletoe" which neither of us wanted to do, according to you, you actually enjoyed it. That's good to know because I kind of thought you did. I just wasn't sure until now.'

'No!' Carole said, feeling herself blushing from the top

of her head to the tips of her toes.

'Really? But I'm positive I heard you say, "Nick is definitely the best kisser" and unless there's another Nick you've been kissing, which I suppose is possible, I rather get the impression you were talking about me. Am I wrong, Josie?'

Josie giggled. 'Nope. You're right.'

'Don't bring Josie into this!'

'I didn't. You did by discussing it with her. Why were you discussing it by the way? I missed that bit.'

'I asked who was the best kisser and–'

'Josie!' Carole glared at her.

'And I won? Wow! Do I get a prize or something? Another kiss perhaps?'

'No! And ... and I didn't say I enjoyed it!'

'Yes, you did,' Josie insisted.

'How dare you eavesdrop anyway?' Carole said, trying to move away from whether she enjoyed it or not.

'You shouldn't talk so loudly if you don't want people to hear you. And you were talking about me, so there's no point in getting all uppity when I respond.'

'Well, we've finished talking about you now so you can go,' Carole snapped.

Nick grinned and moved away from the door without another word.

Carole was furious. 'But to answer your question about which one is best in bed, Josie,' she said, loud enough she hoped that Nick could hear, 'I can say most definitely, Sebastian. He can do things that make your hair curl as well as your toes, and everything else in between.'

'That won't matter quite so much when you're eighty and riddled with arthritis,' Nick called back from somewhere in the hall, 'and as you haven't been to bed with me, I'm not sure you can make that statement.'

'I most certainly can!' Carole yelled.

There was a moment's silence before Nick reappeared at

the door. 'Based on what?' he asked casually.

She hadn't expected him to return. She'd only said it as a parting shot.

'Based on ... lots of things.'

'For example?'

'Oh, I don't know. A woman just gets a sense for such things, doesn't she, Josie?'

Josie grinned and nodded. She was clearly enjoying this.

'Well,' he added. 'If you want to be absolutely sure, just let me know.' He turned and walked away again.

'I can assure you that won't be necessary!' Carole called out. 'I really have no interest whatsoever in going to bed with you.'

'You said you didn't want to kiss me, either,' came the reply, 'but you seemed to enjoy that.'

Carole couldn't think of anything to say, which was probably just as well as she heard her mum's voice in the hall.

'Are you two bringing in this mulled wine today or tomorrow?' Sarah said, grinning as she came into the kitchen.

'Sorry Mum, I got sidetracked.' Carole got to her feet and started sorting out some glasses.

Josie got some plates from the cupboard and Sarah piled them with mince pies, sausage rolls, cheese straws, and some chocolate truffles she'd made.

The three of them carried everything through to the sitting room where everyone was huddled either on chairs, one of the two large sofas or on cushions on the floor. Carole was astonished to see Nicodemus sitting quietly at Nick's feet with Arkenarten curled up on the back of Nick's chair, although the cat did seem to be watching the hound rather intently.

'How on earth did that happen?' she asked, nodding towards Arkenarten.

'They've realised they can tolerate each other after all,'

Nick replied. 'Give it a few more days and we may even see them curled up together in front of the fire.'

'That will never happen,' she said, wondering if there was a hidden meaning in his statement.

'I was just telling everyone about that gorgeous book cover you designed, sweetheart,' Mitsy said. 'Why don't you go and get the printout you did of it. Nick and Jamie haven't seen it and clearly Josie and Aidan haven't. It may be a little too grown up for Jason though.'

'I'm sure it won't be anything he hasn't seen before,' Aidan said. 'The stuff kids can see on TV, in magazines and on the internet these days is unbelievable. Mind you, I don't suppose we were any different when we were his age.'

'No,' Jamie mumbled. 'The only difference is we had to look harder for it.'

'It's not that bad,' Carole said, 'but you really won't be interested in it. It's a book cover for a romance novel.'

'I'd like to see it,' Nick said.

Jamie smiled. 'And so would I.'

'Me too,' Aidan agreed.

Carole tutted and went to get it.

'It's one of those rather racy Regencies.' Carole handed it to her mum to pass to Jamie. 'You know the sort ... or perhaps you don't. Arrogant, powerful hero tries to seduce beautiful but innocent woman. She dislikes him at first but gradually realises she can't live without him and they end up falling into one another's arms in a frenzy of passion. Oops. Sorry Aidan and Jason.'

'That's fine,' Aidan said, smiling at her.

The printout was passed around from Jamie to Aidan to Nick to Josie and it was only when Josie's mouth dropped open and she stared at Carole in surprise that Carole realised they had all been giving her rather odd looks, especially Nick.

'Is ... is it that bad?' Carole asked. 'The publishers love

it. What ... what's wrong?'

'Nothing's wrong,' Sarah said. 'It's gorgeous darling, isn't it, Jamie?'

He nodded several times in quick succession. 'Stunning.'

'You're a very talented artist,' Aidan remarked. 'You can see quite clearly whom you've based them on.'

Carole was surprised. She hadn't based the couple, who were locked in a passionate embrace, on anyone. The only guidelines she'd had were the woman had to have red hair and the man, dark hair. She'd just used her imagination.

'I didn't base them on anyone,' she insisted, taking the printout from Josie and studying it closely.

Suddenly, she saw it. She wondered how on earth she hadn't realised it before. The redheaded woman whose dress barely covered her obviously heaving bosom and who was staring longingly into the eyes of her seducer, was clearly herself, and the dark haired man with one arm wrapped tightly around her, the other hand about to tear the dress asunder, was without a shadow of a doubt none other than Nick.

Carole's head shot up and her eyes met Nick's. He looked as if he had a thousand questions to ask but more importantly, he didn't look pleased. He didn't look at all pleased.

CHAPTER TWENTY-TWO

Carole didn't think she'd ever been more pleased in her life to see Sebastian.

She'd completely forgotten that he'd said during the Christmas tree lighting ceremony, he would be coming around later. There she was standing in the sitting room, all eyes focused on her, not knowing what to say or do when the sound of the doorbell ringing saved her life.

Well, perhaps that was a slight exaggeration but it had certainly saved her from more embarrassment.

Remembering that it was Sebastian, she said, 'That's Sebastian ... for me. We're going out. Don't wait up.'

She dashed from the room, tossing the printout on the hall table, grabbed her coat and bag and ran to the door.

'I don't care where we go, Sebastian but get me the hell away from here as quickly as possible!'

He was only too happy to oblige.

'What's happened?' he asked when they were in the car and nearing the end of the lane.

Carole was lost in thought, going over and over how she could have been so stupid, so blind not to have seen it. The likenesses were undeniable. But why did Nick look so cross, so angry, so ... hurt? Surely he would have been pleased, especially after the conversation in the kitchen where he'd as much as said he'd be willing to sleep with her if she wanted to find out whether he was good in bed or not. She knew he was joking, of course, but that was the point. He found that amusing so why would he find an illustration so upsetting? Perhaps he was just embarrassed? She knew she certainly was. How would she be able to face him again after this?

'Carole? I asked what's happened. What's wrong?'

'Oh. Sorry, Sebastian I ... I just had to get out of there

for a while.'

'Too much of the happy home stuff?' he asked.

'No I ... I just needed some space, that's all. I'm sorry. You said you needed to talk to me earlier. If this is about us then I–'

'It's not. It's about my dad. Well ... Dad and Mum to be precise. They're getting a divorce.'

'What? Why?' As soon as she'd asked. she thought she probably knew the answer to that question.

'They ... they've been having problems for some time now. It's one of the reasons I came back. And in the hope of seeing you, of course.'

'It's okay, Seb. You don't have to pretend you came half way around the world just for me. I know that's not the only reason you're here. I thought it was to take over your dad's business because he's retiring. That's what the village drums are saying. No one has even mentioned any problems between your parents.'

She found that rather astonishing bearing in mind his parents lived in the village, whereas she'd only been back for a few days and rumours about her had spread like wildfire.

'They've been very discreet. What with Dad being a JP and an important part of the village and everything. Things have been getting worse though and Mum said on Friday that enough is enough. She's going to stay with her sister in Eastbourne until the house and business are–'

'The house and business?' Carole interrupted, hardly able to believe what she was hearing.

'Yes. That's what I need to talk to you about.'

He stopped the car and only then did Carole see where they were. It was The Manor Court Hotel.

'W ... why have we come here, Sebastian?'

'You said you didn't care where we went.'

'That's true. But why here?'

'Carole, my darling. Let's just go inside and have a

drink. Just one drink. Please. I really need to be with someone special this evening and there is no one who is more special to me than you.'

He looked so sad and lost that her heart went out to him. He idolised his parents, particularly his dad and this must have come as a real shock to him. The least she could do was to spend a couple of hours with him over a friendly drink, especially if she really did love him. She'd want to comfort him, wouldn't she? And she did want to comfort him.

'Of course, Sebastian,' she replied.

They went inside, past the huge Christmas tree in the reception, which she remembered hadn't been there on Thursday when they'd dined here. She couldn't help but compare it to the tree near the village hall or the ones she'd decorated with Nick and her family at her gran's; somehow it paled in comparison.

They sat by the window in the strangely empty bar and whilst Sebastian ordered drinks, she stared out into the dark, past the floodlit car park and the ornamental bay trees, past the gardens and the tree-lined drive beyond, into nothing but blackness.

She knew what lay beyond the drive but she found herself wondering what it would feel like not to know and she remembered that that was exactly how she'd felt all those years ago when Sebastian had left her. It was as if she were staring past what her life should have been; what she had expected it to be, into a deep, dark blackness that had terrified her.

'I can't stay in the village,' Sebastian blurted out.

His words brought her back to the present.

'What? Why not?'

'Everyone will be talking about Mum and Dad and I really can't face it. Besides, once the business is sold, what would I do? I couldn't face working there, knowing it once belonged to my family.'

'Can't you buy it from your dad? Wouldn't your mum let you keep that anyway?'

He shook his head. 'No. And ... when I said Mum wants the business sold, what I meant was, she wants to get rid of the debts it's accrued. There ... there's no money left. Dad ... Dad's had a few problems and ... well, there's nothing left except the house.'

'Sebastian!' Carole was truly shocked. 'What ... what will you do? Where will you go? Back ... back to Australia?'

'No way! I'll stay in Sussex. Not sure where yet. East or West but somewhere not too far away from Jutsdown. I'll get a job at another estate agents or something. I'm not worried about me. I'm worried about Dad. He's taking it very badly.'

Tears began streaming down his face and he brushed them away with a flick of his hand. 'I'm sorry,' he said. 'You ... you must think I'm a real wimp.'

'No! Far from it. I really feel for you. Truly I do.' She reached out and squeezed his hand and he held on to hers as if he were frightened to let go.

'I love you, Carole. I really, truly love you. I want to spend the rest of my life with you. I want to make up for all the years we lost. I want us to ... have a family together. I know it's difficult for you and I know you have feelings for ... Dominic, but tell me honestly. Do you really love him? Do you really want to grow old with him? Do ... do you want to ... make babies with him?'

Carole felt dazed. She was genuinely moved by his words and his tears and the way he was looking at her and ... and she knew one thing for certain. She loved him more than Dominic.

The honest answers were, yes, she did love Dom but not enough. She had somehow never thought about them growing old together. Never thought beyond hoping he'd propose really and now, giving it some serious thought, she knew that she couldn't see them together in twenty years' time. And children? Dom was more interested in his career than he'd ever be in raising a family. He'd want kids she assumed although now that she thought about that, she realised they'd never discussed it.

'Well?' Sebastian asked.

'No,' she replied. 'No, I don't love Dom enough.'

He took her other hand in his and pulled her towards him, kissing her, not fiercely and possessively this time but more tenderly. The kiss deepened and his arms slid around her. They were both perched on the edges of their seats and balancing awkwardly. Sebastian eased away from her and he got down on one knee.

Holding out the ring he'd offered her twice before he said, 'Carole Ann Singer, will you please do me the greatest honour and say that you'll be my wife? I promise to cherish you and love you and make love to you every day from this day forth until death us do part. Please say yes, Carole, and make me the happiest man on earth.'

And without being absolutely sure of what she was doing, she nodded her head.

'Third time lucky,' Sebastian said, pulling her into his arms and kissing her passionately.

When he released her, he looked deep into her eyes. 'Now let's get a room and really make up for lost time.'

***

Carole spent the early hours of Sunday in a state of bewilderment.

She wasn't completely certain what had happened in the bar at The Manor Court Hotel last night other than Sebastian had proposed and apparently, she'd accepted.

She was certain that he'd said his parents were divorcing. She also knew he'd said he would be moving to somewhere nearby. On that basis, as his wife, she'd no doubt be going with him although that hadn't occurred to her last night.

She was also absolutely certain that she decided she loved Sebastian more than Dom. That meant she'd have to tell Dom it was over. How she was going to do that when he was in London with his mother *and* chickenpox – she had no idea – although to Carole's mind they were one and the same thing. At least she'd made a decision. She should be thankful for that.

And yet, when Seb had said those immortal words, "Now let's get a room" it was as if she'd been snapped out of a deep trance.

'No,' she'd said. 'I'm sorry, Sebastian but I can't. Not tonight. I simply can't. Not until I've told Dom. And I'm not sure when that will be. I don't want to tell him whilst he's ill.'

Sebastian was less than pleased, of course, but even he knew when he was beating a bush with no chance of bagging a bird. He'd reluctantly said that he understood and was prepared to wait. For a few more days.

'Christmas Eve,' he'd said, 'That gives you plenty of time to tell him. Then after the performance of *A Christmas Carol,* you and I will come back here and spend the night. All night. In bed. Together. After that, we can do whatever you want. Spend Christmas Day with your family or whatever but on Christmas Eve, I want you to spend the night with me. I want you to be mine again. Really mine. Is that agreed?'

She had looked into his eyes and was sure she'd seen love.

'Yes,' she'd said. 'That's agreed.'

Now she wasn't quite so sure.

They'd stayed for a few more drinks. He'd tried to talk her into staying the night – again. She'd refused. He'd driven her back to her gran's and they'd kissed goodnight. She'd got out of the car and crept into the cottage. It was late and everyone was in bed. She wasn't sure what time it was and she didn't look at the clock; she just went upstairs, got undressed and fell into bed.

And for someone who had just got engaged to the man she'd loved for more than thirteen years, and was about to change her name from Carole Singer to Mrs Carole Jarvis, she didn't feel anywhere near as happy as she thought she would.

On Sunday morning, having tossed and turned all night, trying to get her head around what she was doing, she left the house early and went for a long walk across the fields in the bitterly cold air, well before the sun was up. She kept on walking in a large semi-circle until she reached her childhood home on the other side of the village at least two hours later.

The Victorian villa looked much the same as it had all those years ago: more than twenty now, when she'd walked through that door with her mother just weeks after her father's death, never to return.

As she stood before the row of metal railings and the gate, which always squeaked no matter how often her dad oiled its giant hinges, she thought of Christmases past. Of the holly wreath the gate had proudly borne and the rows of multi-coloured twinkling lights entwined along the railings. Of the wreath made of thick, dried orange slices, cinnamon sticks, pine cones, holly and chestnuts, tied with a full red ribbon to the blue painted front door.

Of the joy to be found inside: the eight-foot Christmas tree, decorated so that not a single branch was bare; the multitude of presents underneath it; the marble fireplace strewn with pine boughs, cones and cinnamon sticks. The ornate black iron fire basket that could hold a Yule log big enough to burn all night, as all Yule logs should, to ensure good luck for the coming year.

She recalled the smells emanating from the kitchen where she and her mum made the Christmas cake, stirring it three times and making a wish. The Christmas puddings, mince pies and sausage rolls. The pickled onions made using her great, great, grandmother's recipe for pickling spices. The baked hams, cooked slowly in the oven with cloves and honey, mustard and cider. The mulled wine: cups of which were offered to all-comers to the house, including the postman who had finished his round, whistling a merry tune on many occasion.

The house seemed to come alive before her eyes and she was again in the sitting room, playing games and tearing excitedly at the beautifully wrapped presents, singing carols and sitting on her father's knee on Christmas Eve as he read *A Christmas Carol* to her and they drank hot chocolate.

'It's for sale,' said a voice close by.

Startled, she turned to see a man she didn't recognise.

'Oh!' she said, trying to regain her composure. 'Sorry, you gave me quite a fright. I was miles away.'

'I do apologise, my dear. I didn't mean to. I thought you were admiring her. She is a beautiful house.'

Carole blinked several times. The man referred to the house as a 'she' just like her dad had always done.

'She is. I used to live here as a child.'

'Really? I'm from the agents handling the sale. She's just come on the market but she does need rather a lot of work. An elderly gentleman lived here for almost twenty years and I don't believe he's updated her since he moved in. She's selling for a reasonable price and has great potential. Here's my card. I'm Jacob Marley, of Marley and Scrooge estate agents. And yes, my dear, I've heard all the jokes about our names, although my partner is Edward Scrooge, not Ebenezer, so I suppose that's one small blessing!'

'I know about names and jokes. I'm Carole Singer. I'm pleased to meet you, Mr Marley.'

He smiled warmly. 'I was supposed to be meeting a couple from London here early this morning but the wife has gone into labour earlier than expected and they've just called to cancel. Would you like to look inside? I may as well go in anyway whilst I'm here, to check everything is secure, so I'd be happy to have the company.'

She eyed him cautiously for just one second but quickly dismissed the notion that he could be a mass murderer, although she knew such things had happened. But if the same person had owned the house for almost twenty years without updating her, that meant parts of her may be as they were when a fifteen-year old Carole and her mother had left.

'Yes please,' she replied. 'I'd love to look inside.'

CHAPTER TWENTY-THREE

'Where on earth have you been, Carole? We've been worried sick?' Sarah said when Carole returned to the cottage late on Sunday afternoon.

'Why?' Carole asked, rather surprised by her mum's outburst. 'I left you a note.'

'Yes, but all it said was something like 'Gone out, not sure when I'll be back'. We had no idea where. Have you been with Sebastian?'

It was only then that Carole spotted Nick hovering in the background. She wasn't ready to face him and the fact that he was here now, made her angry.

'Mum, for heaven's sake. I'm a grown woman. I told you I'd gone out and I told you I'd be back. Let's face it, that's more information of my whereabouts than you've had for many, many years. And now I'm going out again and I'm not sure when I'll be back.'

She turned and slammed the door behind her, running up the lane as fast as she could. She knew she shouldn't have reacted like that but she'd had such an emotional and bewildering day. Now, all she wanted was time to think. Time to plan. She certainly didn't want to have to talk to Nick.

She wondered where she could go to be alone and as if providence were shining down on her, she saw Bert Threadgold leaving the village hall and locking the door behind him.

'Hello Mr Threadgold,' she called out.

'Hello Carole, dear. How are you? We missed you at rehearsals ... and Sebastian.'

'Oh! I have no idea where he was. Um ... I don't suppose I could ask a favour, could I? I'm going to be rather busy for most of this coming week and I'm not sure how long I'll be able to spend on the remaining scenery. I couldn't ask you to leave me the key so that I can get on with it now, could I? I'll drop it back to you on my way home, I promise.'

He hesitated for a moment before smiling and handing it over.

'I don't see why not,' he replied, 'and don't worry about dropping it off to me later. Nick needs it first thing to come in and shift some things around so I was going to drop it in to him anyway. He's always at Mitsy's cottage first thing in the morning so you can give it to him, and save me the trouble. Goodnight dear.'

'Thank you and good night to you too.'

Carole opened the doors and switched on the lights. She threw her coat on a chair and made her way to the back of the hall where the scenery was still stacked and leaning against a wall. The heating would go off soon she realised but the hall held the warmth fairly well, so she should be okay for an hour or so.

She decided to work on one of the few remaining scenes left for her to finish. It was the one of Scrooge's bedroom. She'd started it days ago but hadn't liked the colours, so she'd left it to come back to. She'd only been working on it for about fifteen minutes when she heard the door open. She assumed it was Bert Threadgold coming back because, as usual, he'd forgotten something.

'I'm back here Mr Threadgold. Did you forget something?'

The only answer was the sound of firm footsteps and they definitely weren't Bert's. She squeezed past the stack of chairs and poked her head around the makeshift stage. She was horrified to see Nick striding towards her with a look on his face more terrifying than that of any of Scrooge's ghosts.

She stood her ground, pushed her shoulders back and stuck her chin out.

'What are you doing here?' she asked as calmly as she could, taking into account the fact that her heart was beating wildly.

'I might ask you the same question,' he said, rapidly closing the distance between them.

'Why? It's really none of your business where I am – or anyone else's for that matter.'

'That wasn't a very nice thing to say to your mum, you know.'

Carole did know but she didn't need him to remind her.

'Again. None of your business.'

'Well, I'm making it my business. Have you spent the day with Sebastian?'

'Nick! It really is none of your business. You have no right to ask where or with whom I spend my days.'

'Or nights comes to that. You spent the night with him, I hear.'

Her mouth fell open. That really did come as a surprise.

'I don't know who told you that but again, none of your business.'

Something in his eyes made her feel the need to keep him at a distance and she turned, adopting the pretence of indifference, and squeezed back past the stacked chairs.

'I can't believe you,' he said. 'I really thought you would come to your senses about Sebastian. It seems I was wrong.'

She turned back to face him. 'Come to my senses! How dare you! You really don't like him, do you? What have you got against him?'

'Nothing. And it's not a matter of liking him. I'm just surprised that you would give him another chance after what he did to you the last time, that's all.'

'And why shouldn't I? Don't you think that people deserve second chances? Everyone makes mistakes you know – even you!'

'I agree. Especially me. Yes, everyone does make

mistakes and everyone deserves a second chance but there are some mistakes that are just too big and sometimes they're not really mistakes, they're decisions made for a reason. Do you want to give him another chance to make the same mistake for the same reason?'

'What's that supposed to mean?'

'He left you on your wedding day without telling you to your face and he went off and married someone else within a year.'

'I know what he did! There's no need to remind me!'

Nick had reached the stack of chairs and it stood like a barricade between them as they stared at one another.

'I think there is,' he continued a little more calmly now, as though he thought a more reasoned approach might have more effect. 'You seem to have forgotten what that experience did to you.'

'I haven't forgotten, believe me, but unlike you it seems, I'm prepared to forgive people.'

'I'm prepared to forgive people too, but I'd think twice before I gave them a second chance to break my heart. You know Mitsy's saying, 'Hurt me once, shame on you, hurt me twice, shame on me'. Do you know why he's getting a divorce?'

'Because he realised he'd made a mistake.'

'After ten years?'

Nick may have sounded calmer but Carole was growing angrier by the minute.

'Okay, it took him a long time to realise it but as soon as he did, he came back and as soon as we saw one another again, it was just like old times. What's wrong with that?'

'Nothing. It's all very romantic.'

'It is! He ... he even kept a jumper I knitted him with a reindeer on it. He wore it last night at the Christmas tree lighting ceremony. You wouldn't keep something like that unless you really loved someone, and wearing it last night was very romantic. He's ... he's a very romantic man.'

She had no idea why the reindeer sweater had popped into her head but it had.

'So you keep saying. Are you trying to convince me, or yourself? But I suppose I can see why you'd admire a man who is brave enough to wear a jumper emblazoned with a cartoon reindeer ... in public.'

'Oh! And what's wrong with that? You ... you had a Santa hat on! I really don't see the difference. Besides, a man will do anything for the woman he loves.'

'I agree. If he really loves her.'

'What's that supposed to mean? Are you now saying that you don't think he loves me? Of course, he loves me. What makes you think otherwise?'

'Have you actually asked him why he left his wife?'

'Yes, I told you. It was a mistake.'

'But what made him suddenly realise that? What made him leave now? Perhaps you should ask him.'

'Why?'

'Because I just don't think he's right for you. Ask him. Outright. And make sure he tells you the truth, not what you want to hear.'

'And now you're calling him a liar!'

'I'm not calling him a liar. I'm just saying that some men will say things they think someone wants to hear. Especially, if it's someone they say they're in love with.'

'Say they're in love with? There it is again. You don't believe he is, do you? Why not? What makes you such an expert on love? Why don't you think he loves me?'

Nick smirked. 'I'm not an expert on love, I assure you. If I were, we wouldn't be having this conversation. And you're asking the wrong man, Carole. You should be talking to Sebastian about this.'

'Yes. I should. And I do know why he came here now but I'm not telling you. I don't even know why I am having this conversation with you. Why you even came here this evening.'

'Because I care about you, Carole. I ... I don't want you to get hurt again. I don't want you to do something else you may regret. I want you to be happy.'

'Something else I ...! Oh, you mean other than sleep with him, is that it? You say you care about me but you don't and all you do is lecture me and ... and judge me. Well, for your information Mr High and Mighty, I did not sleep with Sebastian last night. He asked me to but I said no. So I'm not quite the ... the tart you seem to think I am. And I didn't spend the day with him today either. But I have no idea what makes you think you have the right to involve yourself in my love life anyway. Or why you're so concerned about it. You say you want me to be happy but you haven't the slightest clue as to what would really make me happy. If you did you'd ...'

'I would ...? What is it that I would do to make you really happy, Carole?'

'It ... it doesn't matter.'

'It matters to me. What is it that I would do? What should I do? What do you want me to do?'

He moved the stack of chairs out of the way as if they were sticks of firewood.

'I ... I don't know. I didn't ... I don't ...'

'Are you really sure you love him, Carole? I haven't heard you say it?'

'Yes I ... I'm not going to say it just for you to hear. It's nothing to do with you. It's none of your business.'

'So you keep saying but I told you, I'm making it my business.'

He moved closer to her and their eyes locked. She felt the need to back away. Not from fear of him but from fear of herself. Of how she felt. Of what she might do. She backed herself up against the scenery she'd been working on.

'Nowhere to go,' he said, moving closer still. 'Shall I tell you what I'd like to do, Carole? What would make *me* really happy? No, better still, shall I show you?'

Before she knew what was happening, his arms were wrapped around her, pulling her to him. He tilted her head back with his hand and stared directly into her eyes for a few short moments before his mouth came down on hers in a kiss so passionate that she felt her knees buckle. She threw her arms around him, clinging to him, pulling him closer, kissing him back as passionately as he was kissing her and she shifted her body so that she was pressed hard against him.

She could feel his longing and it matched hers. She tugged at his shirt so that she could slip her hand inside and feel his flesh against her fingers and it felt so good she actually moaned with pleasure. When his hand moved round and cupped her breast, she wanted to feel his hand on her bare skin.

The kiss grew more intense and as Nick began to undo the buttons of her blouse, she reached up and tore at them, all three popping off like little champagne corks. She tugged at the button on his jeans and pulled the zipper down with one quick movement, sliding her hand inside and touching him. He was rock hard and it sent a thrill of anticipation and yearning rocketing through her.

It obviously sent something similar through Nick because he moaned her name before kissing her even more deeply, more passionately. He undid her bra without any help and as his hand caressed her bare skin, she shuddered. She wanted him so badly she could think of nothing else. He fondled first one breast and then the other, replacing his hands with his mouth as his hands moved down across her stomach. He unbuttoned her trousers, slid his fingers inside and stroked her over her panties.

Unwittingly, she drew in a deep breath and let out a little squeal of both pleasure and surprise and it suddenly seemed as if someone had opened the door and let the cold, sobering December air in.

Nick stopped and his head shot up as his eyes met hers. 'I'm so sorry!' he groaned, his voice like course sandpaper scraping across her skin. 'I ... I should never have started this.' He shut his eyes tight, removed his hand from her trousers and pulled back from her.

'W ...what? W ...why?' she stammered, not quite able to catch her breath or to comprehend what had been happening but more importantly, why he had stopped. 'I ... I don't understand. Don't you want me?'

He groaned. 'Of course I do! I've never wanted anyone so much in my entire life.'

'Then ... what's the problem?' Her brows knit tightly together as she tried to control the range of emotions running riot throughout her body. She wanted him so much, it hurt. It actually hurt.

'Apart from the fact that we were about to have unprotected sex pressed up against a scene from the Christmas musical,' he said, nodding towards the scene Carole had been working on of Scrooges' bedroom, 'we both seem to have forgotten that, not only are you living with one man, you're engaged to another, if the gossip is correct. And you've just spent the last twenty minutes defending him. I think that puts me somewhere between a chimpanzee and pond life on the potential boyfriend scale. A quick romp in a fake bedroom may be fine for some men, Carole, but it's not fine with me. And it shouldn't be fine with you either.'

Her mouth fell open in genuine surprise. 'And you've just spent the last twenty minutes telling me I shouldn't be with Sebastian and that he isn't right for me. Are you actually telling me off now for wanting to have sex with you? I don't believe this!'

She tugged at her button-less blouse as tears of frustration and rejection stung her eyes. She wiped them away with the back of her hand and rapidly re-buttoned the top button of her trousers.

'Carole, I ...' His voice trailed off as he zipped up his jeans with a certain amount of obvious discomfort.

'And don't you dare presume to tell me what should and shouldn't be okay for me! If I want to have sex with someone in a fake bedroom, quick or otherwise, I will!'

He reached out for her but she dodged his hand.

'Carole, I'm sorry! For once in my life, I thought I could do what I wanted, instead of having to do what is right. But I can't. It wouldn't be fair to you or to me. Please understand. I–'

'I understand!' she said even though she didn't and swept past him, heading for the door.

She didn't look back when he called her name again, or when the sound of splitting hardboard echoed around the village hall. She just grabbed her coat and ran.

***

She managed to pull herself together by the time she reached the cottage. Taking a deep breath, she stepped inside and headed for the sitting room.

'I owe you an apology, Mum,' she said.

'No, cherub,' Sarah said before Carole got any further. 'It's my fault. You're right. I'm sorry. You're a grown woman. I just ... I just don't want you to get hurt, that's all.' She stood up and took Carole in her arms.

'I know,' Carole said. 'But I have to live my life the way I see fit. I have to make my own decisions. And I've made a decision. Well, more than one actually.'

'We know dear,' Mitsy said, sounding none too pleased. 'Sebastian proposed again and this time you accepted.'

Carole eased herself away from her mother. 'How do you know that, Gran?'

'Sebastian's been here looking for you. He's just left but not before he told us the happy news.'

'Just now? W ... was Nick here?'

'No,' Sarah said. 'He left shortly after you. We wondered if he'd gone to look for you.'

'He had. And he found me. If he'd already left, then how...?'

She wondered what had made Nick say that he'd heard she was engaged. Clearly Sebastian must be telling people.

'I suppose we should say, Congratulations,' Mitsy said.

'Oh yes! Congratulations, cherub.'

'Thanks. But there's no need. It's going to be a very short engagement. And I don't mean in a good way.' She grinned as she saw the confusion turn to relief and pleasure on the faces of her family. 'And let's be honest. You hated the thought of it, didn't you?'

'Yes!' Mitsy exclaimed. 'You can do so much better.'

'Well, we weren't thrilled, cherub, but if it had made you happy, really happy I mean, we would have welcomed him with open arms.'

'Humph! You speak for yourself,' Mitsy said.

'Does this mean ... you're staying with Dominic?' Jamie asked.

Carole shook her head. 'It wouldn't be fair. I love him but ... Actually, I do love Sebastian too, but I've only just realised – about ten minutes ago, in fact – that when you're in love, and I mean *really* in love, you know it. Right down to the tips of your toes and into the very centre of your core, your soul if you like. And you know that even if you don't end up with the one you really love, you certainly don't want to be with anyone else, just for the sake of it. Oh well, I suppose I'd better go and tell Sebastian the news.'

***

She knew Sebastian wasn't happy but although Carole hated to see him hurt even more, bearing in mind the situation with his parents, she couldn't let him continue to believe they would have a future together.

He tried to persuade her of course; tried to make her change her mind; reminded her yet again of how good they were in bed together.

'But that won't mean much when we're eighty and riddled with arthritis,' she said, 'as someone once pointed out to me. This is about the future, Sebastian. Yes, we were good together in the past. But it is exactly that – the past. Because of the way it ended, the way you left, I think I held on to some foolish romantic notion of a lost love. And some part of me didn't want to let you go. When I saw you again in the village, that part of me took over and I didn't really question it properly.'

'Because it was your heart telling you that you love me!'

'No. It was my hurt pride telling me I had to get you back. It was my doubts about the present and my fear of the future. But now I don't have those doubts or fears. I know exactly what I want and even if I don't get it, I know I'll be okay. I have a family who love me and friends who care about me. And one day, if I'm very lucky, I'll be with someone I truly love and who loves me as much as I love him.'

'I love you!'

'Do you Sebastian? Perhaps you do. I don't know. And I'm really sorry but this isn't about you. It's about me. It's about what I want. What I really want. I wish you all the luck and love in the world. But I can't give it to you. I'm sorry.'

'Could ... could we just have sex, just once, for old time's sake?'

Carole almost laughed. 'No, Sebastian, we couldn't. And now I've got to go. I've got a train to catch.'

'But it's nine o'clock on Sunday night!'

'I know it is.' She smiled fondly as she kissed him goodbye. 'But there's no time like the present.'

***

234

Carole knew Mrs Smith wasn't best pleased either, when she arrived home at eleven o'clock on Sunday evening.

'I was just going to bed!' Mrs Smith said, standing in the kitchen as Carole let herself in.

'Hello and goodnight then,' Carole replied. 'I've come to see Dominic, so there's no need for you to stay up.'

If looks could kill, Carole knew she would have been dead on the floor with several knives in her chest. In fact, she thought, after she'd told Dominic what she had to say, she possibly would be. She was fairly positive though that Dominic's mum would welcome the news far more than Dom would.

'Carole! Is that you, babe?' Dom called out from the sitting room.

'Yes,' she said, smiling sweetly at his mother before going into the sitting room and shutting the door behind her.

Dom was sprawled across the sofa watching some football match on TV but to Carole's amazement, he switched it off and sat bolt upright. He didn't have many spots and he didn't look unwell but Carole knew that chickenpox often felt worse than it looked.

'What a lovely surprise!' he said.

'It may not be. How are you feeling?'

His brows furrowed. 'I'm okay. What does that mean?'

'It means we need to talk.'

'I'm not sure I like the sound of that.'

Carole sat on the armchair opposite him and smiled weakly. 'There's no easy way to say this Dom, so I'll just say it and I'm sorry for being so blunt and for the timing, but it's best that you know now.'

'If this is about me not being romantic,' he said, 'I can be romantic.'

She had no idea where that had come from. She shook her head.

'It isn't. Well not exactly. It's about us. I don't see us having a future together, Dom. I'm truly sorry but I don't.'

He seemed to let the words sink in before he said, 'Why not? What's happened since you've been at your gran's to make you change your mind? We were fine before you left.'

'Were we? Were we really? Can you honestly say that you saw us spending our lives together? I'll admit, before I went to Gran's I wanted nothing more than for you to propose but part of that was me being an idiot about my name.'

'I can propose. I was going to propose this weekend in fact and then this happened. I'll do it now. Let's get married, Carole. I know your gran doesn't like me but we can work around that and I know Mum thinks I can do better but she'll come round. We've got a good home and a pleasant life. We should get married.'

'As lovely as that sounds, Dom, no we shouldn't. I want more than a good home and a pleasant life. I want passion and togetherness. I want a family and a husband who'll be there bringing up our children beside me.'

'I want those things too. I haven't been able to stop thinking about sex since you've been gone, and I want kids.'

'Sex and passion are two different things, Dom, at least in the way I mean them. As for you wanting kids, I'm sure that's true but you'd be at the office all day and possibly half the night and I'd be here at home waiting for you.'

'What's wrong with that? We could work something out.'

'This isn't a negotiation, Dom. And we couldn't. I'm sorry but this just isn't what I want and I don't think it's really what you want either if you're completely honest with yourself.'

He let out a long, meaningful sigh. 'And there's nothing I can say or do to make you change your mind?'

She shook her head again. 'No, Dom. I'm sorry.'

'Well ... I assume you're going to stay the night anyway. It's too late to get a train back now. Let's sleep on it and see how we feel in the morning. Perhaps tomorrow you'll feel differently ... and the spot on my dick has gone already!'

Carole gasped. Why was it, she wondered, that everyone wanted to have sex with her except Nick?

'Oh!' she said, 'I'm ... glad to hear that, but no, I won't be staying the night. I called a friend who lives nearby and I'm spending the night there. I'll come back tomorrow and sort out my things if that's okay with you or I can leave it until you're fully recovered. Let me know which you'd prefer.'

'There's no rush. Leave it until after Christmas.'

'It's got to be done, Dom. We both need to get on with our futures.'

***

Carole stayed in London for two days before returning to Jutsdown. She needed the time to sort things out, to visit clients, to get her finances in order and to think things through, away from the village and its distractions. Away from Nick.

She had a lot to do if her plans were going to succeed, and she really wanted them to. The moment she had stepped inside her old family home with Jacob Marley on Sunday morning, she'd felt it. She knew that whatever else happened, one thing was certain. She had to buy that house.

She had some savings, which would cover the deposit. The house was a real bargain and although it needed work, it was mainly with regard to updating the interior; the house itself was structurally sound and in fairly good repair.

Her business was thriving and she had several years' worth of certified accounts so getting a mortgage wouldn't be a problem, the bank assured her. She was sure it would all work out. She just had a really good feeling about it. After all, it was only a week until Christmas – a time when miracles happened.

CHAPTER TWENTY-FOUR

'I can't believe Christmas Day is only one week away, can you?' Josie asked when she and Carole arrived at rehearsals on Wednesday.

'No,' Carole replied. 'I've hardly done any Christmas shopping. Do you fancy going to Brighton for the day on Saturday?'

Josie pulled a face. 'Well ... we could I suppose.'

'Don't sound so enthusiastic! Oh, of course. I'd forgotten you and Aidan are inseparable. Fine. I'll go on my own.'

'Aren't you helping out at the garden centre on Saturday anyway? It's the weekend before Christmas and the place will be heaving.'

'Well, it'll have to 'heave' without me. I won't be setting foot in that place again until hell freezes over. I've already told Gran, and Jamie has very kindly offered to continue to stand in for me.'

'So you haven't seen Nick since the two of you attempted to bring your delightful romance cover to life?'

'Very amusing, Josie.' Carole made a fake grin. 'I'm trying very hard to forget that.'

'What? The fact that you drew the exact likeness of you and Nick locked in a passionate embrace without even realising you'd done it, or the fact that you were locked in a passionate embrace ... and still didn't do *it*.'

'You've missed your vocation. You should be on the stage.'

'Which is exactly where I shall be ... in three minutes' time. Are you working on the scenery tonight?'

'Yeah. I heard Bert Threadgold telling Gran that Nick wasn't coming tonight, so I figured it was safe. I'll finish the rest during the day, tomorrow and Friday and that's me done. I won't have to be here again until the big night.'

'You can't avoid him forever you know, Carole. Besides, from what you told me about it, once he knows the competition's out of the running, he'll be happy to ... resume discussions, shall we say.'

'No, I think he just used that as an excuse.'

'Why? What makes you say that?'

'Various things. The way he looks at me sometimes, as if I make him really cross or something. The way he lectured me. The way he tried to avoid kissing me under the mistletoe, but most importantly, the fact that he didn't come after me on Sunday night.'

'But ... he was the one who kissed you on Sunday. He made the first move. He said he wanted you but he didn't want to be in the queue of boyfriends or some such thing. Now there's no queue. Now you're on your own.'

'Precisely. If he was really interested in me he'd have told me on Sunday and asked me to dump the others and be with him. He didn't. And now that I'm free, he still hasn't. The entire village must know about Sebastian by now, and Gran must have told him about Dom. He hasn't called or been near. No. It was just one of those spur of the moment things and he regretted it afterwards. In fact, he regretted it during! That's the real reason he stopped.'

'Perhaps,' Josie said. 'Or perhaps he was just giving you some space on Sunday. Maybe he didn't want to add to your confusion. Or maybe he was frightened you'd add him to your list and then reject him later. And there's a chance he hasn't heard you're ... now open to offers, a slim one I'll admit but a chance. And anyway, you've only been back for one day. I think you should go and talk to him, at the very least.'

'Maybe next year,' Carole replied, heading off to continue working on the scene for *The Ghost of Christmas Yet to Come.*

There was no way Carole was going to talk to Nick, no matter what Josie said and whether by chance or by design, they didn't see one another until the Saturday evening. Even then it took the considerable efforts of Mitsy, Sarah and Jamie working together to pull off a meeting and they only managed that with Matilda's help.

'Run these mince pies over to Matilda would you, cherub?' Sarah asked. 'I promised her I'd drop them in earlier and it slipped my mind completely.'

It was another bitterly cold night and Carole wanted nothing more than to stay where she was, curled up in front of a roaring fire with Arkenarten purring on her lap, but she moved the cat, much to his obvious displeasure, put on her coat and grabbed the Christmassy tin.

'Fine,' she said, 'but if she asks me again whether I've got a boyfriend yet, I'll hit her with this tin.'

Carole had been back for four days and whilst it was clear that everyone and his dog, cat and parrot knew she was now a single woman, nearing thirty-five – and therefore probably on the shelf – Nick still hadn't been near her or called her or even sent her a note. She was beginning to realise that she had been right about him and he had no intention of being in her future, romantically or otherwise, it seemed.

'Oh hello dear,' Matilda said, beaming with Christmas joy. 'Have you–'

'No! I haven't got a boyfriend yet,' Carole interrupted, 'and frankly I don't think I want one.'

'Oh! Well, that's a shame, dear,' Matilda said, grabbing her hand and pulling her into the hall, 'but I wanted to ask you whether you've got a few minutes to spare. I would like your opinion on something. Thank you dear, you're such a sweet girl. One day, you'll make some lucky young man very happy, I'm sure of that. We're in here.'

Before Carole could say a word, Matilda pulled her into the sitting room, closed the door behind her and stood with her back pressed firmly against it, blocking Carole's exit.

Carole's mouth fell open in surprise. Her shock was matched by Nick's who was standing in the centre of Matilda's sitting room. He was dressed as Santa.

'Well dear,' Matilda said, 'what do you think?'

Carole was furious and then she remembered her comment about boyfriends, which Nick must have heard and she blushed crimson.

'About what?' she managed to say after several seconds.

'About Nick! Do you think he'd make a suitable substitute Santa? Justin Jarvis has said that he can't perform this year so we're a Santa short.'

Carole slowly surveyed a scowling Nick. The trousers were far too tight and about four inches too short, revealing the top of Nick's boots, two bands of sock and about an inch and a half of two firm calves. The jacket tugged across his broad shoulders and strained across his chest. The only items that did fit were the hat and the beard. She just couldn't help herself. She burst out laughing.

'I'm glad you find it funny,' he said, glowering. 'Matilda, I think we've established I'm not a suitable stand-in. As I said in the beginning, I really feel Bert Threadgold would be far more suitable for the part.'

'Bert Threadgold!' Matilda repeated as if the thought hadn't occurred to her. 'Of course! Now why didn't I think of that?'

'I think we both know that you did,' Nick replied. He seemed far from amused. 'Even before I suggested it ten minutes ago. I'm not sure what you're playing at but if this is some ploy to get Carole and me together, I think you've wasted your time and ours. Now if you'll excuse me, I'd like to get out of this ridiculous outfit.' He removed the hat and beard and tossed them onto the chair.

'There's no need to be quite so rude,' Carole snapped. 'It

was a silly idea I agree, but don't shout at Matilda. I think we both know who's behind this, and don't worry, I'll tell Gran and Mum to mind their own business in future. You've made it perfectly clear you have absolutely no interest in me and I don't know why they thought this would make you change your mind. Excuse me please, Matilda.'

'*I* have no interest in you and this won't make *me* change *my* mind?' Nick sounded angry and confused.

'Okay!' Carole exclaimed. 'There's no need to emphasize the fact. I got the message loud and clear, thank you very much!'

'What message? What are you talking about?'

'Matilda! Please will you excuse me?' Carole asked again, her anger rising rapidly.

Nick was beside her in an instant. 'I asked you what message? I didn't send you a message.'

'No! You didn't. And by not doing so, you did. Loud and clear.'

Nick shook his head. 'Run that by me again.'

Carole tutted, pursed her lips, crossed her arms in front of her and tapped one foot as she scowled at Matilda. She couldn't manhandle the little old lady out of the way and she hoped her body language would do the trick.

It didn't.

'This is really none of my business,' Matilda commented, 'but what Carole is saying, Nick dear, is that she hasn't heard from you and despite being single and quite clearly available for several days now, you haven't even asked her out.'

Carole seethed quietly. She saw Nick frown, stare at Matilda, frown again, stare at her and finally, open his eyes wide as if a huge bright star hung over his head lighting his way to comprehension.

'Oh! There seems to have been a bit of a misunderstanding.'

Carole glared at him. 'Misunderstanding? What's that supposed to mean?'

'Matilda?' he said. 'Would it be too much trouble if I were to ask you to kindly give us five minutes alone, please?'

'Of course not, dear,' she replied, 'you take as much time as you need.'

She opened the door, shot out and closed it behind her before Carole had time to open her mouth.

'I'd rather not ... Oh! How did she move so fast?'

Carole stepped towards the door but Nick beat her to it and leant against it.

'You'd rather not ...?' he asked.

'I'd rather not discuss this now.'

'Well, that's a pity because I would. Have I understood this correctly? Are you saying you've been waiting for me to call you and ask you out?'

'No! I'm saying nothing of the sort.'

'But you've been expecting me to?'

'No. Far from it.'

'But you wanted me to?'

'Absolutely not!'

Once again, she stuck her chin out and put her shoulders back. He studied her face and she met his eyes. She saw the smile spread across his mouth and light up his dark eyes.

'Oh!' she said as he grabbed her arm and pulled her to him.

'Well, let's see if you get this message.' Within an instant he'd wrapped his arms tightly around her and was kissing her deeply. The near silence was broken only by the sound of several seams of Santa's suit, ripping apart.

It was several minutes before Nick spoke again. 'I suppose I'd better get out of this before all the other seams burst.'

'I'd offer to give you a hand,' Carole replied, 'but it might give Matilda a heart attack!'

'If that kiss was anything to go by,' he said, looking into her eyes, 'it'll be me who has the heart attack.'

She smiled wickedly. 'I'm not that sort of girl anyway. I never have sex *before* my first date.'

'Just as well we stopped when we did last Sunday then,' he said, grinning.

'*We* didn't stop. *You* stopped. Why was that?'

'I told you. You were dating two other men. I'm not that sort of guy. I had to wait until you decided what you wanted. Who you wanted. I hoped you'd decide you didn't want Sebastian or Dominic but I still wasn't sure you'd want me.'

'What would you have done if I'd chosen one of them?'

'I'd like to think I'd have tried to be your friend if you really loved either of them but there's a very strong possibility that I would have abducted you and locked you up in a tower or something until you came to your senses and chose me.'

'Oh really? But ... why didn't you ask me out? When you knew I'd finished with both of them. Why didn't you call me or come and see me or anything? And just now, you said Matilda was wasting her time trying to get us together.'

'I thought you needed time. I thought you wanted time. I thought if you wanted me, you would come and see me, to tell me in person that you'd finished with them. When you didn't and then you seemed to be avoiding me, I thought you'd decided you didn't want me either. It was only just now, when I saw you were hurt and angry that I realised I was wrong.'

'So does that mean you're going to ask me out then?'

'Absolutely.'

'When?'

'As soon as I get out of these clothes but first ...' He pulled her closer and another seam gave up the ghost.

***

On Sunday morning after her first date with Nick, Carole asked Jacob Marley if she could show Nick her old family home and he happily agreed. He said that he had to be in the village anyway to look at the offices of a former estate agency called *Jarvis and Jarvis* which he and his partner Mr Scrooge were thinking of taking over, so it was no problem to show them around.

Carole was very nervous and she wasn't sure what Nick would think but the moment he walked through the gate she knew that it would be fine. Better than fine. It would be perfect.

'I'll have to put some oil on these hinges,' he said.

'Now I don't want you to say you like it just because I do, Nick. I want you to be honest.'

He pulled her to one side smilingly sheepishly as Jacob Marley opened the door.

'I've got a confession to make,' he said. 'I drove past this house yesterday and I phoned to get the details. I didn't know this was the house you grew up in. I ... I was looking for somewhere to buy so that I can move out of the cottage I'm renting.'

Carole couldn't believe her ears and when they went inside and she told him about her Christmases here as a child, she could tell from the expression on his face that he was picturing Christmases of the future.

'I know we've only had one date,' she said, 'and I know anything could happen but if things work out with us ... if...'

'Are you proposing to me, Carole?' he asked jokingly.

'No!' Just thinking that ...'

'The answer's yes, whatever the question is.' He took her hand and they explored each room excitedly. When they left, he stood at the gate. 'She's beautiful,' he said, 'and so are you.' Then he kissed her just to prove it.

Snow began falling just before dawn on Christmas Eve and it didn't stop for three hours.

By the time the village hall opened its doors for the performance of *A Christmas Carol,* as Bert Threadgold had decided the musical would now be called, several inches covered the ground.

Mitsy was concerned that she wouldn't be able to get there because of the heavy snow but Nick and Jamie strapped the wheelchair onto one of the larger sledges Nick had for sale in the garden centre and they were able to get her to the hall with no trouble at all.

The audience received a mince pie and a glass of mulled wine on arrival. There were soft drinks for the children and as the village hall filled up, it seemed as if every member of the population of Jutsdown had come out on this snowy Christmas Eve.

Carole and Josie rather cynically, thought that it had more to do with wanting to discuss the bizarre events of the last few days than it had with watching the Christmas musical but whatever the reason, the hall was full to bursting and Bert Threadgold's position as the kingpin of the village was firmly established.

This was the position formerly held by Justin Jarvis, but since he, his wife and even his son, Sebastian, had left the village rather suddenly four days ago, Bert's role was undisputed.

The villagers were certain that Bert Threadgold would not turn out to be a secret pervert, unlike Justin Jarvis whose nefarious activities only came to light when a young woman reported him for making lewd remarks and groping her in a queue at the post office stores. Several other women came forward with a similar complaint and Josie discovered she was just one of a very long list of women. In fact, Carole began to wonder what was wrong with her, as she was one of only a few whom Justin Jarvis had *not* attempted to seduce.

She even asked Nick but he replied, 'Nothing my darling, you are absolutely perfect,' and as he took every opportunity he got, to touch and look at, kiss and caress every inch of her, and had done since their first date on Saturday, she trusted his judgment completely. And … she could say the same about Nick.

Everyone remarked on Carole's 'lucky escape' and what a good thing it was that she'd fallen so deeply in love with Nick and dumped Sebastian before discovering he was more like his father than anyone guessed.

Sebastian's soon-to-be-ex-wife Julia, was currently 'trashing' him on various social networking sites, as were three of his mistresses. When a young woman of twenty-six came to the village just two days ago with a ten-year-old daughter, looking for Sebastian, Carole realised exactly why he'd left her at the altar ten years ago and gone to Australia.

She thanked her lucky stars that he had.

Carole and Nick were sitting back stage watching the audience take their seats. Nick would be helping move the scenery during the musical and Carole would be dressing the stage between sets.

'By the way,' she said, 'you still haven't told me your surname and you did promise to tell me on Christmas Eve. This morning you said you'd tell me after you'd opened your birthday presents but you didn't.'

'Well that was your fault. Firstly, for giving me all those presents and secondly, for giving them to me when we were still in bed.'

'Well, you'd better tell me soon, the musical is about to start. I still don't know why you've been so secretive about it.'

'There's a reason for that. I've told you that I started to fall in love with you before we'd even met because of the photos Mitsy showed me and the stories she told me about you.'

'Yes. And that was why you tried to pretend you were indifferent to me, because I had a boyfriend.'

'Two boyfriends.' He kissed her on her nose and grinned. 'Well, she also told me how you'd come to hate your surname since your father's death and how desperate you were to get rid of the 'Christmas' connection. I wanted to wait until you got to know me. I was hoping that, when you did, it wouldn't matter. Of course, I couldn't be sure that you'd dump your boyfriends or that you'd fall in love with me but that first night we met, I knew I didn't want any more obstacles in the way.'

She eyed him anxiously. 'What wouldn't matter? What obstacles? Your name can't be any worse than *Carole Singer*, surely?'

Nick nodded. 'I'm afraid it can.'

'*Really*? What is it?'

He hesitated for a moment, took both her hands in his and looked her directly in the eyes. 'Please don't get mad and please say it doesn't matter. It's only a name, after all. All that matters is we love each other.'

She nodded and held his gaze. 'Nick. Tell me.'

'It's ... Christmas. My name is Nicholas Christmas.'

Carole didn't answer. She just stared at him and then smiled broadly. 'So ... if this relationship lasts, and assuming you do actually propose to me, and on the basis that you don't leave me standing at the altar, I would go from Carole Singer to Carole Christmas! Nick. You really should have told me!'

'Are you really cross? It's just a name, Carole. Just a silly name.'

Carole caught a glimpse of the children from the village school exchanging anxious but excited looks as they prepared for their big opening. They were to sing a carol before the start of the musical and the adults would sing one at the end.

A mischievous smile spread across her mouth. Nick was right. It *was* just a name and what did it matter if people made silly jokes about it? There were far worse things in life. Like not being with a man you adored.

'You're right,' she said, moving closer to him and slipping her arms around his waist. 'Why the Dickens should I care about a name? Mrs Carole Christmas isn't that bad. In fact, I think I could get used to it. In fact ... I could keep my name as well and be Mrs Carole Christmas-Singer! I rather like the sound of that!'

'Do you know what?' he declared, beaming with love, pride and happiness, 'So do I, and I think the sooner we do that, the better.'

He swept her into his arms in a long, lingering kiss. When he finally released his embrace, he smiled lovingly, staring into her eyes. 'You know, as far as name's go, we got off pretty lightly really,' he said, undoing the top button of her blouse. 'Don't forget my sister's name is Mary, so she was really keen to get married.'

'What's wrong with ...? Oh good grief!' she exclaimed. 'Mary Christmas!'

His lips twitched with merriment. 'Precisely! And a Merry Christmas to you too, my darling.'

He kissed her again and she knew that wishes made on shooting stars really did come true as his arms held her in a way that assured her this would be a truly wonderful Christmas – and not just this Christmas but every *Christmas Yet to Come*.

The carol singers boomed out the opening lines of *We Wish You a Merry Christmas* and Bert Threadgold encouraged the audience to join in. But neither Carole or Nick heard them. They were far too busy getting into their own Christmas spirit.

THE END

Win! Win! Win! There's a competition on my website with some lovely prizes. Pop over and enter for your chance to win.

To be the first to hear about new releases, competitions and other news, why not subscribe to my newsletter via the 'Sign me up' box, whilst you're there?

You can also see more of my books, or contact me by clicking the website bookmarks and it would be great if you want to send me a friend request on Facebook or 'like' my Facebook author page. I'd also be thrilled if you have the time to write a brief review on Amazon.co.uk and/or Amazon.com. Reviews really do mean a lot to us writers!

Thank you so much for reading this book. I really hope you enjoyed it.

***

Author contacts :

http://www.emilyharvale.com

http://www.twitter.com/emilyharvale

http://www.facebook.com/emilyharvale

http://www.facebook.com/emilyharvalewriter

http://www.emilyharvale.com/blog

http://www.pinterest.com/emilyharvale

http://www.amazon.co.uk/Emily-Harvale/e/B007BKQ1SW

A SLIPPERY SLOPE

Love shouldn't be an uphill struggle

Verity Lawton expects a big surprise from her husband, Tony for her upcoming fortieth birthday but telling her he's leaving, isn't what she had in mind. To make matters worse, their daughter, Lucy has landed a job as a chalet girl for the ski season so Verity will be facing her marriage breakdown alone, and that's not a pleasant prospect.

Twenty-one year old Lucy doesn't want to leave her heartbroken mum, so when her co-worker drops out, she persuades Verity to take her place. It'll mean they can have some 'together time' in a luxury chalet in the up market ski resort of Meribel, France and Verity will have time to consider her options. Her cooking may be more 'bleugh!' than cordon bleu but how difficult can it be to make crème brûlée? She's about to find out.

But being a chalet girl involves a lot more than sitting by a roaring fire watching snow fall as her employer, Josh Calder tells her – repeatedly. He owns several chalets in the French Alps and expects his staff to be exceptional, not set the kitchen on fire, ignore the rules, take in stray dogs and snap at him every time he opens his mouth. Verity Lawton has to go. He just has to find a way to tell her and why that is proving to be so difficult, he has no idea.

Verity's on a slippery slope and when her own mother arrives, she knows things can only get worse. Add to the mix some raucous holidaymakers, two sexy ski instructors, her repentant husband and a mountain rescue dog that clearly doesn't understand its job description and you've got a recipe for more than just upside down cake. Will things work out for the best or is it all downhill from here?

Printed in Great Britain
by Amazon.co.uk, Ltd.,
Marston Gate.